One Hell of a Vacation

By

Tara Tannenbaum

II

One Hell of a Vacation ©2023 by Tara Tannenbaum

Donald, Henry, Carol and Jane Publishing, LLC

Cover art © 2023 by ElderLemon Design

www.elderlemondesign.net

All rights reserved.

This book is a work of fiction. Names, characters, places, and incidents are either products of the author's imagination or are used fictitiously. Any resemblance to actual events, locales, or persons, living or dead, is entirely coincidental. No part of this publication may be reproduced or transmitted in any form or by any means, electronic or mechanical, without written permission from the author.

IV

TABLE OF CONTENTS

Chapter 1	1
Chapter 2	6
Chapter 3	12
Chapter 4	16
Chapter 5	21
Chapter 6	26
Chapter 7	32
Chapter 8	37
Chapter 9	43
Chapter 10	49
Chapter 11	54
Chapter 12	59
Chapter 13	64
Chapter 14	69
Chapter 15	74
Chapter 16	80
Chapter 17	86
Chapter 18	91
Chapter 19	97
Chapter 20	103
Chapter 21	108
Chapter 22	113

Chapter 23	119
Chapter 24	125
Chapter 25	130
Chapter 26	136
Chapter 27	141
Chapter 28	146
Chapter 29	151
Chapter 30	156
Chapter 31	160
Chapter 32	168
Chapter 33	173
Chapter 34	177
Chapter 35	183
Chapter 36	187
Chapter 37	191
Chapter 38	196
Chapter 39	201
Chapter 40	206
Chapter 41	210
Chapter 42	215
Chapter 43	219
Chapter 44	224
Chapter 45	229
Chapter 46	234

Chapter 47	239
Chapter 48	243
Chapter 49	247
Chapter 50	251
Chapter 51	256
Chapter 52	261
Chapter 53	266
Chapter 54	270
Chapter 55	275
Chapter 56	280
Chapter 57	285
Chapter 58	290
Chapter 59	294
Chapter 60	298
Chapter 61	302
Chapter 62	307
Chapter 63	313
Chapter 64	317
Chapter 65	328
Chapter 66	330
Chapter 67	338
Chapter 68	349
Chapter 69	358
Chapter 70	368

Chapter 71 — 383

Chapter 72 — 388

Epilogue — 391

In memory of my father,
Robert B. Poore
1954-2014

Chapter 1

"Congratulations Caller Number Five! You've got Wild Man Stan on the line and it's time for you to answer a trivia question for a chance to win a fabulous prize! Where are you calling from this morning, Caller Number Five? Can you tell us your name?"

"Sharon Stone and I'm calling from New Canaan, Connecticut." *Wait for it,* she thought.

"Caller, are you sure your name is Sharon Stone?" Wild Man Stan laughed obnoxiously.

Sharon rolled her eyes and tucked a spiral curl behind her ear as she sat at the stoplight. "That's the name on my driver's license the last time I checked, Stan."

"All right, all right. I believe ya. Ready to answer a trivia question for the chance to win a big prize?"

"I'm ready."

"Okay Sharon. Who was the female lead in the 1992 blockbuster hit *Basic Instinct*?"

Sharon cringed. She thought about hanging up. This guy was a total asshole. She had other things to worry about this morning and was running late for work. Was it her fault she became Sharon Stone when she got married? She'd wanted to keep her maiden name, but her husband, Maxwell, would have thrown a fit. Besides, she was nothing like the actress. For instance, she was half black, and her skin was the color of caramel, her eyes, the shape of almonds, and her hair, dark and curly.

"Clever, Stan," she said. "Very clever, indeed. That's not the real trivia question, am I correct?"

He laughed again. "You're absolutely right. That's not the real question. I'm just having a bit of fun with you and our audience. It's not every day I get to have a conversation with Sharon Stone, babe!!"

"Then what's the real question?" Impatient, she contemplated just ending the call. *That'd show him and his audience*, she thought.

Wild Man Stan got more serious. "Okay, here we go. *Sanditon*, which she began writing in 1817 but did not finish before she died the same year, was the last novel by what English author?"

Sharon rolled her eyes again. Such an easy question. "Jane Austen."

"Correct! Wow, Sharon, how did you get it so fast? You didn't cheat, did you? Maybe you did a little Googling?"

"Maybe it's because I'm an English Literature professor. If you want the truth, that question was a bit easy for me. You should pick something a little more difficult next time." She smiled at her smug reply. *Serves him right.*

"All right, Ms. Smarty-Pants! Well, well, well! I guess today is your lucky day -- You've won an all-expenses paid vacation to the Czech Republic! Since it's October and only two weeks until Halloween, we here at KX101 thought it would be fun to have our winner stay at a haunted castle. And guess what, Sharon?! You and a guest will be staying at not just any haunted castle, but *the most* haunted castle in arguably all of Europe, Houska Castle! What do you say to that? Aren't you excited?!

She wasn't sure Stan even took a breath while telling her all of that. Her brain was still processing it. She replied, "That sounds interesting. I'm looking forward to it."

Whether she actually *was* looking forward to the trip or not was still undetermined, but due to the current state of her marriage, she knew that a trip away from daily life might help.

"Wonderful! It's been a blast having you on the show today. Even though you aren't *the* Sharon Stone, I'm sure you're just as hot, babe!"

Sharon felt like she was going to throw up. She couldn't wait to get off the phone. "Thanks for the opportunity, Stan."

"Sure, no prob, babe! Just stay on the line; our production assistant will take it from there! Have a good one and thanks for listening to KX101!"

Sharon heard a click and then, a seemingly annoyed monotoned woman came on the line.

"This is Denise. I'm a production assistant. Can I get your full name and the name of your guest, along with both of your birth dates and addresses, please?"

Wow, Denise sounds like she's the one who needs a vacation. Sharon rattled off the information. After another couple of minutes, Denise had the trip booked and had hung up before Sharon had a chance to thank her. The call ended.

***

ONE HELL OF A VACATION

Sharon pulled into the university parking lot and wheeled her car into a faculty spot. As she walked to her building, she thought more about the trip. Could it really give her and Maxwell a chance to work things out? Talking at home always led to fights, but maybe in a foreign setting, it would be different.

Sharon hoped so. After waiting fifty-one years to find the love of her life, she didn't want to give up so easily. Sure, marriage wasn't made in heaven; every couple struggled. It didn't mean that Maxwell didn't love her, or that she didn't love him.

She'd thought their wedding day was going to be the happiest day of her life, a day of hope and new beginnings.

How could she have known it'd take a wrong turn so soon? She hadn't meant to upset Maxwell.

Upsetting Maxwell was the last thing she wanted to do, because if Maxwell wasn't happy, no one was.

Chapter 2

One Year Ago

"You may now kiss the bride."

Maxwell leaned in, but Sharon, always a bit shy about public displays of affection, kept her lips closed, so that the most he got was a polite little peck.

When he pulled back from her, she knew by the look on his face that a storm was coming.

She smiled meekly, hoping to lighten the mood, but as he grabbed her hand to lead her back up the aisle, she knew it was no use. The minute they entered the foyer at the front of the church, he let go of her hand and stomped off. Sharon shook her head as she opened her dressing room door.

The reception was lovely. There were flowers and balloons everywhere, and the champagne was flowing. Everyone was laughing and having a good time.

Everyone except for Maxwell, who zeroed in on Sharon the second she stepped into the room and wouldn't take his eyes off of her no matter where she went. Sharon tried to ignore it. She visited with their guests, and engaged as much as she could but it was hard to concentrate.

Finally, she made her way over to the drinks table, where Maxwell was standing. He continued to stare at her.

"I'm so happy," she said, trying to break the ice and maybe pull him out of his mood.

"Yes, you seem to be quite pleased with yourself, making me look like a fool."

Sharon scrunched her nose. "What are you talking about, Maxwell?" She reached out to touch his arm, but he jerked away.

"What the fuck was that stunt you pulled at the altar? I try to kiss my new wife, and she behaves like I have some sort of disease? What the fuck were you thinking?"

"I didn't do it on purpose. You know I get nervous. Being in front of a crowd, and the center of attention? Even if it was just our friends and family? I couldn't help it." Sharon again reached for his arm.

This time, he grabbed her wrist and marched her towards the bathroom. She knew if she resisted it would cause a scene so she willingly followed behind him.

As soon as they were inside, he shut and locked the door, then spun her and shoved her against the wall. She managed to brace with her palms to keep from going face-first into it and hurting herself.

His breath hot in her ear, he whispered, "If I want something, you're going to give it to me. Do you understand that, you little bitch?"

"Maxwell, calm down, please. It's our wedding day!" Sharon pleaded.

"It sure is, and now I feel like taking what's rightfully mine."

He yanked up the back of her dress and undid his pants. She begged him to stop, but he wouldn't. He rammed himself inside of her and began pounding furiously. Tears fell down her cheeks.

When he was done, he zipped his pants and let Sharon's dress fall back down over her. She watched him as he went over to the sink and washed his hands.

Then, he turned toward her. "Don't you ever embarrass me again."

He opened the door and walked out.

Sharon rushed over and locked it again.

ONE HELL OF A VACATION

I just need to calm down, she thought. *Everything is alright. He is my husband. I deserved that. I shouldn't have embarrassed him.*

She fixed her hair and makeup, straightening her dress and making sure she looked like a happy bride. She noticed her wrist was bruised where he'd grabbed her earlier.

Oh well, the bruise would fade.

When she was ready, she went to rejoin the party. The first face she saw when she entered the reception hall belonged to Graham, Maxwell's older brother. He smiled at her, but his smile turned to a look of concern and he started heading her way.

Shit, she thought.

"Sharon, you look lovely," he said.

"Thank you so much, Graham."

"But you also look sad. What happened?" Graham had an eye for when things were out of place. He always had.

"Don't be silly. Everything is wonderful! This reception is every bride's dream. Donna did a beautiful job with it. I couldn't be happier." She knew he didn't believe her.

9

"Is something wrong with Maxwell? He seemed a bit off earlier, and he's knocking back drinks one right after the other."

"He's fine. We just took a moment to discuss something in private." She looked away.

Graham's expression suggested he wasn't convinced. "Sharon, you're my sister now. I have your best interests at heart. I will protect you from harm, even if that harm is my little brother. I know he has a temper."

Sharon continued to look anywhere but at her brother-in-law. "I'm fine. It's no big deal. We had a small disagreement, but I apologized and we made up."

Graham's eyes widened. "What in the world could you have had to apologize for on your wedding day? Listen Sharon, I don't know how else to say this, but my brother is...well, he's not what you deserve. I've held back in saying that, but it's true. You deserve so much more than him. I know you're married now and I wish you the best, but God help me, I won't let him hurt you."

Sharon gave her brother-in-law a hug and a kiss on the cheek. "Thank you," she said, "but I'm sure everything will be fine."

ONE HELL OF A VACATION

Then she moved off in the direction of the other guests, before he could say anything more.

Chapter 3

On Tuesdays, Sharon didn't have any afternoon classes. Normally she stayed to grade papers or work on lesson plans, but today she thought she'd catch the afternoon train and surprise Maxwell at the office.

The ride flew by, aided by a book she'd brought, and it was only a short walk from Grand Central Station to Mega Trust Bank, where Maxwell was CEO.

She loved New York City, with its hustle and bustle and bright lights. It was such a big contrast to New Canaan. She stopped in at two shops she liked to frequent, but didn't see anything that she thought she simply must have.

As she made her way to the bank, she sipped on the coffee that she'd picked up along the way and thought about what she would say to Maxwell regarding the trip. She wasn't sure if he would be excited about it, or if it was something else that would cause another argument.

The doorman opened the big double doors for her and she set her handbag down on the conveyor belt to go through security. An officer waved a wand over her body. When she was cleared, she walked into the lobby, retrieving her handbag from the belt.

Riding the elevator to the 25th floor, Sharon closed her eyes and listened to the pleasant music coming from the speakers. It soothed her ears and cleared her mind.

Before she knew it, she heard the familiar ding of the bell. The doors opened and she stepped out into another lobby. Behind the reception desk sat a woman Sharon didn't recognize, with red frizzy hair and glasses.

"Can I help you?" she said.

"Hi, I don't believe we've met." Sharon extended her hand. "I'm here to see my husband, Maxwell Stone. I'm Sharon, his wife."

The other woman didn't take the offered hand, so Sharon smiled, hoping to relieve some of the awkward tension.

She didn't return the smile, either. "I'm Bonnie. I'm a temp. Monica is out for the day. Mr. Stone isn't here either. He left for lunch and he's not back yet."

"Oh. Okay. Then I will wait awhile." Sharon took a seat. She didn't mind waiting; she'd just read some more of the book she'd brought along.

An hour later, Sharon glanced at her phone. Bonnie appeared to have forgotten that she existed. She was surprised to see how much time had passed. She sent Maxwell a text. HI LOVE. I'M HERE AT YOUR OFFICE. WANTED TO COME SEE YOU. HAVE SOME GOOD NEWS. ARE YOU COMING BACK SOON? XX SHARON.

After thirty more minutes and no reply, she tried to call him. It rang once and went straight to voicemail. Frustrated, she sent another text. I GUESS YOU MUST BE IN A MEETING SOMEWHERE. I'LL TELL YOU THE NEWS AT HOME. LEAVING NOW TO GO CATCH THE TRAIN. LOVE YOU.

Bonnie didn't even look up from what she was doing as Sharon returned to the elevator. The music didn't have the same effect it had earlier. There was still no reply from Maxwell.

She couldn't help a nagging feeling that something wasn't right. Even though she knew Maxwell was a busy man, she didn't think he would be out of the office for such a long amount of time. And furthermore, he could have at least sent her a short text back to let her know he wouldn't be back, so that she wouldn't have had to sit and wait forever for no reason.

By the time she'd gotten back to Grand Central, she was in a bad mood. What she'd hoped would be a pleasant afternoon had been anything but, and she still had an hour train ride ahead of her in order to get back home.

She tried not to think about it. She boarded the train and found a seat and plopped down, closing her eyes and contemplated the upcoming vacation. She prayed it would be a chance for her and for Maxwell to get on the same page, and perhaps, to fall in love again. She felt so lonely most of the time. Maxwell often didn't come home until late at night. They barely spoke, and when they did, it was usually to argue.

She needed this to work. She needed him.

Only as she was getting into her own car and setting her handbag on the passenger seat did she hear the familiar noise alerting her of a text.

She dug out her phone and looked at the screen.

The message was from Maxwell. It said: FOR FUCK'S SAKE SHARON! I'M BUSY!

Sharon started the car and drove home in silence.

Chapter 4

Maxwell rolled off of Monica, bringing the sheet up to wipe the sweat from his chest and forehead.

There's nothing like an afternoon lay, he thought to himself. He might even be able to get in another one before he had to go home. At least, he hoped he would.

"Go turn the fan on," he ordered. "It's hot as hell in here."

Monica got up from the bed and strolled across the hotel room. She flipped a switch on the wall and the ceiling fan began to spin. Maxwell admired her nude body. Twenty-three, with perky tits and a flat stomach. She had long blonde hair and baby blue eyes.

And, best of all, she followed Maxwell's every command. *She's exactly what I want and the opposite of what I have,* he thought.

She laid back down on the bed, took his cock in her hand, and began to stroke it.

"Is this okay, baby?" she asked him.

"It's okay, but I wish it was your mouth."

ONE HELL OF A VACATION

She immediately obliged. He closed his eyes and focused on what her mouth was doing to him. He felt himself already starting to get hard again, which was amazing, considering he'd turned sixty in July.

Over on the dresser, his phone buzzed. He ignored it. Probably someone from work.

Monica removed her mouth from him and slid one leg over so that she was straddling him. She positioned his cock to go inside of her, then lowered herself back onto him.

He could have helped her, but he didn't feel like it. He enjoyed watching her do all of the work.

She moved up and down, leaning forward so that her hair was tickling his chest. He grabbed her breasts and she moaned.

"Oh, you like that, huh?" he asked her playfully.

"You know I do." she replied.

She bounced faster and he began to thrust as he neared orgasm. He listened to her cries of joy as she reached it before him and then, he was spent.

Monica crawled off of him, kissing his shoulder as she did, and curled up next to him. He loved how she worshiped him. That innocent dumb expression she wore. He couldn't get enough of it.

"I wish we could do this every day and every night," she said.

Maxwell chuckled. "Me too, baby. But we do what we can, right?" His phone buzzed again. He rolled his eyes. He hated being bothered.

Reluctantly, he picked up the phone to check his messages. Both were from Sharon. What the fuck? She was at his office? Then he remembered it was Tuesday. She didn't have classes Tuesday afternoon. Still, she never came to the city to see him. What the hell could she possibly want?

Thoroughly annoyed, he swung his legs over the side of the bed and put on his pants. Monica retrieved her bra and thong from a nearby chair.

When they were both fully dressed, she put her arms around his neck.

"I can't wait until I have you all to myself," she said, pouting.

"Baby, I'm doing the best I can right now, you know that. I have some stuff to work out first. Then I'll be able to leave

Sharon, and we can run away together, anywhere you want to go. You just have to give me some time."

He meant every word, which surprised him. He didn't care that she was dumb as a rock. She was beautiful and loyal as a dog. That's what he needed.

He slapped her on the rear playfully, then went into the bathroom, shook a bit of cocaine from a bag, and cut a couple of lines with a razor. Taking a Benjamin from his wallet and rolling it up, he snorted them and instantly felt better.

The money he'd 'borrowed' from work needed to be replaced, and he still needed to figure out how to get rid of Sharon, but none of that seemed to matter right now. He'd come up with a plan, and could then be with Monica, preferably someplace with sunshine and sandy beaches.

He donned his Rolex. It was 4:45pm. The city would be packed with people, all trying to get home from work. And the prospect of riding a crowded train all the way to New Canaan? He didn't feel like dealing with any of that right now.

Walking back out of the bathroom, he smiled at Monica as he unbuckled his belt and started to unbutton his shirt. She looked at him curiously, then the lightbulb went off in her head. She eagerly took off her dress and unhooked her bra.

TARA TANNENBAUM

It's not time to go home yet, he thought, as he pulled down Monica's thong underwear and bent her over the bed. *It's time for Round Three.*

Chapter 5

Sharon woke before the sun was up.

She looked beside her; no Maxwell.

Of course not. It had been happening more and more frequently lately.

She climbed out of bed and went into the bathroom to wash her face and comb her hair. When she passed the extra bedroom, she saw Maxwell sprawled on the bed, his clothes strewn all over the floor. She rolled her eyes. He was exactly where she thought he'd be.

She went downstairs to the kitchen, started the coffee maker, then stepped out onto the back porch. She took a deep breath, enjoying the cool but not cold weather, and sat down in the rocking chair to watch the sun rise.

When the coffee was ready, she poured herself a cup and popped a piece of bread in the toaster. As she turned around to get the butter out of the refrigerator, Maxwell was standing in front of her.

"Did you sleep well?" she asked.

"I got in late, so I took the extra bed."

"I figured." The toast popped up and she spread butter over it.

"What's that supposed to mean? Are you insinuating I do this all the time?"

Sharon could tell that he was getting irritated, so she tried to defuse the situation. "No, I wasn't insinuating anything. I just assumed, since you weren't in our bed, that you'd stayed in the extra bedroom, that's all."

Maxwell poured himself a cup of coffee and sat down at the table. "So, what did you need to tell me yesterday? Was it so urgent that it couldn't wait until I got home? You felt you needed to hop the train to the city and come to my work to tell me about it? Did we win the fuckin' lottery or something?"

"In a way, I guess we did," she said, sitting opposite him. "We won a paid vacation!"

"What? How?"

"I answered a ridiculous question correctly on the radio and won a trip to some castle in the Czech Republic."

"Who the fuck would want to go to the Czech Republic for a vacation?" Maxwell laughed.

"It has to do with Halloween." She shrugged. "The castle is supposedly haunted. The radio station thought it would be fun for the prize to be something spooky."

Maxwell crossed his legs. "Well, when is this trip? Because I am very busy at work and I don't know that I can just take off whenever I feel like it." Although, even as the words came out of his mouth, he wondered if a vacation could help get him out of the jam he was in. It might be the perfect opportunity to flesh out a plan.

"The flight out's this Saturday. It's already booked, and everything's paid. I've gotten someone to cover my classes. All we have to do is get on the plane and go enjoy ourselves."

He frowned, so she kept trying.

"Oh, come on, Maxwell," she pleaded. "This could be good for us. We never go anywhere. Please don't say no."

Maxwell reached out. Sharon had practiced not flinching for over a year now, so she didn't move a muscle as he touched her arm. "I suppose if it means that much to you, I can find the time to get away for a few days," he said.

She was shocked, but she didn't show it. She expected a much bigger argument, and instead she'd hardly had to do any coaxing at all.

"Where were you yesterday, anyway?" she asked, knowing it risked ruining the mood, but it had been bugging her and she couldn't help herself. "I waited for quite a while in your office. Did you have a meeting or something?"

Maxwell frowned. "Did I not already tell you that I was busy? I'm pretty sure I sent you a text to that effect, after you kept bugging the shit out of me."

His face was getting red, and she knew she was on thin ice.

"I just wondered. Normally, when I try to get you on the phone, I don't have a problem. I was worried."

"Really, Sharon? What were you worried about? I was with some of the board members. We had a meeting across town. Afterward, we went to a bar. I didn't answer your call because I couldn't hear my fuckin' phone." Maxwell stood up, and slammed his coffee cup down on the counter.

"Okay," she said, feeling like a bus was headed straight for her. "It's no big deal, I was just worried about you."

"I don't need you to worry about me. I worry about myself." He poked a finger into her chest. "You need to worry about *you*, Sharon."

"I'm sorry I bothered you. I know I shouldn't have." Her voice was trembling.

He grasped her upper arms and urged her from the chair to her feet. She could tell he loved the look of fear on her face.

"Oh baby, I know," he said. "You just ask me ridiculous fuckin' questions all the time because you have nothing better to do. But now, baby, now you have to worry about this trip and getting my things packed and ready for Saturday, so maybe you won't be asking me any more questions. I don't like to have to get annoyed with you."

He lowered one hand to her breast, then pinched her nipple. Hard. She yelped. Then he turned and left the kitchen.

Sharon let out a breath she hadn't realized she'd been holding. She took her plate to the trash and dumped the uneaten toast.

Maxwell was right. She wasn't going to ask him any more questions. At least not today.

Chapter 6

The eleven-hour flight to Prague was long and uneventful. Maxwell slept for a good portion of it. When they landed, Sharon looked out the airplane window and what she saw amazed her.

What a beautiful city! She wasn't sure what she had been expecting, but it certainly wasn't this. There were so many bright colorful buildings of all sizes, and gothic looking churches ... she could even see a body of water too, although she couldn't identify it.

She nudged Maxwell, and he stirred and mumbled but closed his eyes again, until the plane had come to a full stop and they were ready to disembark.

On their way through the airport, Maxwell told Sharon he needed to stop off at the bathrooms before they hailed a taxi. Sharon agreed to watch the luggage while he was gone.

***

Maxwell hurried into a stall, pulled out his cell phone, found Monica's name, and pressed CALL. The phone rang twice before she picked up.

"So, I take it you've landed?" she said.

"Hi baby, yeah, a few minutes ago. I'm holed up in the bathroom. I told Sharon I had to piss before we got on the road."

Monica sighed. "How long are you going to be gone again?"

"Only a few days. But if you think you'll miss me too much, come visit."

"How would that work? You don't think Sharon would mind sharing a bed with both of us?"

"I could put you in a hotel here in Prague. It's only an hour or so from the place where we are staying. I'm betting there isn't any internet there and maybe no cell phone service, so I'd have a great excuse to travel into Prague at least every other day. I'll just tell Sharon I have to work. She won't think twice about it."

"I'd love to come see you, but who's going to manage the office?"

"Get that Bonnie chick again. She practically orgasmed at the opportunity the other day. She loves being in charge." Maxwell let out a loud laugh.

"I might be able to convince her," Monica said, still sounding unsure.

"How 'bout this? I'm your boss, and I'm ordering you to get your sweet little sexy ass on a plane and come, ahem, assist me."

"I can't disobey a direct order now, can I?" She giggled. "What exactly would you like me to assist you with, Mr. Stone?"

"Stop teasing me, Mon. We've got to cool this kind of talk. I can't go back out there with my dick hard." He adjusted himself.

"Okay, fine. We'll save the fun for when I get there," she said.

"I'll book you a flight as soon as we get off the phone and email you the information."

"Can't wait. Hey, Maxie, I love you."

ONE HELL OF A VACATION

There's not a chance in hell he would let anyone else call him Maxie. He wouldn't even let anyone call him Max. But she was different. "I love you too, baby doll. I'll see you soon."

He hung up the phone and began to search flights from New York City to Prague. Within five minutes, he had Monica booked on one of them. He searched for the nicest hotel in Prague and booked her the largest room, then called the hotel to make sure they would have a dozen roses and a bottle of champagne waiting when Monica arrived. Only the best for his girl.

Maxwell unbuckled his belt and dropped his pants and boxers. He really did have to take a piss. But first, more importantly, he needed something else. He pulled his butt cheeks apart and removed the small bag of white powder he'd had tucked up there for the entire flight. Laying his wallet flat, he sprinkled a fine line of cocaine onto it, then snorted with a rolled-up twenty. Rubbing some on his teeth afterward, he took a couple of breaths. Much better.

He aimed his dick over the toilet and relieved himself, shaking it once before pulling up his pants. Then he picked up all of his belongings, shoved the bill and little bag into his wallet, and put it back in his pocket.

Sharon had an annoyed look on her face when he exited the restroom.

Well, too fuckin' bad. She'd really be annoyed if she knew I just booked my girlfriend a room here in Prague while we're on vacation, he thought.

***

They wheeled their bags outside and found a cab. Soon, they were on the road to Blatce. Sharon asked the driver about the body of water she'd seen from the plane and he told her it was the Vltava River.

The hour in the car flew by. Soon, they were turning onto a winding road that twisted and turned. Surrounding the road were nothing but trees. After another fifteen minutes or so, they caught their first glimpse of the castle.

It didn't really look like the picture in Sharon's head. It was beautiful and old, but didn't stand out, like other castles she had seen in photographs or on the internet.

The cab came to a stop and a woman who looked to be about the same age as Sharon emerged to meet them

"Welcome to Houska. My name is Klaudie," she said.

Sharon offered her hand to Klaudie and introduced herself. Klaudie smiled at her warmly, leading her toward the castle. Maxwell followed along behind them, as a younger man hurried to help the driver unload their bags.

"This place is beautiful." Sharon said.

"We think so, but then again we didn't build it." Klaudie laughed lightly. The man with their luggage also chuckled. "Let me show you to your room first to let you freshen up. Dinner will be in an hour."

She leaned forward and kissed Sharon on each cheek and gave her a hug, surprising her.

"I am so happy you are here," said Klaudie. "I think we will be great friends, yes?"

Sharon had the same feeling.

Chapter 7

After freshening up in their whimsical, charming room, Maxwell and Sharon made their way downstairs for dinner, Maxwell still complaining about how he'd been ignored when they'd arrived.

Sharon listened to him rant and just nodded her head in agreement to placate him.

They found other guests already gathered around the dinner table. A man and woman sat together at one end, and two men were on the left side. Sharon and Maxwell sat down at two empty chairs on the right.

Klaudie came in and stood formally at the head of the table. "Good evening," she said. "I'm so pleased all of you are here. As you can see, you are not alone." She smiled at each of them, then gestured to the man and woman. "Nigel and Laila Fisher, who reside in Essex, United Kingdom." She then gestured to the two men. "Xander Chen and Dwayne Waters, visiting from Detroit, Michigan." Then she turned and smiled at Sharon. "Last but not least, Sharon and Maxwell Stone, of New Canaan, Connecticut."

ONE HELL OF A VACATION

"I know what all of you are thinking," Maxwell interrupted. "You're thinking, hey, that ain't Sharon Stone!" He threw his head back and laughed. "I agree! She's not what I think of when I think of Sharon Stone either."

Sharon dipped her head in embarrassment. The other guests remained silent, but Nigel's eyebrows were raised and Laila spared Maxwell a disapproving look.

The man who'd helped with the luggage rolled in a cart of silver trays, plates, and silverware.

"This is Marek," Klaudie said. "He is our chef, and will be preparing all of the lovely meals you'll be eating while you are here as our guests. One thing you will notice later when you explore the castle, is that it was built without a kitchen, and no original water supply. But that should not be a concern to any of you. We dug a well, and now have water for bathing, and plenty of bottled water for drinking. Meals will be prepared remotely and brought in for you to enjoy. Dishes and laundry are sent out to be cleaned. Are there any questions so far?" She looked around at the guests.

Again, Maxwell spoke up. "Could we eat our food before it gets cold?" He folded his arms and smirked at her. "I'm pretty hungry."

Klaudie bit her lip, turned to Marek, and nodded her head. He took the cue and started placing the silver trays on the table. Once everything was in place, Klaudie raised her hands and said, "Dinner is served. Please enjoy yourselves."

The food smelled like heaven and Sharon couldn't wait to taste it. Prime rib, roasted potatoes, salad, and what looked like fresh homemade bread were calling her name.

Maxwell looked at her plate and said, "Are you really going to eat all that, Sharon? Jesus, that's a lot of food."

Sharon, not being at all overweight, recognized this as the tactic it was. He liked to have control of her at all times, and so, he would say things to shame her, especially in front of other people. Like the comment about her name, and the way he loved to point out she wasn't blonde or white, like the famous actress.

She sometimes wondered why he married her to begin with. Maxwell was the definition of a Greek god, with wavy silvered "good" hair, and worked out every morning to maintain a perfect body. While Sharon didn't work out every day, she knew she was desirable. She had the black girl butt most white girls could only achieve through surgery, and nice firm breasts. She liked the way she looked. But when Maxwell said cruel things, it still hurt her feelings.

"Hey mate, why don't you give it a rest, eh?" Nigel shot Maxwell a look. Laila was still glaring at him as well.

Maxwell gave Nigel an evil grin. "Why don't you mind your own fuckin' business, 'mate'?"

Nigel's face went red. Laila set a hand on his arm so he wouldn't do anything stupid. Xander and Dwayne exchanged wide-eyed glances. Sharon focused at her plate.

Just then, Klaudie re-entered the room. "How are you finding dinner? Is everything all right?"

"It's wonderful, thank you," Sharon said.

"Perfect," Laila said. The others nodded in agreement.

"I'm pleased you are enjoying the food. After dinner, I'd like to show everyone around, but for now, I'll leave you to enjoy the rest of your meal." She left the room again.

After a moment, Xander asked, "Have any of you researched this place?"

"We were visiting Prague and it was suggested to us as a tourist attraction, so we decided to book a few nights before we leave for home," Laila said.

"I won a vacation on a radio show," Sharon said.

"Oh wow, that's awesome," said Xander. "My husband and I are here because we like to explore haunted locations." He rested his hand on Dwayne's shoulder and Dwayne covered it with his own hand, smiling.

"Haunted." Maxwell rolled his eyes. "It's all a load of shit. I can't believe anyone thinks ghosts are real." Having finished his meal, he threw his fork down on the table.

"Well, I'm interested in hearing more of the history about this place." Nigel said.

Marek, who'd come into the room to gather empty trays and load them back onto the cart, paused to glance at Maxwell.

"Do not be so quick to judge," he advised. "What Klaudie is about to share with you might change your mind."

Chapter 8

"Klaudie, that dress is lovely!" Sharon exclaimed.

Their hostess had rejoined her guests after dinner. She now wore a long blue form-fitting gown, with her long dark hair pulled up into a bun. Her alabaster skin seemed to be glowing.

"You are too kind," she said. "Thank you. I made it myself."

"You certainly have talent," Laila agreed with appreciation.

Klaudie smiled. "I would like to apologize to you all. When I was making introductions earlier, I forgot to properly introduce myself. I am Klaudie Dvorak, and I am the caretaker of Houska. I've been working here for the last fifteen years and this castle has come to feel like my home. Now, is everyone ready to take a little tour?"

They followed, even Maxwell holding off on commentary for the time being. The large room she ushered them into had high wooden ceiling beams and was heavily decorated with animal heads, skins, chairs made of animal bones and similar furnishings.

"This is the trophy room," Klaudie said. "I think it speaks for itself."

Sharon looked around in awe. It was indeed a trophy room. But something just seemed off about it. Various old-fashioned and medieval weapons were also prominently featured, making the place look rather dangerous.

The room directly adjacent to the trophy room housed more weapons, mostly swords, displayed on the walls, along with at least two dozen family crests. An antique iron chandelier hung from the ceiling.

Sharon was definitely ready to move on and get away from all of the weaponry, and was glad when Klaudie led them into a beautiful open courtyard with flags all around it. They walked across it and entered what appeared to be an old chapel. There were strange murals on the walls, an altar, and a few scattered chairs.

A young woman, a girl no older than twenty, turned as they came in. She held a duster and appeared to be cleaning.

"This is Amalie," Klaudie said. "She is a caretaker here at the castle. She makes sure things stay neat and clean. Please help her by picking up after yourselves while you are here as our guests. And, as you can see, this of course is the chapel. It was built along with the castle in the thirteenth century, so it is quite old. Let us move on, for now. It's late, and I will give you further details in the morning at breakfast."

They followed Klaudie downstairs to the basement. It was cold and damp. At the far end, stairs led up to a platform, which held a chair. It almost looked like a throne of some sort, with bones tied to it in various places.

Sharon glanced at Klaudie, who appeared visibly uncomfortable. Xander and Dwayne seemed fascinated, Nigel and Laila as well.

Maxwell, clearly bored, climbed the steps to the chair and sat down.

"This room is better known as Satan's Office," Klaudie said. She scowled at Maxwell, her hands shaking. "And you, sir, are sitting on His throne."

Sharon caught his eye and shook her head, letting him know she didn't approve, but all he did was smirk at her

***

When the rest of the group plodded back upstairs, Maxwell followed reluctantly.

He'd really liked that throne thing. He felt like a king sitting in it. He wondered if he could sneak out of their bedroom later, after everyone went to bed, and go back down there and sit in it again.

Maybe even jerk off in it.

So far, otherwise, this trip was a bust. The only things halfway decent were the food, and that hot, young maid he'd seen in the chapel. He couldn't stand that Klaudie bitch, and could tell she didn't like him either.

Then there was that prick from England, who thought he could tell Maxwell how to speak to his own wife? Well, Maxwell would show him who was in control.

Plus, there were the queer ghostbusters. *Give me a break*, he thought.

He glanced at his watch. It felt like forever until Monica would arrive in Prague. He pulled out his phone and found he actually did have cell phone service, which surprised him.

HEY ANGEL, he texted. HOW'S MY FAVORITE GIRL?

ONE HELL OF A VACATION

WHO'S THIS? HEE HEE

CUTE. ARE YOU AT THE AIRPORT?

JUST GRABBED A COFFEE FROM STARBUCKS AND NOW HEADING TO MY GATE. ARE YOU HAVING A NICE TIME?

ARE YOU SERIOUS? OF COURSE, I'M NOT HAVING A FUCKIN NICE TIME. I'M ON A GHOST TRIP WITH MY WIFE, WHO I CAN'T STAND TO BE AROUND. I'M MISERABLE.

WELL NOT TOO LONG AND I WON'T BE FAR AWAY FROM YOU. I CAN MAKE EVERYTHING BETTER. <3 <3

I'M COUNTING ON IT. HEY MON, WHAT COLOR THONG DO YOU HAVE ON?

MAXIE, WHO SAYS I'M WEARING ONE?

Maxwell grinned. Monica could always pull him out of a rotten mood.

"Maxwell?"

He glanced up. It was Sharon.

"Everything all right?" she asked.

"Yeah, everything's fine. Just a work thing." He quickly shoved his phone back into his pocket.

"Oh. Well, the rest of the group is getting pretty far ahead."

"Okay, okay I'm coming," he said, mumbling under his breath, "Can't even have a fuckin' minute to myself?"

Chapter 9

All of the guest rooms were on the second floor, so Klaudie led them to the third. It looked to be uncared for and in disrepair.

All of the doors were closed. Xander wished they could stop and open them to see what was inside, but figured it might be rude to ask. As they reached the end of the hall, yet another flight of stairs led to a door at the top.

Klaudie turned. "We are about to enter the attic," she announced.

When Xander stepped inside, he felt the temperature drop by at least twenty degrees. He reached for Dwayne's hand, but grasped nothing but air. He looked to his right, where he thought his husband was standing, but instead, Dwayne was halfway across the room, with Nigel and Laila.

The attic was empty, except for some broken toys, an antique radio, and other scattered litter. Xander felt more uneasy in here than he had anyplace else so far. He went over to Dwayne and they shared a knowing look, both feeling the same strange energy.

Xander continued to scan the room. That asshole who was married to Sharon -- he didn't remember his name -- was leaning against the doorframe with a bored expression. Sharon stood next to him, clearly uncomfortable. Xander caught her eye and gave her a little wave, gesturing for her to come join him. She walked over.

"This attic gives me the creeps," she said, shivering.

"Right?! I get the same vibe, Dwayne too." Xander glanced to him for confirmation, but Dwayne was clear at the far end of the attic again, with Nigel and Laila. *Oh well,* he thought. *At least he's made some friends.*

"Have you lived in Detroit all of your life?" Sharon asked.

"No, I'm originally from Austin, Texas. I moved to Detroit about three years ago for a job opportunity. I met Dwayne six months later, and six months after that, we got married."

"Oh, wow. So, you are practically newlyweds! Maxwell and I have only been married for a year. To be honest, I thought I would end up staying single my entire life. Never thought I'd find love after fifty, but here we are." She smiled.

He smiled back. *That's right, the prick's name is Maxwell. You should have stayed single, girlfriend,* Xander thought.

ONE HELL OF A VACATION

"What type of work do you do?" she asked.

"I'm a biochemical engineer. I know, not hard to believe, since I'm Asian, right?" He laughed.

Sharon chuckled. "Oh, you go ahead, now!" She high-fived him. "Let me ask you, do I look like an English Lit professor?"

Xander raised his eyebrows. "I had you pegged for a model."

Sharon laughed, looking like she was finally enjoying herself. "You're too kind."

"Aww thanks." He glanced at Dwayne again. At the far end of the room, he, Nigel, and Laila all appeared to be interested in something on the floor. Xander jerked his head in that direction, and, with Sharon following, went over to see what it was.

***

"There's a loose board," Nigel said, now on his knees, as Xander and Sharon joined them. He brushed away some dirt, then pulled a pocket knife from inside his jacket, and worked the end of its blade into the crack. Using the knife as a lever, he pried the board from its spot.

Everyone tried to lean in for a look.

"Is everything alright over there?" Klaudie called from the doorway. She appeared to have been attempting to engage in conversation with Maxwell, but he didn't seem very interested.

Nigel called back, "Everything's fine, just thought I saw a mouse." He reached into the gap beneath the floorboard, picked up what looked like a book of some sort, and hurriedly tucked it into his jacket. Holding his finger to his lips, he whispered, "We'll look at it later."

The others nodded, and followed him back to Klaudie, who led them all downstairs to the front room.

"It's late, and I know that all of you must be exhausted. Let us retire for the evening. Breakfast will be at 9:00am." She bowed and took her leave.

Once she had gone, Nigel said, "I think I saw a mini bar in the trophy room. I may go have a nightcap. Anyone care to join me?"

"I could use one too," Dwayne said.

The rest of them, even Maxwell, agreed. In the trophy room, Nigel lined up glasses and poured a neat finger of whiskey into each one. He passed them out, then reached into his jacket and produced the book.

"What's that?" Maxwell asked.

"Something we found in the attic," Nigel said. He opened the book. "I believe it's written in Hebrew, but there are handwritten notes in the margins in German that seem to be translating the meaning." he said. As he flipped through the pages, some papers fell out. He picked them up, seeing a Swastika at the top of each. *Nazi documents,* he thought.

No one else had noticed. He shoved the papers back into the book and closed it.

"It's late," he said, finishing his drink. "I'll try to decipher some of this before I turn in for the night, and let you all know what I find out in the morning."

With that, they all headed upstairs to their bedrooms.

Nigel waited until Laila was in the bathroom before he pulled the book out and opened it again.

Beneath the printed title were several handwritten words. His German may have been rusty, but was serviceable enough.

JEWISH MYSTICISM: A BOOK OF SPELLS.

He closed the book and put it on the nightstand.

Interesting, he thought, and began undressing for bed.

Chapter 10

Maxwell couldn't sleep. So many thoughts ran through his mind. Like his problems at work. He had no idea how he was going to replace that $500,000. Eventually, an audit would catch the discrepancy, and he'd be exposed. He was terrified of going to prison.

Then there was Monica. She was truly spectacular. If he went to prison, she'd have nothing further to do with him. He closed his eyes and imagined her there beside him instead of Sharon.

To think, she'd applied to be a teller in the bank lobby, but he'd seen her waiting to speak to the manager and offered her a job as his personal receptionist on the spot. By the time the manager came out to get her for the interview, she was already upstairs in Maxwell's office.

She'd been with him three months now, and they were the happiest he'd ever had. He couldn't wait for her to get to Prague.

Thinking of Monica and how long it might be before he got to see her was depressing, so he shifted to wondering about the book Nigel had shown them earlier. What the fuck was that about? He hadn't really been paying attention in the attic, had been leaning by the door hoping to rest his eyes for a minute. That is, until Klaudie the pest had to disturb him, suggesting he explore the attic with the others. He'd shut her down pretty quickly.

He wished they'd all just leave him alone. The only cool thing he'd seen since being here was that throne in the basement.

His mind focused on the throne, and his earlier notion of returning to the basement to sit in it again. He looked over at Sharon, who was fast asleep. *What the hell,* he thought, *they wanted us to explore, right?*

He got out of bed and put his slippers on, grabbing his jacket to wear over his pajamas. It was cold in this place. Creeping down the hall, he noticed that Nigel and Laila's door wasn't fully closed, so he slowly pushed it open and peered inside.

Nigel and Laila were both asleep. The book on the nightstand caught Maxwell's eye. It was the same one Nigel had shown them downstairs. Silently, he made his way into the room, picked it up, and carried it back to the door. He grinned as he pulled the door closed behind him. He was still pissed off about how they'd treated him at dinner, so, taking the book gave him immense satisfaction.

Of course, he didn't speak Hebrew or German, but figured maybe there were some cool pictures in it or something. *Hell, maybe it's worth something*, he thought. That would be the funniest thing ever, if it was worth a couple of million. It'd solve his problem at work, he could file for divorce, and start over somewhere else with Monica, Costa Rica maybe.

The house was quiet as he headed downstairs. When he got to the basement door, it was closed. Not just closed; a padlock hung on it.

Son of a bitch, he thought. He'd really been looking forward to going down there, kicking back on the throne for a while.

He was pretty sure he'd seen an ax among the weapons in the trophy room. That would take care of the padlock, but left him with two problems. The first was, of course, Klaudie would know it must have been one of the guests. The second was that hitting the lock with an ax would make a lot of noise. Probably wake everyone up. He didn't want to risk getting caught. *No, that won't do*, he thought.

He hung his head in disappointment. Now where would he go? Not back to the room. He needed some light if he was going to look at the book, but the light would wake Sharon.

Then, he had an idea, heading back upstairs and making his way out into the courtyard. The moon was full as he crossed it, reaching the chapel entrance.

Yes, this is where I'm supposed to be, he thought.

On the altar, candelabras awaited him. Someone had even left a lighter conveniently nearby.

He lit the candles. *There, plenty of light,* he thought. He dragged a chair over. The candlelight danced on the walls, making strange shadows.

The unusual murals caught his eye. He walked around the chapel, looking at them. The scenes they depicted were ones of extreme violence, and the figures all appeared to be peering malevolently at him.

It made him slightly uncomfortable, so he went back to the chair and sat. He took a deep breath.

Excitement rose in him as he pulled the book out of his jacket. He had an odd feeling that whatever was in it might be the answer to all of his problems. Briefly closing his eyes, he said a silent prayer to a god he didn't believe in, hoping he'd be able to understand what he was about to read.

Then, Maxwell opened the book.

Chapter 11

Shit! he thought. He couldn't understand any of it. He flipped through its pages. All more of the same, foreign words with very few pictures. *What a waste.*

He tossed the book to the ground. When it landed, it flopped open. Maxwell glanced at it, seeing an image he couldn't believe he'd missed.

The drawing depicted a very vivid image of Hell. Humans were writhing in misery, while demons tormented them, beneath some rough, arched surface with a ragged crack in it. Maxwell guessed this was to show that the people and demons were below the surface of Earth.

Although he didn't believe in any of that stuff, the drawing intrigued him. Below the picture were lines of text in Hebrew, and handwritten German beside it. He wasn't able to read the Hebrew at all. *What a stupid looking language,* he thought to himself. He began trying to sound out the translation, stumbling on the words.

Denn unter der Erde ist die Hölle, der Ort, wo Dämonen wohnen. Der Grat zwischen Gut und Bose ist sehr schmal. Wir müssen vorsichtig sein mit den Worten, die an diesem Ort gesagt werden, wo die Oberfläche dünn ist. Du wirst niemals die Worte sprechen, um diese Oberfläche zu öffnen, oder die Hölle wird auf der Erde sein. Die verbotenen Wörter, die nicht laut ausgesprochen werden dürfen, sind: 'FAC TIBI SUPERFICIEM TUAM, DOMINE TENEBRAE, ET EDUCAM EXERCITUM TUUM, ET SERVIAM TIBI IN AETERNUM'. So steht es geschrieben!

Frustrated, Maxwell shrugged, and dropped the book again. What a load of nonsense. Why whoever wrote the thing to begin with didn't bother to just write it in fuckin' English so people could understand it was beyond him.

He knew it had to mean something important, but how was he supposed to know what it was?

Suddenly, he heard a low rumble as the ground began to shake. *Oh shit! Earthquake?*

Jumping from the chair, he pressed himself to the back wall behind the altar and watched in amazement and horror as a gap opened up in the floor of the chapel.

When the ground stopped rumbling and all was silent, Maxwell stepped forward to get a closer look. The gap was about six inches across, and five feet long. An eerie light shone through it.

Suddenly, three darkly transparent shadows flew up, and Maxwell heard an ear-piercing shriek. He stumbled over his own feet, falling hard on his butt, and continued to scoot backward 'til his back was against the wall.

He covered his ears and squeezed his eyes closed. After a few seconds, it seemed the noise stopped. He hesitantly opened his eyes and looked around.

The shadowy figures were gone, and the crack wasn't glowing anymore.

Maybe I imagined it? he wondered. No, he couldn't have imagined all of it; because the gap in the floor was still there. But maybe the excitement of the quake had caused his mind to play tricks on him.

Getting up, telling himself it was over, his gaze fell on the book, which was still laying on the floor by the chair. A lightbulb went off in Maxwell's head. He couldn't believe it hadn't dawned on him earlier.

He opened the book to the page he'd attempted reading from, placed it on the altar, then pulled his cell phone from his jacket pocket. Downloading a translation app took a few minutes, but when he successfully typed in the letters, and hit 'Translate,' The words came up in English:

ONE HELL OF A VACATION

"For below the Earth is Hell, the place where demons dwell. The line between good and evil is very thin. We must be careful with the words that are said in this place, where the surface is thin. You shall never speak the words to open the surface, or Hell will be upon the Earth. The forbidden words that must not be spoken aloud are: <Translate doesn't recognize this text as German. Suggested translation language: Latin. Would you like to proceed with the suggestion?>"

Maxwell scratched his head. *Latin? I guess the British bastard didn't notice this when flipping through it earlier,* he thought. Shrugging, Maxwell selected 'Yes' and the words that popped up next on the screen made his eyes go wide.

"PART THY SURFACE FOR THEE, MASTER OF DARKNESS, AND I SHALL BRING FORTH YOUR ARMY, AND SERVE YOU FOR ETERNITY."

Oh shit, Maxwell thought. *Did I do that? Did I make the ground open up?*

His mind raced. He wasn't thinking straight. There was no way he could have done that, just by speaking some words out of a stupid old book. He took a deep breath, gathered himself, picked up the book and stuck it inside his jacket. He'd had enough for one evening.

As he started to leave the chapel, one of the murals caught his eye again. It was one he'd already looked at, but something seemed different now.

He changed direction and went over to it. Like before, all of the figures in the mural appeared to be looking directly at him ... but instead of malevolent peers, now they were smiling.

The hair on Maxwell's arms stood on end as he looked around at the other murals. It wasn't just this one. The figures in all the other murals were also smiling at him.

Without further delay, Maxwell rushed from the chapel, across the courtyard, through the first floor, and up the stairs. He didn't stop until he'd reached the safety of his own room.

He took off his jacket and climbed into bed, shaking all over. As he lay there, he gradually began to calm down.

By the time he went to sleep, he'd convinced himself he'd imagined the whole thing.

Chapter 12

Maxwell woke up to the sound of Sharon humming. Why she couldn't just be quiet and let him sleep, he'd never understand. He heard water splash and realized she must be in the bath.

Intense pain shot through his skull as he sat up. Great, just what he needed. Another headache to deal with. He got out of bed and went over to the chair where he'd left his pants the night before. He pulled out his wallet and opened it up, retrieving the little bag of cocaine he'd brought along for the trip.

Listening to make sure that Sharon was still in the bathtub, he sat on the edge of the bed and sprinkled some of the coke out onto the nightstand, cutting the powder into two lines.

Sharon called, "Maxwell, are you up yet?"

Maxwell quickly rolled up a twenty-dollar bill. "Yeah, why?" He snorted the first line.

"I thought I heard you get out of bed. What time is it?" she said.

He looked at his Rolex. "It's 8:30." He snorted the other line of coke, put everything away again, and laid back on the bed to enjoy the rush of the drugs in his system. His headache could fuck off and not come back.

When he got up again and went to the window, he saw it was pouring rain. In the distance, thunder boomed and lightning flashed, a real thunderstorm. He dressed in a lightweight sweater and some jeans, clean socks, and boxers. He'd really wanted to have a quick wash before going to breakfast, but Sharon was taking her time in there.

She came out of the bathroom draped in a towel, smiled at him, and leaned over to give him a kiss. As she did so, he turned his head so it landed on his cheek. She didn't seem to mind.

He watched as she dropped the towel and pulled on clean clothing. She had a nice body, but it was nothing compared to Monica's.

In a dress, with a cardigan tied around her waist in case she got cold later, she twisted her curly hair into a French knot and secured it with pins, little spiral curls escaping at the base of her neck and around her face, softening the look.

"Where did you go last night?" she asked as she began putting on her makeup.

"What do you mean?"

"I mean, where did you go? I woke up and had to use the bathroom and you weren't here."

Maxwell thought for a moment. "I went downstairs to see if I could find a snack in the kitchen."

"Klaudie told us yesterday that there isn't a kitchen in this castle." She folded her arms, doubt written across her face.

"Which is what I was going to say if you had given me a minute to finish my sentence." He rolled his eyes. "I went down there, then remembered what that woman said, so I came back."

"You were gone for over an hour."

"God damn it, Sharon, what is this? Did you time me with a stopwatch? Why do you fuckin' care where I went?" He could feel the headache creeping back.

"I was concerned, that's all. We're in a foreign country, in a castle in the middle of nowhere. I was just worried you might have gotten lost."

For whatever reason, on impulse, he decided to tell her the truth. "You know that book Nigel had last night? The old one he found in the attic?"

"Yes." She scrunched her nose.

"I took it. I took it and I was going to go down and see that throne thing again in the basement, but the door was padlocked shut. So, I went to the chapel instead. I sat there for a while, that's all. This place gives me the creeps though, that's for sure. There was some kind of earthquake, too, and now there's a crack in the floor. I swear Sharon, it was the weirdest thing."

Just saying it out loud made him feel stupid. He wasn't sure he would believe it himself if he were the one hearing it. She probably thought he was making all of it up.

"Why did you take the book?" she asked.

"I just wanted to know what was in it."

"Did it have anything to do with yesterday at dinner?"

"No, Sharon, it had nothing to do with that. I simply wanted a chance to look at the book and Nigel took it with him, which I didn't think was fair, but no one else objected. It's fine. I'll put it back in his room later today. It was all just fun and games."

"What about the crack in the chapel floor?"

"Honestly, it might've already been there. This place is super old, it was dark, and I don't remember looking at the floor before in the first place. It had nothing to do with me reading from the book."

Shit. He hadn't meant to share that last part.

"Reading from the book? I thought it was in German or Hebrew?"

Maxwell covered his tracks quickly. "It is. I tried to pronounce some of it and failed miserably. It was all a joke. No big deal. Aren't you done getting ready yet? I'm hungry."

"Yes, I'm ready," she said. "Let's go down to breakfast."

Chapter 13

Laila woke up to the sound of rummaging. She rubbed her eyes and sat up. Nigel was practically tearing their room apart.

"What are you doing?" she asked.

"I'm looking for the book, it's gone missing."

"Gone missing? What do you mean?"

"It's not where I left it last night."

"But it must be, Nigel. Where would it have gone?"

"I left it on the nightstand, and it isn't there. Did you move it?"

"No, my love, I didn't. I don't think I even knew you left it on the nightstand. You came to bed after me."

Nigel covered his face with his hands. "Yes, that's right. I'm sorry, Laila. I just don't understand what could have happened to it. Books don't get up and walk off by themselves."

"Was it really so important?"

"I was curious. I wanted to read some before going down to breakfast."

"Did you check underneath the bed? Maybe it wasn't sitting properly on the nightstand and fell to the floor." She went around to his side of the bed and got down on all fours, scanning underneath. "Hand me your keys, please?" she asked, knowing he carried a mini-torch on his keychain.

Nigel did so, and she shined the light under the bed, seeing nothing but a few dust bunnies.

Once Laila was standing again, she crossed her arms and looked at her husband. He wore a puzzled expression. "Nigel?" He looked at her. "Are you positive that you left it on the nightstand? You didn't leave it in the lavatory, perhaps?"

"Yes, yes, I'm sure. Why would I leave it there? It's a mighty strange place to leave a book, don't you think?"

"Not necessarily. What if you carried it in there with you when you brushed your teeth last night, and forgot it?" Hoping to solve the mystery, she went into the lavatory and looked around, but again, didn't find the book. "No, nothing in here."

"I told you I didn't take it in there. Are you just looking for ways to prove I'm mad and have me committed?" he teased.

"That's exactly what I'm doing, you old coot! You've caught me!" Laila playfully stuck out her tongue at him.

Nigel slapped her lightly on the rump and leaned in for a kiss. Laila obliged. Then they both laughed.

"Well, we can't worry about a missing book right now, my love," Laila said. "Breakfast is at nine and it's half past eight now. Let's get dressed and get going. We can look some more later."

"I suppose you're right," sighed Nigel. Feeling defeated, he went over to his suitcase, pulled out pants and a long sleeve button down, and began to strip off his pajamas.

Laila admired him while she watched him change into his trousers. Twenty-five years together, and she loved him more every day. Sure, they had disagreements sometimes, but they always managed to work through them.

"So, what do you think of the others?" Nigel asked.

"They all seem pleasant, except for that Maxwell. I really am fond of his wife, though. God bless her for having the strength to put up with him. He needs to be taught a few things about manners, and respect for women. She looked like she wanted to crawl under the table last night at dinner. I wonder how many times he's cracked the same remarks about her not being as good looking as the actress? If you ever said anything like that to me, you'd be wearing my handprint on your cheek."

"I wouldn't dream of ever saying something so cruel, my dear, and you know it. How long do you think they've been together?"

"I gathered not long, but I don't have any supporting facts." Laila retrieved a pair of pearl earrings that had once belonged to her mother from her jewelry pouch, and clipped them on her ears.

"I quite like the other couple, the two men. They seem like nice chaps," said Nigel.

"Oh, me too! That Dwayne has quite a sense of humor, and Xander is just as delightful. I'm looking forward to visiting more with them today and getting to know them better."

"As am I." Nigel checked his watch. "I wonder what we are having for breakfast? I am famished!"

"I could eat something too," said Laila, putting the finishing touches on her hair. She didn't want to fuss with it much today, since it was raining.

She walked back into the bedroom and over to the door to slip on her shoes, and retrieved her glasses from the dresser. "Are you ready to go downstairs, my love?" she asked him.

"Yes, I believe so."

They left their room together, making their way to the stairs arm-in-arm.

As they descended, Laila glanced over at her husband, and could tell his mind was still on the missing book.

He'll never let this go until he solves the mystery, she thought.

ONE HELL OF A VACATION

Chapter 14

A breakfast of omelets, bacon, fruit and toast had been laid out, and Klaudie joined them, as they took their seats.

"I trust everyone rested well, yes?" she asked. Seeing their nods, she smiled. "Wonderful, that makes me very happy. So, today, as promised, I will provide you with some history on the castle while you eat this wonderful breakfast Marek has brought to us."

"Is there any more bacon?" Maxwell interrupted.

Without a word, Xander passed the tray down to him, his eyes never leaving Klaudie.

Klaudie resumed speaking. "In the 9th century, a fort stood upon the very ground where we are sitting. It had fallen into ruins by the time this castle was built, four hundred years later. Its purpose remained somewhat of a mystery. Why build a castle in the middle of a forest, with no water supply, and no kitchen? Then there was the matter of the windows. You may not have noticed, but over half of them are fake, appearing as windows from the outside but only plain walls from within."

"That is rather strange, indeed," said Laila, as several of the others glanced around the structure.

Klaudie paused to take a drink of water. "Most castles are designed to keep enemies or unwanted people out," she continued. "Houska appears to have been built almost the opposite. Almost as if, it seems, to keep someone or something inside.

"There is a legend about this place, regarding the chapel. When the castle was first built, the chapel wasn't there. Instead, it is widely believed that a large pit existed there. It was dark and deep. Many people threw stones and other objects inside and waited for the items to hit the bottom in hopes of finding out just how deep the pit actually was. However, the items never reached the bottom, or if they did, it was so far down that the human ear couldn't hear them hit the bottom.

"At one point, a deal was offered to certain prisoners, the deal of a lifetime to those serving life sentences. All they had to do was agree to be lowered into the pit and report what they saw, and they could go free, their debt to society paid in full."

"Must've been tempting, given the likely conditions of prisons at the time." said Nigel.

Klaudie nodded. "One man did agree, and was lowered into the pit, but within a matter of seconds, he began screaming at the top of his lungs. They quickly pulled him up, and what they saw was shocking. The prisoner, a young man when he went in, appeared to have aged forty years in an instant, his hair turned white as snow. He had also gone completely mad. He was sent to a madhouse, where he died only a few days later."

Sharon pulled her cardigan close around her. "What happened to the pit?" she asked.

"Everyone who'd witnessed it became convinced the pit was a portal to Hell itself. They laid a great slab over it, and built the chapel atop, to keep the evil contained. According to legend, the pit remains hidden under the chapel floor."

Maxwell shifted in his seat. He caught Sharon's gaze, but didn't say anything.

Klaudie looked around at them all. "But an alleged portal to Hell isn't the only legend surrounding this castle, ladies and gentlemen. In the 17th century, during the thirty-year war, forces from the Swedish army seized and occupied the castle. They were led by one Commander Oronto, who was said to be a most despicable man, committing numerous rapes, animal sacrifices, and demonic rituals in the chapel."

Sharon wasn't the only guest to shudder at such a grim revelation.

"After he died -- shot and killed in the front hall by his own men -- the Swedes vacated the castle, and it stood empty until the Nazis took control of it during the 20th century. Legend has it they conducted human experimentation on Jewish hostages. No one knows for sure if that is true, but the Nazis *were* here, and used this place for something.

"Several ghosts are said to reside in this castle," she told them. "Witnesses report having seen a little girl roaming the halls, and a headless man who often appears in the courtyard, as well as several accounts of flying shadowy figures."

"Have you seen any of these things, Klaudie?" Xander asked eagerly.

"Oh yes, many times."

"Aren't you scared?" asked Dwayne.

"I've worked here for many years. I've seen many strange things, some of them very frightening, but I've never been harmed in any way. If I believed there was danger, I would never let guests come here."

The door opened and Marek rolled the cart in to pick up the empty trays and dishes. "I've fresh pots of tea and coffee brewing, which I'll bring in a few moments."

"Thank you, Marek," said Klaudie.

"So, you believe we're all safe and have nothing to worry about?" Nigel asked.

"Yes, yes, of course! You are all perfectly safe. I want you to have a fabulous time here at Houska. Today, the plan is to explore the castle more in depth; I'm sure you didn't get to spend as much time looking around as you all would've liked last night. Also, it was dark, which made things harder to see. Does anyone have questions or particular requests?"

"Actually, yes," Nigel said. "I have something I'd like to discuss."

The others all turned to look at him.

Chapter 15

Nigel cleared his throat. "As some of you know, last night, I found a book in the attic."

Klaudie's forehead wrinkled. "Really? I don't remember seeing a book up there before. What type of book was it?"

"There was a loose floorboard at the far end of the attic. Dwayne and I began messing with it, and when it popped up, the book was hidden inside it."

Dwayne broke in. "We didn't damage anything; the board was already loose. We just used a pocketknife as a lever, and it came right up."

Klaudie nodded, her attention still on Nigel. "But what was this book?"

"It appeared to be written in Hebrew, with a handwritten German translation. I speak German, so my intention was to take a closer look this morning before breakfast. I was exhausted last night, so I left the book on the nightstand, and when I woke up, it wasn't there."

"What do you mean, it wasn't there?" asked Xander.

"I mean exactly that," Nigel said. "It was gone. Laila and I searched our room and didn't find it. It's a mystery to me."

"We are going to look for it again, later," said Laila, and patted her husband on the back. "A book doesn't just walk off on its own, after all. It has to be up there somewhere."

Sharon looked over at Maxwell. He looked back at her, warning her to keep her mouth closed. He'd already told her he would put the book back in the old man's room when no one was around. Then it would simply seem like Nigel had just misplaced it, or was going senile.

"Did you have the chance to learn anything else?" asked Dwayne.

"I only had a chance to look at the title page. According to the translation notes, it's a book on Jewish mysticism," said Nigel. "A book of spells, specifically."

"Spells?" asked Xander.

"As in, witchcraft?" Dwayne shared an excited look with Xander.

"Yes, I believe so." Nigel replied.

Xander and Dwayne exchanged a high-five.

"We love all this occult stuff," Dwayne said, by way of explanation.

Xander nodded, grinning. "Our first date was to a haunted house in Detroit. I mean, okay, maybe ghosts are real, maybe they're not, but it's fun to investigate, a hobby we can enjoy as a couple."

Sharon seethed in guarded silence. She was furious with her husband for taking the book from Nigel's room, and at having to pretend she knew nothing about it, essentially making her an accomplice in the theft.

Then there was what he'd told her about what had happened in the chapel, especially considering the history Klaudie had just related. Not knowing that the book he'd stolen contained spells frightened her. Sure, he'd insisted it was just a dream or exaggeration, but how could he know?

And a crack appearing in the chapel floor that Maxwell claimed he didn't remember being there before? What if it was all somehow connected?

She decided to stay quiet for the moment, but the minute she was alone with Maxwell, she would encourage him to put the book back in Nigel's room, like he'd promised, and let the whole thing drop.

"I certainly hope this book is found," said Klaudie. "I'd like to have a look at it myself."

"Absolutely. Once we find it, you'll be the first to know," Nigel said. "It certainly wasn't our intention to keep the existence of the book a secret from you. We only just found it last night, right before bed."

With a discreet tap on the door, Marek brought in the tea and coffee on his cart, along with spoons, cups, creamer and sugar.

Everyone gladly helped themselves to the carafes of caffeine, with no more to be said at the moment on the subject of missing books.

***

Outside, the wind had picked up, and it was still raining buckets. Laila stared out the window and a shiver ran down her spine. She was thankful to be inside, enjoying her tea with the group.

She could feel the tension in her husband beside her. He clearly was still quite upset that the book was missing.

Maybe he hadn't misplaced it. Maybe someone took it.

She looked around at each of the people sitting at the table. It couldn't have been Klaudie, of course. She hadn't even known about the book until a few minutes ago. Xander and Dwayne were excited about the book's contents, but if they'd taken it, what would've been their motive? As far as Laila knew, neither of them could speak Hebrew or German, so they wouldn't have been able to read it. *No, they hadn't taken it,* Laila thought to herself.

Which left her with Sharon and Maxwell. Sharon was the sweetest woman; there was no way she'd have done anything of the sort. Maxwell, on the other hand? First, there had been that small altercation between him and Nigel at dinner the night before ... maybe Maxwell had taken the book to get back at Nigel for defending Sharon? That seemed plausible. But she very much doubted Maxwell spoke any foreign languages either, so the book would have been useless to him. Unless he'd taken it thinking it was worth money? She had no idea what the book was worth, but it was old, and might bring something to a collector.

Had Sharon said what he did for a living? Laila didn't think so, but they didn't look like they were hard up, not with that Rolex on his wrist.

ONE HELL OF A VACATION

Klaudie stood up. "Is everyone finished? If so, maybe we should look around some more, now that we have time and daylight, yes?"

Xander and Dwayne practically jumped out of their chairs. Sharon and Maxwell were next, followed by Nigel and Laila. They followed Klaudie back into the hall, for a more thorough exploration of Houska.

Chapter 16

Having already seen all of this shit yesterday, Maxwell quickly found himself bored as Klaudie went rattling on about the symbolic crests in the room adjacent to the trophy room.

No one cares, Maxwell thought. He rolled his eyes.

He glanced up and saw Laila watching him. This was the third time he'd caught her. He knew he was good looking, but wasn't interested in her, if that was what she had in mind. He decided to tease her a little anyway, lifting his hand to give her a mini secret wave and a wink. She quickly looked away from him. He laughed to himself.

Strolling ahead of the group, he pulled out his phone to text Monica, but she'd beaten him to it.

THIS HOTEL ROOM IS AMAZING, BABY! I CAN'T WAIT TO SEE YOU. XXX

Maxwell smiled. NOT AS AMAZING AS YOU ARE, SEXY. I'M GLAD YOU LIKE IT. WHAT ARE YOUR PLANS FOR THE DAY?

I THOUGHT I'D GO OUT AND EXPLORE THE CITY A LITTLE. SEE IF I CAN FIND THEIR MAIN SHOPPING AREAS. LOL

ONE HELL OF A VACATION

LOL. OF COURSE. I KNEW YOU'D ZERO IN ON THE SHOPPING. HOPE YOU FIND SOME WONDERFUL STUFF. YOU HAVE THE CREDIT CARD WITH YOU, RIGHT?

It was a Discover card Sharon didn't know about, which he'd given to Monica. Easier than remembering to give her cash all the time, so he just paid the bill every month. She never spent large amounts on it anyway.

YEAH. I HAVE IT WITH ME.

FIND SOMETHING PRETTY TO WEAR FOR ME, OKAY?

I THINK I CAN MANAGE THAT. ANY SPECIAL REQUESTS?

SOMETHING BLUE, I THINK.

I'LL SEE WHAT I CAN FIND. ANY IDEA WHEN YOU WILL BE ABLE TO GET AWAY FROM THERE?

I'M WORKING ON IT.

OK MAXIE. IT'S JUST THAT THIS BED IS SO BIG AND EMPTY WITHOUT YOU HERE. IT'S RAINING HERE TOO, SO IT WOULD BE A PERFECT DAY TO SNUGGLE UP WITH YOU IN THE ROOM.

I KNOW IT. I'LL TRY MY HARDEST TO MAKE IT THERE BY EVENING. WE'LL GO SOMEWHERE FABULOUS FOR DINNER, THEN SPEND THE REST OF THE NIGHT IN BED. OR IF IT'S STILL RAINING, WE'LL JUST ORDER ROOM SERVICE. I MISS YOU.

I MISS YOU TOO, MAXIE. LOVE YOU. XXX

LOVE YOU TOO, MON.

Instead of putting him in a better mood, the text conversation with Monica had made things worse. He wanted out of here, and fast. He looked around. The group must've moved on to some other place without him.

He found them a few minutes later, in the basement. Which, Klaudie was explaining, was apparently subject to a ton of paranormal activity. About six out of every ten people who visited it claimed to have had strange experiences.

Weirdos. Maxwell loved the basement. And he loved that throne. He walked over to it, admiring it. He took a seat. Yes, there it was, that same wonderful feeling he had last time he'd sat here.

The others stared at him. He ignored them, and sat with his eyes closed, almost in a trance.

Until, of course, Sharon had to run her mouth. "Maxwell, I don't think you are supposed to sit there."

He opened his eyes, annoyed. "Why not?"

"It just seems ... disrespectful. It looks old. What if you damage it?"

"It's a chair! Or throne, or whatever. It's meant to be sat on by someone. Why shouldn't that someone be me?"

"I'm quite surprised you'd want to sit there, " said Klaudie. "Most people are too afraid."

"Yeah, well, I'm not afraid of anything," said Maxwell.

But he got up and headed for the stairs, hoping it would get the tour moving along again. Then it would be over sooner, and he could find an excuse to get the hell out of there.

***

Instead of crossing the open courtyard, they skirted the covered walkway all the way around to avoid being soaked by the rain.

Klaudie opened the door to the chapel and everyone went inside.

It looked much as it had before, except for a chair which had been in the corner now being over in front of the altar.

Then they all noticed the crack in the floor.

"Oh, my goodness, what in the world?" wondered Laila.

"It was not like this," said Klaudie, seeming troubled.

"Maybe the thunder shook the building, causing the ground to destabilize," Dwayne suggested.

"Or maybe the pit to Hell has opened," said Xander, laughing.

When no one else laughed, his face turned pink with embarrassment. Dwayne took his hand for reassurance.

"A small earthquake?" Nigel offered. "Do they have earthquakes here, Klaudie?"

"I'm sure we must, but none I've felt, and certainly none that have caused damage." Her forehead wrinkled with concern.

Sharon shot a look at Maxwell. He shrugged and rolled his eyes. She gestured with her eyes towards Klaudie. Maxwell shook his head.

Stubborn man, she thought. So, the crack was new, and her husband may have had something to do with it. *Great.*

Klaudie circled the rest of the chapel, looking for more damage, but couldn't find any. The others were still in the middle of the chapel, inspecting the crack. Nigel had pulled out a measuring tape.

He looked up. "Six inches wide. But it doesn't go the entire length of the floor, which I assume it would if it had been an earthquake."

"Let's go somewhere else," Klaudie said. "Until the floor is inspected, it might not be safe for us to be in here."

Chapter 17

As everyone trudged up the stairs toward the attic, Maxwell figured it would be his best chance to deal with the book.

"Sharon, my head is killing me," he said. "I think I'm going to skip the rest of the tour and go lay down for a bit."

"I have some Paracetamol if you'd like," offered Laila.

"What's that?" he asked.

"It's Tylenol, dear. The English version," Sharon told him.

"Oh. Yeah, that would be great. Thanks."

Laila reached into a pocket of her skirt and pulled out a little travel-sized packet, and handed it to him.

Maxwell took it, thanked her again, and headed to his own room.

Once inside, he waited a bit to give them a chance to get upstairs, then retrieved the book, checked the hallway, and hurried to Nigel and Laila's room. Thankfully, the door was unlocked. A chair piled with what looked to be the clothes Nigel had worn the previous day seemed a promising place, where the book might have been easily overlooked.

With that taken care of, he could work on an exit plan. As bad as he would like to, he didn't think he could get away this evening. With the rain, and all that had gone on with the crack in the chapel etc., he was tired. He didn't want to go see Monica just to fall asleep early, defeating the purpose of going to see her in the first place.

He figured he better call her, talk to her over the phone rather than text. With no one around, it was the perfect opportunity.

He dialed her number and she answered quickly. "Maxie? Are you on your way?"

"Hey, Mon. No, baby. I think I'm going to have to wait until tomorrow." He knew she was going to be disappointed.

"But why?" she whined. "This day is already turning out to be super shitty. I went out to get a cab to go shopping and got splashed by water and soaked to the bone, so I came back to the hotel to wait for you. That's all I care about anyway."

"I'm sorry, Mon. I really want to come and see you. There's just been a lot going on here. Some weird stuff. Sharon is a little freaked out, and if I leave right now, she'll be suspicious. I don't need to have a big fight with her today. I just don't think I can handle it. I didn't sleep very well last night, and

I'm tired. If we wait for tomorrow, we'll have a much better time together. You don't want me to fall asleep right when I get there, do you?"

"I guess not. I'm just bored. Now I have no idea what to do for the rest of the night."

"Call room service and order some champagne," he said. "Get undressed and take a nice long bubble bath. Listen to some soft relaxing music, and imagine I'm there. What do you think of that idea?"

"It might not be a bad idea," she pouted. Then, with hope in her voice, "But Maxie, you promise you'll be here tomorrow? If you leave me stuck in this hotel room all by myself the whole time, I will go insane."

"I promise, baby. I'll be there tomorrow, just as early as I can get away."

"Okay. I trust you," said Monica.

"That's my girl. I'll talk to you soon. Love you."

"I love you more." Monica giggled and made kiss sounds before she hung up.

I'm a lucky man, Maxwell thought. He lay back on the bed with his arms folded underneath his head. Yes, tomorrow morning would be a good time to get away. He'd just have to find out what the plan was, so he'd have a better idea of when to leave. *Hell, I might not come back,* he thought.

Since he didn't get much sleep the night before, it didn't take long for him to drift off into dreamland. Visions of Monica naked danced through his head, along with piles and piles of money. He was on the verge of things finally working out. This trip was the key. What happened with the book, well, it must have been a sign. This place was trying to tell him something. He just didn't know what that something was yet.

It would all work out. It always did.

When he awoke, Sharon was there with him.

"Hey dear, just wanted to check on you," she said.

"I'm feeling a lot better."

"You've been asleep for hours. You slept all the way through dinner. But I brought you a plate."

He looked over and saw a plate sitting on the dresser. "Thanks," he said, rolling over.

"I'm going back down to have tea with Nigel and Laila. I'll be back in a bit."

Maxwell didn't reply. He was already almost asleep again.

Chapter 18

Sharon found Nigel and Laila already having tea. Laila poured her a cup and handed it to her. She took a seat and added some creamer. None of them said anything, content to have silence for a moment.

Finally, Laila spoke. "How was Maxwell?"

"He was still asleep. I woke him up briefly to let him know I'd brought him a plate of food. He went right back to sleep after that."

"Do you know if he had a fever?" asked Nigel.

"I didn't check. But he must be sick to have slept all day long. Either that, or the long trip exhausted him, and he needed the extra rest."

Klaudie peered in. "Having tea?" she asked.

"Yes," said Laila. "Would you like some?"

"That would be wonderful," Klaudie said, joining them as Laila poured her a cup "Thank you."

"We were just talking about Maxwell," said Sharon. "He's still sleeping."

"However," Nigel said brightly, "I have news! We went back to our room to give it another quick once over, and guess what?!" He was so excited he could hardly stand it.

"We found the bloody book," said Laila, laughing. "It was underneath Nigel's pile of dirty clothes on a chair."

"I'm sure that's not where I left it, Laila, like I told you before," he said.

Laila patted his knee. "Well, it hardly matters. What matters is that we've found it." She took the book from her bag and held it out toward Klaudie, who looked but didn't touch, so then she passed it to Nigel.

He flipped through, stopping now and then to examine certain passages, then looked up at them.

"It does indeed claim to be a book of spells," he said. "There seems to be a spell for everything you can think of in here. Whether you want to fall in love, have money, hurt someone, or grow a rather impressive garden, this book will tell you how to do it."

"Couldn't something like that be dangerous?" asked Klaudie.

"Well, assuming magic is real." Nigel chuckled. "Since we found it hidden in the attic, it does lead one to assume that it is historically authentic. But that leads to another question: Who put it there?"

Sharon stayed silent, sipping her tea. The guilt was eating her alive. If magic *was* real, and there were spells in the book that could have caused the crack in the floor of the chapel, she knew she should tell Klaudie. Maxwell had had no idea what he was doing and might have unknowingly put all of them in harm's way.

"A good question," said Klaudie, answering Nigel. "Maybe the Nazis left the book behind. That seems plausible."

They all agreed. Nigel set his empty cup on the table and folded his arms, deep in thought.

"What are you going to do about the crack in the chapel floor?" Laila asked.

"I'm not sure yet," she replied. "We may need to figure out what caused it to begin with, before we can see how to fix it."

"Are we *sure* it wasn't there last night?" asked Sharon, almost woefully. She really hoped they had overlooked it, perhaps because it was dark. Anything to get Maxwell off the hook for causing it.

"We couldn't have missed a crack like that," said Laila. "Even if we hadn't noticed it, Klaudie surely would have. Or Amalie, the maid, who goes in there to clean."

"Yes, she does," said Klaudie. "And yes, we would have noticed it, had it been there last night."

Nigel yawned. "Well, on that note, I believe we should retire to our room."

"My goodness, it's half past nine!" said Laila. They both got up. "What time is breakfast?"

"Same as today, 9:00am," Klaudie said. "It's not supposed to rain tomorrow, so after breakfast, maybe we will take a tour of the grounds. My brother, Jakub, will be here to guide us."

"Perfect! I'm looking forward to some fresh air after having been cooped up inside all day today," said Nigel.

Laila nodded in agreement. After bidding Klaudie and Sharon a good night, they headed upstairs.

Sharon wrestled with her thoughts. Now was the perfect opportunity to tell Klaudie what Maxwell had done. But something was holding her back.

What if Klaudie got upset at her?

She'd have no reason to, Sharon told herself. *I have no control over what Maxwell does*. Finally deciding, Sharon sat up straight and cleared her throat.

Just then, Amalie came into the room. "Sorry to interrupt," she said. "I came to clear the cups if you are through with them. Marek is about to leave for the evening and wants to take them with him for washing."

Klaudie smiled. "You're not interrupting at all, dear. Of course, you may take them." She paused, in thought. "Actually, you showed up at the perfect time. We were speaking about the crack in the chapel floor."

"What crack?"

Klaudie glanced at Sharon. "Never mind, dear."

Amalie gathered the cups quickly and left the room.

"Well, that settles it. The crack wasn't there yesterday, or Amalie surely would have noticed it," Klaudie said.

Now, thought Sharon. Before she could talk herself out of it again, she said, "Klaudie, I have to tell you something."

Chapter 19

The words flew out of her mouth like vomit. "I should have mentioned this before, I really should have. I'm sorry. I think my husband did something. Something bad. Maybe. I mean, I'm not sure." She was out of breath.

Klaudie gently patted her arm. "Slow down, slow down!. What has you so frazzled? I'm sure we can take care of whatever the problem is, dear."

Sharon looked Klaudie in the eyes. She saw warmth. It gave her strength to keep talking. "Last night, I woke up some time in the middle of the night, and Maxwell was gone. I couldn't go back to sleep right away, because I was worried, thinking he had wandered off and gotten lost. He was gone for more than an hour. But eventually, I dozed off before he came back. This morning, I questioned him, and he made up a story about going looking for something to eat in the kitchen. Of course, I remembered you told us there wasn't a kitchen, so I knew he wasn't telling the truth. I confronted him and he caved and told me where he'd really been."

"And what did he say?" asked Klaudie.

"After I fell asleep last night, Maxwell got up and went to Nigel and Laila's room. He said the door was open, so he snuck inside and took the book. He told me he'd planned to go down to the basement to read it, but when he got there, the door was closed, with a padlock on it. Not wanting to come back to the room and risk waking me up, he decided to go to the chapel instead."

Klaudie's expression suggested she had a bad feeling she knew where this story was going, but she continued listening.

"He told me he looked at the book, but obviously he doesn't know Hebrew or German. Joking around, he tried to stumble through a couple of paragraphs aloud. Afterward, he heard a rumbling sound and a high-pitched scream, and he saw the crack open up on the floor."

Klaudie kept listening, somberly.

"I'm pretty sure he was scared out of his mind when it happened, but he'd never admit it. After the screams and rumbling quit, he thought the same thing Nigel did, that maybe it had been an earthquake. But it seems like a big coincidence that the crack appeared when he read a passage from that book of spells."

"Do you know which passage it was?" Klaudie asked.

"No. And now he's saying it was all a joke or a dream, and he's certain the crack was already there."

"I know he's not feeling well, Sharon, but it's important we find out."

"Okay, let's go talk to him," said Sharon.

***

The last thing Sharon wanted to do was wake Maxwell up again, but she couldn't argue with Klaudie.

When they got to the room, though, Maxwell was actually awake, still in bed and picking at the plate she'd brought him. He looked up, irritation creasing his brow.

"What?" he asked.

"I told Klaudie about what happened last night," Sharon said in a rush, eager to get it over with.

"What the hell, Sharon? I knew I couldn't trust you to keep your big mouth closed."

"Maxwell, I need to know which passage you read from the book," Klaudie said. "Do you remember?"

"No, I don't remember. It was late, and I was just fooling around. I don't understand why everyone is making such a big deal about some old book."

"It may be important," pressed Klaudie.

"Fine," he grumbled. "Hand me my phone, Sharon. It's on the dresser."

Sharon retrieved Maxwell's phone from the dresser and handed it to him. He typed in his password and opened the translation app he'd downloaded the night before, the passage and translation saved in its memory.

He handed the phone to Klaudie, whose face turned ashen as her eyes scanned the screen. She handed the phone to Sharon, who examined the passage as well. She looked up at her husband in horror. "Oh Maxwell, what have you done?"

He snatched his phone away and turned it off. "It's not a big deal, okay? You can't tell me either of you actually believe me reading from the book had anything to do with the crack. That's absurd."

Klaudie looked at him. "Mr. Stone, I understand that in your culture, God is not a high priority. Americans don't believe in much, except their right to bear arms, apparently. In this country, it's a different story. We believe in God. Some of us believe in more than one God, and some of us believe in spirits. But one thing is consistent: we all believe in evil. The history of the chapel has a bad reputation, and now, you may very well have unleashed something because of your careless actions. Please do not insinuate that what I believe is ignorant."

With that, Klaudie turned and left the room.

Sharon covered her face with her hands. "Oh Maxwell, what have you done?" she repeated. "Now Klaudie is upset with us. You should have left all of this alone."

"No, Sharon! You should have kept your fuckin' mouth shut like I told you to! But of course, I should have known that you wouldn't. If anyone is to blame, it's you."

She flinched from his words and his tone.

"If you'd been the least bit considerate last night, you might have thought about me for once. Here we are, on vacation, and what do you do? Oh, that's right, you curl up in the bed and go to sleep. What a fine wife you are. You never even thought about my needs. When was the last time we fucked? Do you even remember?"

"Maxwell, please! I don't want to fight with you. I just want to go to bed," she said, warily, heading for the bathroom to take off her makeup.

Chapter 20

Klaudie paced back and forth with her phone in her hand, trying to calm down. She couldn't believe what that idiot, Maxwell, had done!

Finally, she sat down on the edge of the bed and called her brother.

Jakub answered on the third ring. "Klaudie? What's wrong? Why are you calling so late?"

"I think I have a big problem here," she said.

"What's happened? Do you need me to come over? Mother is asleep, so I can get away if you do."

"The guests," she said. "One of them found something in the attic. An old book, under a floorboard. He took it to his room, meaning to study it. But then another guest -- a very obnoxious man -- stole it during the night and went down to the chapel. He read a passage out loud and now, there is a crack in the floor, right in the center. Right in the center." Klaudie took a breath.

"But that's where the..."

"I know."

"Who is this man? And what did he read, exactly?"

"Maxwell is his name. He's been nothing but trouble since he arrived. He makes everyone uncomfortable, including his wife. And yes, he just showed me what he read."

She told him, and heard long silence from the other end of the phone before Jakub finally spoke again. "Klaudie, this is bad. Very bad. What are we going to do?"

"I don't know. Maybe the crack is a coincidence, nothing to do with --"

"You don't believe that any more than I do," he said.

"What time will you be here tomorrow?" Klaudie asked.

"As soon as I can. I have to feed Mother, and take care of some of the chores around the farm, but then I'll be there," Jakub said.

"How is Mother?" Klaudie asked.

"About the same. She sleeps mostly, and eats less than a bird. But she's happy."

"I need to come visit, but it's hard to get away because of the guests," she said.

"I know, Klaudie. Stop worrying. You'll get down here to see her eventually. In the morning, I'll call Irenka and ask if she can come stay with Mother while I'm at the castle."

"Thank you, Jakub, I'm so sorry to ask for your help on this. I don't know what else to do."

"Don't worry about it, my sister. I'm always here to help. I was coming anyway to lead your guests on a tour of the grounds; might as well stick around awhile. If for nothing else, to keep this Maxwell person in line."

"I'll let you get some sleep now," said Klaudie.

"Goodnight," Jakub said. "I'll see you in the morning."

Klaudie ended the call, and laid the phone on her nightstand. At her vanity table, she unpinned her long, silky, raven black hair and brushed it smooth.

Her thoughts went back to the book again, and the passage. As hard as it was to believe that Maxwell may have opened a portal to Hell, that was exactly what she feared.

Klaudie picked up a blue jar from the vanity and unscrewed the lid. Night cream was her favorite. She carefully and purposefully rubbed it in circles onto her face. She began to relax.

Jakub would help her make things right. He always knew what to do.

She screwed the lid back on the night cream and rose from her seat at the vanity, unbuttoning her dress. She stepped out of it, leaving it in a pile on the floor. She was too tired to pick it up tonight.

Naked, Klaudie went to the bed and pulled back the thick quilt and sheets. She stretched her arms above her head and twisted from side to side, hoping to release some of the stress of the day. She may have been pushing sixty, but she'd always taken care of herself.

Ready for bed, she slid beneath the cool sheets, her skin tingling from the sensation. She closed her eyes and concentrated on her breathing, just as she'd been doing for the last thirty years. She pretended her head weighed nothing against her pillow.

All of the thoughts that had plagued Klaudie's brain floated away and she finally slept.

She wasn't aware of the shadowy figure slipping under her door. She wasn't aware when it floated under her cool sheets and wrapped itself around her, sliding in and out and underneath and between, violating her body.

ONE HELL OF A VACATION

As the dark entity moved, Klaudie lay perfectly still, but her eyes twitched beneath their lids and a frown appeared on her face, as if she were having a bad dream.

But it was no dream. It was real. Something evil was in bed with her.

She woke with a start, breathing heavily, but nothing was there.

The shadow figure was gone, having vanished back into the night.

Chapter 21

Jakub awoke the next morning with a sense of dread.

He was going to the castle today. He got out of bed and put on his trousers and boots. Setting about doing his morning chores around the farm, he tried to keep his mind off of what was to come.

Last on his list of chores was the hen house, where he gathered fresh eggs for breakfast. He wasn't hungry, but knew he needed to eat, and more importantly, so did his mother.

Walking back into the cottage, he put the eggs on the table and went to check on his mother. She was still sleeping peacefully. He hated waking her, never knowing if she would remember him, or if she would be having a bad day. The bad days were awful and broke his heart.

"Good morning, Mother," he said in a soothing voice, taking her hand.

She opened her eyes and looked at him. Slowly, a smile came over her face. Thank God; it was going to be a good day. He wasn't sure he could've handled the other, especially knowing he was leaving her to go to the place he hated the most.

Jakub helped her out of bed and over to her favorite chair. Once she was comfy, with her favorite blanket in her lap, he asked, "Are you hungry, Mother? Would you like some eggs for breakfast?"

She nodded. He put some music on for her to listen to while he prepared the meal. As he was finishing up, the door opened and his sister, Irenka appeared. He asked her if she wanted some and she told him no. He prepared two plates and quickly ate his portion in three bites before taking the second plate into the bedroom.

Irenka came into the bedroom and took the plate from him. "Go, Jakub," Irenka said. "Klaudie needs you at the castle. I will take care of Mother."

Without another word, he leaned in and kissed his mother on the forehead, gathered his things, and went to the barn. He mounted his horse, Blesk, and they took off in the direction of the castle.

***

Marek had just served breakfast to the guests when Jakub arrived.

Klaudie ran to the stable to greet her younger brother. He picked her up, swinging her around in a circle, as she laughed at him to put her down. He hugged his sister tightly. She was closest in age to him, and they'd always shared a special bond.

"Are you still hungry? The guests just sat down to eat," she told him.

"Of course, I'm still hungry!" Jakub quickly secured Blesk and followed her inside.

Six people were gathered around the table when they walked in. Klaudie ushered Jakub to take a seat, fetched a clean plate from the cart, loaded it with bacon, eggs and a roll, and set it in front of him.

"Thank you, Klaudie," he said.

"This is my brother, Jakub," Klaudie told her guests. "He will be taking you on a tour of the grounds this morning."

As he picked up his fork, scanning the faces of the others in the room, his gaze landed on the most beautiful woman he'd ever seen in his life. He set his fork down.

Her skin was a buttery caramel color. Her hair hung in long flowing dark tendrils. And her eyes ... well, Jakub would become lost quickly in them. He had to tear his eyes away from her to avoid seeming rude.

ONE HELL OF A VACATION

In that moment, he felt like a young boy. Klaudie did a round of introductions, while he tried to recover his wits. Two men, one of them Asian, the other black, appeared to be a couple. An older white couple looked to be in their late seventies or early eighties. A grumpy white man seemed to be giving him dirty looks.

And then there was the goddess sitting across from him. Jakub's dream woman.

Several said hello to him and he tried engaging with everyone as he ate, but his eyes kept being drawn back to her. When she politely asked if he lived nearby, Jakub felt his face heat up. He wasn't sure he would be able to answer, but Klaudie helped him out.

"Yes, very close," she said. "What does it take, thirty minutes by horse?"

Jakub nodded. What the hell was the matter with him? He was behaving like a child. He needed to get out of there, at least for a moment, to gather himself.

"Speaking of horses," he said, getting up, "I'm going to go check on Blesk and get him some water."

He quickly exited, and didn't stop until he was safely outside of the castle walls.

***

Sharon wasn't sure what to make of the man she'd just met. His stare made her uncomfortable, but not necessarily in a bad way. She sat silently, waiting for everyone to be finished with their breakfast.

When they were done, Klaudie addressed them.

"Do any of you need to change clothing or get anything from your rooms before the tour?" she asked.

"Let me just go up and grab my scarf," Sharon said.

Maxwell tagged along with her, but by the time she'd found the scarf and wrapped it around her neck -- *Much better!* -- she turned to see him lying down on the bed.

"Maxwell, come on, they're waiting for us," she said.

"I'm not going," he told her. "My headache has come back. I'm just going to stay here and get some more sleep."

Not wanting to argue with him, Sharon kissed him on the cheek before leaving the room.

Chapter 22

Maxwell's presence was not missed during their tour of the grounds. Although it was still cloudy, the rain had stopped, and it was a pleasant outing. Jakub kept a close eye on Sharon, making sure she didn't linger too far behind. Once, he even saved her from falling in the mud, which she was ever so grateful for.

The tour took just under three hours, and although everyone had a good time, they were more than ready to get back and have a bite to eat for lunch. Klaudie waved at them from the front steps as they walked the last few hundred feet up the road.

"Did you have a nice time?" she called.

"It was awesome!" said Xander. Dwayne and the others nodded.

"Wonderful! Perhaps you'd all like to freshen up and meet down in the front room in half an hour for some lunch?" Klaudie asked them.

Again, everyone eagerly agreed. The others followed Klaudie back into the castle, but Sharon lingered behind. She watched Jakub as he brushed his horse and fed him an apple.

"What's his name?" she asked.

"Blesk."

"That's unusual. Is it Czech?"

"Yes. It means Lightning. He's a very fast horse."

"He's beautiful," Sharon told him.

Jakub turned to look at her. Again, he felt himself drowning in the depth of her brown eyes. He couldn't speak.

"Well, I guess I'll go in and check on my husband," she said after a moment. "I'll see you inside."

***

Such a sweet man, Sharon thought as she headed for the stairs. She hoped he would hang around for a bit so she could get to know him better.

Reaching her room, she quietly turned the knob, in case Maxwell was still sleeping.

He wasn't in bed.

"Maxwell?"

The bathroom door was closed. Sharon knocked softly. "Maxwell, honey, are you in there?"

No answer. She opened the door, and the bathroom was empty.

Turning around, she noticed all of Maxwell's things were gone, including his suitcase. Sharon frowned, and left the room. She found the others downstairs and immediately headed over to Klaudie.

"Klaudie, have you seen Maxwell?" she asked.

"No ... I thought he was in your room, resting."

"As did I. But he isn't. I just went up to check on him, and he's gone. And not just him, all of his belongings too." Her hands were shaking and she felt like she was going to start crying. This was supposed to be their vacation, and a chance to fix their marriage. So why would he leave?

"But where could he have gone, dear?" asked Laila. "He couldn't have left on foot, surely; did someone pick him up?"

"I didn't hear any cars arrive," said Klaudie. "Let me go ask Marek and Amalie."

Nigel wandered over. "What's the matter? Why the long faces?"

"Maxwell has disappeared," Laila told him.

"Disappeared? What do you mean?" he asked.

"I went upstairs to check on him after we got back from the tour, and our room was empty. He and his things are gone." Not being able to hold back any longer, Sharon began to cry.

Just then, Jakub walked in, asking cheerfully, "What's for lunch?" He immediately noticed Sharon crying and went over to her, as did Xander and Dwayne.

Laila led Sharon to a chair, where she sat and put her head in her hands, as Laila explained to the others. Moments later, Klaudie returned, followed by Amalie.

"Neither Marek nor Amalie saw or heard anything, either," Klaudie said. "Did he leave a note or anything?"

"I don't know." Sharon sniffled. "I saw that he and his things were gone, and I came downstairs straight away." She felt a bit foolish for not thinking of it herself

"I'll go look," Nigel volunteered.

"We'll go with you," said Xander, Dwayne by his side.

Jakub brought a cup of tea for Sharon. She gave him a half-hearted smile. Laila and Klaudie sat with her.

"What if they don't find a note?" asked Laila. "Do we notify the authorities?"

"In America, we have to wait twenty-four hours before the police will take a missing persons report," said Sharon, staring into the teacup.

"It's not like that here," said Jakub. "We will let the authorities know he is missing, but that he also took his belongings, and they will then keep an eye out for him."

Nigel, Xander and Dwayne came back into the room, shaking their heads. "We searched the whole bedroom. There wasn't a note," Nigel said.

"Klaudie and I will go call the police," Jakub said.

***

As soon as they were out in the hall and alone, Klaudie turned to him. "Why do you think he would have left?" she asked.

"I don't know," said Jakub.

"It's either because they are having problems, or because of what happened in the chapel, one of those two things. That's what I think," said Klaudie.

"I hardly had any interaction with him at all," said Jakub. "But what I wonder is, why is a woman like Sharon with a man like Maxwell in the first place?"

"Trust me, we've all wondered the same thing," Klaudie said dryly, as she went to her room to get her phone.

Chapter 23

Dinner, like lunch, was eaten in mostly silence. Sharon sat and stared at her plate, but hardly touched her food, no matter how much Laila and Klaudie encouraged her.

As expected, the police hadn't had much advice to offer. They promised to send an officer out to patrol the grounds, but because Maxwell's things were missing, they could only presume he had left on his own, and didn't feel he would be found in the vicinity of the castle.

Jakub had called Irenka and asked her to stay the night with Mother, to which she'd gladly agreed. Amalie was making up a spare room for him.

Meanwhile, Xander wouldn't stop fussing over Dwayne. He seemed to have a rash of some sort and couldn't stop scratching his arms. Xander told the others he suspected that Dwayne had gotten into something poisonous while out touring the grounds. Xander himself also complained of a raging headache, which some of Laila's Paracetamol didn't even take the edge off of.

Klaudie had announced that this evening, the group would be free to do whatever they wished. Sharon knew that

Klaudie had done this out of consideration for her situation with Maxwell being gone.

As Marek came in to clear the dishes away, Sharon heard her cell phone make its familiar noise. She quickly picked it up, and saw a text from Maxwell.

HEY SHARON, I'M SURE YOU'RE PISSED OFF AT ME. I HAD TO GET SOME WORK DONE, SO I DECIDED TO LEAVE FOR A DAY OR TWO BUT I'M CLOSE BY. I'LL BE IN TOUCH. DON'T WORRY ABOUT ME. - MAXWELL.

She felt her blood begin to boil. Worry and sadness turned to anger. How dare he just up and leave her without notice, without a word? While they were on vacation?! In a foreign country, no less!

"Sharon, are you alright?" asked Jakub.

She handed her phone to him without a word. Jakub took it and read the text. His eyebrows raised. He set the phone down on the table as he chewed the side of his face. "Asshole," he muttered, under his breath but not so far under his breath for her not to hear.

Sharon picked up the phone and typed out a hasty reply to her no longer missing husband.

YOU ARE A SELFISH PRICK. WE'LL NEVER WORK OUT OUR PROBLEMS IF YOU ARE ALWAYS ABSENT.

She re-read it, quickly deleted what she'd written, and tried again.

MAXWELL, PLEASE COME BACK. I'M WORRIED ABOUT YOU. US. OUR MARRIAGE. WE NEED THIS TIME TO FIGURE THINGS OUT.

This time she hit 'Send' and abruptly stood up from her chair, tipping it backward onto the floor with a clatter. "Will you all please excuse me for the evening? I'm going to lie down," she said.

Before Sharon could take her leave, Dwayne stood up from his chair and announced that he would be returning to his room as well. Xander looked up at his husband with a confused expression, before standing and following Dwayne out of the room. Sharon hurried off behind them.

***

Jakub knew he shouldn't, knew it was a bad idea and none of his business, but couldn't help himself, as he went upstairs and knocked on Sharon's door.

"Come in," she said, her voice muffled.

He opened the door and saw Sharon, lying on the bed. It was obvious she'd been crying.

"I'd ask if you are feeling any better, but I already have my answer," he said.

She sighed. "I'm fine. Just tired. I thought this vacation would be a chance to make things better with Maxwell. It looks like I thought wrong. I'm so tired of fighting the inevitable. Also, I'm sorry to unload all of this on you. I barely know you."

He smiled warmly. "Come now, we know quite a bit about each other already. You know the name of my beloved horse and the meaning behind it, yes?"

Her soft laugh was like music to Jakub's ears.

Jakub took her hand. He drew a chair to the bedside, and sat. "There is something else I wanted to talk with you about. Klaudie has told me about Maxwell reading from the book of spells. I'm very worried it could have ... well ... done something." He looked into her eyes.

"Something?" asked Sharon.

"A portal," he said. "A portal to the underworld. To Hell, specifically."

She sat up, wiping her eyes. "I don't know what to say. You don't think it's more plausible an earthquake caused the crack?"

"I guess that's possible, but the timing, Sharon, the timing is everything. And the place the crack occurred, what about that? Right on top of the exact spot, legend has it, was covered to hide a bottomless pit? That, to me, is a pretty big coincidence." said Jakub.

"So, what do we do about it?" she asked, in a tone that said she could hardly believe she was having such a conversation. "If he did open a portal to the underworld, how do we close it?"

"As of yet, I don't have a solution. Klaudie and I are trying to figure out what to do. But, for now, it's obvious you need to rest. I just wanted to make sure you were alright. Shall I bring you a cup of tea?"

"No, thank you. More caffeine will just make me jittery. I'm going to close my eyes. I'll be able to fall asleep in no time. My mind is utterly exhausted."

"Then that's what you shall do. And I will watch over you, until you fall asleep," he said.

"Oh no, that's not..." she started, but he raised a hand, not letting her finish.

"Don't be silly," he said. "You'll be asleep in no time, like you said, and when you are, I will go back downstairs."

She didn't argue with him.

Instead, she closed her eyes, aware of his comforting presence.

And, soon, she drifted off to sleep.

Chapter 24

Dwayne sat up in bed. His whole body felt like it was on fire. He scratched his arms, his stomach, his legs. When he went into the bathroom, closed the door and flipped on the light, he saw he was covered in open sores, oozing pus and blood. He winced in pain as his fingers grazed one of the wounds.

Worried about infection, he found some antibiotic ointment in his Dopp kit and lightly coated them as best he could. In the morning, he would ask Klaudie if she had any bandages, but this would have to work for now.

He got back into the bed with Xander, and laid there, thinking of everything that had happened since their arrival. The most interesting thing, of course, was the crack in the chapel floor. He wasn't quite sure what to make of it.

He heard what sounded like whispers in the dark, though he couldn't make out the words. The hairs on his neck and arms stood on end.

"Hello?" he whispered back. "Is anyone there?"

He'd always been a believer in ghosts. He loved scary movies and anything that had to do with the paranormal, so this didn't strike fear in him. He was excited; turned on, even.

He climbed back out of bed and went to the door, reaching for the doorknob. But the door opened by itself, its hinges creaking. A tingle went down Dwayne's spine. He stepped into the hall and tried again. "Hello?"

Thinking he saw movement near the stairs, he headed that direction. He didn't even have his slippers on, but there was no time to go back and get them now.

When he got to the end of the hall and looked down the stairs, he was sure he saw a shadowy figure moving toward the trophy room.

Dwayne hurriedly descended, wishing he had his phone so he could document this, and show Xander.

The shadow figure disappeared through the door that led into the courtyard.

Dwayne followed, just in time to see it slip into the chapel. He thought of the story Klaudie had told them, and wondered if the shadow had come from the crack in the floor.

His eyes widened when he opened the chapel door. The crack in the floor had grown wider, emitting a strange glow. He stepped inside. Whispering voices swirled around him, making him dizzy. On the walls, all of the images within the murals were moving as if they were alive. A half-human, half-goat creature smiled at him, putting a finger to its lips as if telling Dwayne to keep their secret.

His arms itched like crazy, so he scratched them, ripping the sores wider, blood dripping to the floor. But it no longer hurt; instead of making him weaker, the bloodletting made him stronger.

The whispering voices urged him to come closer to the pit. Slowly, he began to walk towards the glowing light, feeling calm, yet powerful. The energy in the air was like a drug.

When he reached the edge, he stopped. The shadow figure he'd seen earlier floated up, curling around him, through his legs, around his head, behind his back. Three more came out of the pit, and all of them felt warm and welcoming.

Looking down, he saw hundreds -- no, thousands, or hundreds of thousands -- of the shadow figures. They reached toward him, inviting him to join them.

It was how he imagined it would feel to be famous. Until he met Xander, he'd felt alone his entire life. Unwanted, weird, different. He'd just wanted to fit in. Xander made him feel that way, but to most people, he was still a nobody.

He couldn't resist this opportunity, telling himself Xander would understand.

Then thoughts of Xander, his home, his dog, his parents and anything else that had previously mattered were erased from his brain. The shadow figures reached into his eyes, *through* his eyes, down his throat and grabbed his soul.

What was previously Dwayne was no more.

The light from the pit faded. The shadow figures were gone.

But the thing that was not Dwayne was still there. It turned toward the door of the chapel, and, taking small, slow steps, it began to walk, seeming to be relying on muscle memory to stay upright.

The thing that was not Dwayne crossed the courtyard and went to the trophy room, picking up an intricately carved hunting knife from the displayed weapons.

He turned it over and over in his hand, admiring the beautiful carvings and the way it felt in his hand. He slowly climbed the stairs to the second floor, walked down the hall, and went into the bedroom Dwayne and Xander had shared.

Xander was still fast asleep.

The thing that was not Dwayne went to the edge of the bed, then sat down, staring straight ahead.

The shift on the mattress caused Xander to stir. "Baby, what are you doing? Everything okay?" he mumbled. "Come back to bed."

The thing that was not Dwayne laid down, and Xander cuddled close, already falling asleep again.

Chapter 25

As they walked along the shore of the river, something crawled from the river and grabbed Dwayne's feet. The panic on his face made Xander cry out. He clung to Dwayne's hands, but whatever held him was too strong, pulling Dwayne from his grasp.

Xander's eyes shot open and he sat up, gasping. He looked, and saw Dwayne's familiar figure beside him.

A dream, an intense one but only a dream. He laid his head back down on the pillow and drifted back to sleep.

He could hear Dwayne screaming, but didn't know where he was. It was pitch dark, and Xander was freezing, huddled on the cold ground. Dwayne continued to scream. Feeling helpless, Xander blundered around in the dark until he stumbled through a doorway. He groped for a light switch.

When he found one and switched it on, he wished he'd stayed huddled on the ground and never moved from that spot.

Dwayne, still screaming, lay on a table, bloody stumps where his hands and feet had been. Xander ran to him, tears streaming down his cheeks. When he got there, he saw empty sockets where Dwayne's eyes had been torn out, and his gaping mouth was missing its tongue.

Again, Xander jolted up, breathing hard.

Dwayne was still beside him, appearing not to have moved.

This is getting ridiculous, he thought.

Lying back down, he fell asleep again, and this time, he dreamed of nothing at all.

***

Maxwell swung Monica around the dance floor.

They'd been out all evening. She had been so excited when Maxwell first arrived, he wasn't sure she would even want to leave the hotel room.

But the sheets soon needed changing, so they'd taken a shower and gotten dressed to go out, calling for maid service before they left.

Maxwell knew Sharon was going to be pissed, but he couldn't stand being at that place any longer. The boredom, for one thing. And all that stuff about the book and the chapel, for another.

Anyway, he wasn't going to think about that now. He was going to enjoy his time with Monica. They'd gone out to a fancy dinner in downtown Prague, and then to a club their waiter had recommended.

They'd both had way too much to drink, and as the song ended, Monica stumbled off in search of the bathroom.

Maxwell headed back to the bar for another round, then sat down at their table. He picked up his glass, savoring the alcohol as it slid down his throat. He watched Monica appreciatively as she crossed the room.

"My God, it's hot in here!" she said, taking her seat.

"Agreed," said Maxwell. "But you know what's even hotter? You." He reached over and pinched her nipple. She squealed with delight. "Do you want to go back to the dance floor or would you rather sit this one out?"

"I need a breather," she said.

"I was thinking the same thing."

It was three in the morning. The bars didn't close here in Prague like they did back home. The bars didn't close at all. He stifled a yawn.

"We can go back to the hotel now if you're tired, old man," she teased, then threw her head back and laughed.

"Baby, I can keep up with you any day," he said. "But if you're ready to go back to the room for other reasons, and you're just too shy to say so, give Maxie a little nod, and away we'll go." He winked.

Monica contemplated his offer. "I do really love that thing you do with your tongue," she said. She leaned forward and whispered, "You know, down *there*."

"Say no more, my love. Let's get out of here."

He wrapped her coat around her -- she looked so damn good in her short red dress, but it was cold outside -- and ushered her toward the door. He hailed a taxi, and soon, they were snuggled up inside. Monica moved her legs apart so Maxwell could access her hot spot, rubbing her crotch, loving the silky smoothness of her satin panties.

After making sure the driver wasn't paying attention, he worked his hand into her panties, finding that she was already slick with excitement. She moaned in his ear as he began rubbing her clit in circles, then slid two fingers deep inside of her. With his other hand, he squeezed her ass.

Tempted to encourage her to straddle his lap, he glanced up, and caught the driver taking a peek in the rearview mirror. He removed his hands from her body and smoothed her dress over her legs.

"Why'd you stop?" she asked him.

"We have an audience," he whispered, nodding toward the driver.

Monica smiled. "So?"

While he wasn't entirely against starting things up again, they were only a minute from the hotel now, so it would be pointless.

They pulled up to the curb. Maxwell paid the fare and helped Monica out of the car. The driver rolled down his window. "You give me no tip?" he said in broken English.

"Here's a tip," Maxwell said. "Maybe next time you see a couple in your back seat trying to have a private moment, you keep your eyes on the road and mind your own fuckin' business."

ONE HELL OF A VACATION

With that, he put his arm around Monica and guided her through the front door of the hotel.

Chapter 26

At breakfast, Xander watched his husband closely while picking at his food. He wasn't hungry. Apparently, neither was Dwayne, who hadn't even taken one bite, but just sat there, staring straight ahead.

Xander had noticed something was wrong from the moment he woke up. As he'd stretched, and gotten a clean towel, preparing to take a bath, he'd noticed Dwayne still lying on his side, but his eyes were open.

"Hey," he'd said.

Dwayne only shifted his gaze to Xander, saying nothing. He just laid there, staring.

Xander, exhausted and still suffering from his headache, didn't make an issue of it, but it had made him uncomfortable, so he went on into the bathroom. Maybe the nightmares he'd had during the night and the constant waking had something to do with it.

He took his time in the bath, enjoying the hot water. Not hearing a peep from the bedroom, he figured either Dwayne had fallen back asleep, or he'd gotten dressed and gone downstairs already. He let his head slowly go under, eyes closed, exhaling through his nose, hoping to relieve some of the pressure from his headache.

He stayed under for a good twenty seconds, then broke the surface and opened his eyes ...

And saw Dwayne, standing over the bathtub, watching him.

Xander jumped, water sloshing. "Jesus Christ, Dwayne! You scared me to death. I didn't hear you come in."

Dwayne just stood there, with no expression on his face. His arms hung limp at his sides and his eyes looked glazed over.

"Dwayne? Are you alright?"

Now more than just a little uncomfortable, Xander got out of the tub and wrapped the towel around his waist. Even though Dwayne was his husband, he felt weirdly vulnerable in his present state, and hurried into the other room to get dressed.

After what felt like an eternity, Dwayne came out of the bathroom, still expressionless, still staring.

"So... are you mad at me?" Xander asked. "Because, if you are, I'm not sure what I've done, so I'm going to need you to tell me."

Dwayne said one word, his voice oddly flat. "No."

"Okay, whatever," said Xander. Obviously, trying to talk was pointless at the moment.

They'd gone downstairs in silence.

Xander tried to make pleasant conversation with the others at breakfast, pretending to listen to Nigel and Laila as they told a story about their travels two years ago to Iceland. But if someone were to ask him to summarize what he'd just heard, he wouldn't have been able to do it. He kept thinking of Dwayne.

When he couldn't stand it any longer, he tapped Dwayne on the arm.

"Follow me, we need to talk," Xander murmured. He led Dwayne out, aware of all eyes on them as they left the room.

"This has gotten ridiculous," he said, stopping well down the hall, out of earshot. "I don't know why you're upset with me, or why you're acting like this, but I need you to tell me right now. What's wrong?"

"Nothing."

"Nothing?! What do you mean, nothing?! You've been a zombie since you woke up. In fact, I think you've only spoken about two words to me all morning. So don't tell me that nothing is wrong. I'm not stupid, Dwayne."

Dwayne didn't speak. He only stared back at Xander with a blank look.

"Fine, have it your way. When you are ready to talk, come find me. I'll be with the rest of the group." He turned on his heel.

Dwayne just stood there.

Of course, the others had noticed, and Xander soon found himself venting to the sympathetic ears of Sharon and Laila.

"I must've made him mad somehow, but I don't know how."

Laila patted Xander's hand, while Sharon offered up some advice.

"Give him some space," Sharon said. "When he's ready to talk, he'll let you know. Maybe he's not mad at you. Maybe it has nothing to do with you. He might just be having a bad day."

Xander sighed. "Maybe. I sure hope he's over it soon, though, because I'm ready to slap that stupid zombie expression right off his face."

Chapter 27

As soon as she was able to get away discreetly, Sharon headed upstairs to change into her boots and grab a heavier coat. She needed some fresh air. The events of the morning had already proven to be too much for her. Poor Xander was a mess, and Dwayne acting so strange? She just needed to get outside.

It still felt weird walking into her room and being all alone. She was grateful to Jakub for staying with her until she fell asleep the night before, however odd it might've been given they'd only just met.

Before she reached the front door, she heard his voice from behind her.

"Sharon? Where are you going?"

She turned, seeing a concerned look spread across Jakub's face.

"Nowhere. I mean, nowhere important. I was just going for a walk to get some fresh air."

"One moment?" Jakub went to say something to Klaudie, then removed his coat from the back of the chair he'd been sitting in at breakfast and returned. "Okay, let's go."

Sharon wasn't about to argue with him, though she'd wanted to go on her walk alone. It felt claustrophobic being around the rest of the group for so much of the time.

"I can't let you go alone," he said, like he'd been reading her mind. "Too many dangerous animals around here, and the chance you'd get lost. I couldn't let that happen. I'm sorry."

"I didn't think about any of that. You're right, I don't want to go by myself now." She said it, and she meant it.

They went outside, walking down the path toward the barn.

"Tell me about your family," Sharon said.

"What would you like to know?"

"Everything."

"That might take a while, but as you wish." Jakub pulled a brush from his saddlebag and began to groom Blesk. "I've lived in Blatce my entire life on a farm. I still live on the same farm with my mother. I'm the youngest of six children. I have five older sisters. Let's see, what else would you like to know?"

"Five sisters?! I bet that was fun growing up. Did they all pick on you?"

"Oh sure, but they also protected me fiercely. They'd run off any girl I tried to date. Klaudie was the worst. She stuck to me like glue. I couldn't get away with anything without her knowing." Jakub threw his head back and laughed. "I love all of my sisters, but Klaudie and I are the closest. I wish so much she didn't work at this godforsaken place." He put the brush back in his saddlebag, took out some carrots and fed some of them to Blesk.

Sharon gave Blesk a kiss on the nose. "You're a good boy," she told him.

"So, what about you? Tell me about your life." Jakub stood back, watching Sharon as she stroked Blesk's mane.

"There's not much to tell. We live in Connecticut. I teach English Literature at a private school. Maxwell works at a bank in New York City."

"What about your parents? Do they live near you? Do you have any brothers or sisters?" asked Jakub.

"My parents are both deceased, and no, I was an only child. I do have a second cousin who lives nearby, though."

"That must be rough to have lost your parents. I'm sorry."

"I'm okay with it now. It was tough when Mom died, a few years ago. But then I met Maxwell, so I didn't feel so alone after that." She looked down at the ground, avoiding eye contact with Jakub.

"I didn't realize you'd only been together a short time."

"We've been married for a year, actually." Sharon continued to concentrate on the dirt. "It's been a long one," she admitted. "I was beginning to think I'd never be married. I'm fifty-two now. If this doesn't work out, I think I'm done for good." She laughed, trying to make a joke of it.

"Hey, I'm fifty-six, and I still haven't met the right person." A lie; he felt like that person might be right in front of him. "I am sorry it's difficult, though."

"Well, it's my own fault. I think I rushed into it. Maybe because my mom had just died, and I was grieving in my own way. I still have hope that things will work out with Maxwell ... but the hope is fading fast. How can we fix things if he's missing in action? It's kind of humiliating, to be honest."

""The way I see it," Jakub said as they resumed their walk, "you're not the one that should feel humiliated. He left you all alone in a foreign country, among people you barely know, to fend for yourself. Forgive me for sounding rude and speaking ill of your husband, but he is, from what I can tell, the very definition of an asshole. I couldn't stand him the minute I saw him."

Sharon covered her mouth to hide a smile. Even though what Jakub said about Maxwell was unkind, every word was the truth. Feeling much better than she had before leaving the castle, she reached out and took Jakub's hand.

"Thank you for coming with me. I really appreciate it."

"I am glad to. I enjoy your company very much, Sharon." Jakub paused, as if there was more he wanted to say. But, after a moment, he continued walking, still holding her hand.

Chapter 28

After breakfast, Laila went back upstairs and changed into a cozy house robe and slippers, planning to curl up with a good book for a few hours while Nigel amused himself downstairs.

She dug through her suitcase for her reading glasses and the new Ruth Ware mystery she'd been itching to start. Stealing extra pillows from Nigel's side of the bed, she propped them all behind her and settled in. She definitely needed some relaxation after the morning's stress.

She felt sorry for Xander; the poor young man was torn up over whatever was going on with Dwayne. Laila wasn't convinced it had to do with Xander at all, though. Dwayne had been acting very strange. Not only was he not speaking to his husband, he hadn't said a word to anyone else either, and the eager and excited expression he normally wore had been absent.

Then there was Sharon; Laila felt awful for her, too. While she couldn't stand that bloody Maxwell one bit, she certainly knew Sharon was devastated he'd left her there all alone with strangers. How someone as sweet as Sharon would be married to such a creep to begin with ... Ah well. Maybe this would be the eye opener that Sharon needed to get rid of the scum and move on to someone who deserved her.

Laila shook the thoughts from her mind and opened her book.

A noise jolted her awake. She wasn't sure how long she'd been sleeping. Her book was open on her lap and she still had her reading glasses on. She took them off and rubbed her sleepy eyes. When she looked up, she saw someone standing in the corner of the room.

"Nigel?"

They didn't answer.

"Nigel? Is that you?"

The figure that looked like Nigel still didn't speak. He crossed the room to the open door, and went out into the hall. Laila was sure she'd closed the door when she came up earlier. After all, she'd changed clothes, and she wouldn't have done that with the door wide open.

Swinging her legs over the side of the bed, Laila went out into the hall, with the intention of finding out what her husband was up to.

She looked to her right, and then to her left, and she saw Nigel climbing the stairs to the third floor. She followed. He didn't appear to be in a hurry.

"Nigel? What are you doing? Where are you going, love?" Laila called.

He paused on the steps and turned to look at her. He had no expression on his face. He continued climbing.

Something was wrong, very wrong. Why wasn't he speaking to her?

He went all the way up to the attic. The door opened with a long creak. Laila waited 'til he'd walked through before climbing the stairs herself. She no longer wanted to call out to him. The hair on her arms was standing on end.

When she reached the landing, she saw Nigel at the far end of the attic, standing in the corner, facing the wall. This was bizarre; she wondered if she were still asleep after all, and dreaming. She felt like screaming and crying and running away all at once.

As much as she didn't want to, she tried to speak to him again. "Nigel? Can you hear me? What's going on, love? Why are you up here in the cold, dark attic?"

This time, when Nigel turned toward her very slowly, Laila saw that what she'd thought all along was Nigel ... wasn't. Whatever it was, it was in human form, and had managed to fool her into believing it was her husband. But now it had chosen to reveal its true identity.

Its eyes glowed, and its teeth showed razor sharp when it smiled. Laila felt like her heart was going to beat out of her chest. Her instincts told her to run, but she couldn't seem to get her legs to move.

It started toward her, which seemed to be the trigger her legs needed. She took off down the stairs as quickly as she could, hearing the thing she'd mistaken for her husband chasing after.

She dashed down the next flight of stairs to the second-floor hall, her pursuer breathing hard close behind. She burst into her room, slamming and locking the door.

From the other side, she heard nothing. She leaned her forehead against the door, trying to calm herself down.

She was safe. It was over.

She felt a tap on her shoulder.

She turned and saw Nigel, screamed, and covered her eyes. He grabbed her around the waist ... but it was to keep her from falling to the floor as he held her, concerned.

"Laila, my love, what's wrong?" he said, stroking her hair.

Was she losing her mind? Faltering, she explained what had happened. Thankfully, he sat and listened to every word, and when she had finished, he hugged her tight.

"I don't think you're crazy, love," Nigel said. "I believe everything you just told me."

Chapter 29

Leaving Sharon safely with Klaudie, Jakub saddled Blesk, knowing he needed to go home and check on Mother. He promised Klaudie he'd be back before dinner.

The farm quickly came into view in the distance. Jakub hadn't spoken to Irenka that morning, so he had no idea if their mother was lucid. He hoped she would be.

When he reached the house, after putting Blesk in the barn, he saw Irenka sitting on the front porch, knitting what looked to be a scarf.

"How's Mother?" he asked.

"The same as yesterday," said Irenka.

He went inside and found his mother in the rocking chair in her bedroom, looking out the window.

"Jakub my son, come closer," she said.

He did so, kneeling at her side so that she could see him. "How are you feeling today?"

"I'm feeling just fine. I'm a little tired. Why is Irenka here? Where have you been?"

"I had to go see Klaudie," he reminded her gently.

"I don't want you at that place, Jakub. It's evil. You need to make your sister come back home. She should never have agreed to work there."

"Mother, she's been there for a long time, and nothing has happened. She just has an unruly guest that she needs help with." Jakub put his hand on her shoulder.

"I visited the castle, once when I was young," she said.

Jakub had never heard her mention it before, so he listened closely.

"I was around the age of ten. Your Grandpap went to Houska for a concert they were hosting in the courtyard. I tagged along with him. But the concert proved to be more of a grown-up event, so I asked if I could go and play with the other children, and he gave me his permission."

She stopped her tale, visibly shaken.

"Go on, Mother, it's alright. I'm here," Jakub told her.

Mother continued. "This is hard for me. The only person I've told before now was your father, may he rest in peace." She wiped a tear from her cheek. "I followed two other children into the castle. We had decided to play a game of hide and go seek. This was the obvious game of choice, because the place was so massive, and there were hundreds of good spaces to hide."

He held her hand, nodding to encourage her.

"The boy, he hid his eyes and started to count, and the other girl and I took off in opposite directions. I ran up stairs and down hallways as fast as I could, until I reached the highest door I could find, went through, and closed it behind me. It must have been the attic. It was pitch black, and the air was very cold."

Jakub shivered himself, in sympathy.

"As I rubbed my arms, trying to keep warm, I felt someone breathing on my neck. I asked who was there, but no one answered. Then I heard a low growl. I've never been more scared in my life. I reached for the doorknob but it wouldn't turn. I was stuck."

"Oh, Mother, how frightening for you."

"I started to scream, Jakub, as loud as I could. I screamed and screamed and kicked the door. The growling turned to maniacal laughter. I felt my bladder let go. I remember being so terrified that I wasn't even ashamed that I'd wet myself."

He patted her hand soothingly.

"It seemed like forever before they found me. The little boy who'd been seeking heard my screams, but was too scared to open the door, so he ran to get his father for help. Then the men went around the attic with torches and searched every inch, but found nothing. They decided I'd let my imagination get the best of me." She looked at him with a pleading expression. "But, Jakub, I know what I felt, and I know what I heard, and it was evil. That's why I'm begging you to please get Klaudie away from that place."

He hadn't heard his mother speak more than a few words at a time in over a year, because of the dementia she suffered so badly. Yet she'd managed to share this full story with him, an entire memory from long ago.

"I'll watch over her, Mother, I promise." And he meant his promise. He would never let anything happen to Klaudie. He would protect her at all costs. "I'll go see her right now."

He leaned over and kissed his mother on the forehead, then left the house. Irenka was still on the porch, knitting.

"Are you going back to the castle?" she asked.

"Yes," he replied.

ONE HELL OF A VACATION

"Any idea how long you'll be gone this time?"

"I'm not sure. Do you mind staying with Mother while I'm gone?"

"No, I don't mind a bit."

Irenka lived by herself since her husband had died, and her children were all grown and had places of their own. Jakub often thought that Irenka enjoyed the company of their mother. She would sometimes come to stay with the two of them for a week or more, which was a nice break for Jakub.

Jakub bent and kissed his sister on top of her head. "Call me if you need me," he told her.

"Please be careful," she replied.

Chapter 30

Xander had no idea where Dwayne had disappeared to, and at the moment, he didn't care. He'd just longed for the comfort of his pillow, needed a nice quiet lie down. His headache was pounding inside his skull.

He'd kicked off his shoes and climbed into bed, pulling the covers up. It didn't take long for him to drift off. Unlike last night, his sleep wasn't plagued with bad dreams, and he rested peacefully.

Sometime later, Xander opened his eyes. He stayed on his side, facing the wall, letting himself wake up completely. He felt well rested, and his headache seemed to have eased up, which was a relief.

He had a weird feeling though, that feeling one gets when they aren't alone.

Xander rolled over onto his back, and saw Dwayne standing over him. His eyes were glazed, and he held something in his hand, but Xander couldn't see what it was.

Well, maybe he's ready to talk, Xander thought.

"Hey. Everything alright?" he asked.

Dwayne didn't reply. He just stood there, staring.

Xander rolled his eyes. *Fuck this shit*, he thought. *I've had enough.*

He sat up, but Dwayne pushed him back down. He sat up again, and Dwayne reached to push him down again, but Xander dodged and got out of bed.

"What the fuck is your problem?" Xander asked, angry now.

Dwayne had never raised a hand to him. This sudden shift in behavior was super odd. And, more importantly, unacceptable. Before he could stop himself, he shoved Dwayne away.

Dwayne showed no reaction whatsoever, but that didn't stop Xander from immediately apologizing.

"Dwayne, I'm so sorry. I don't know what came over me. It's just... you ... I don't understand! Everything was fine and now nothing makes sense." Xander ran his hands through his hair.

Dwayne still didn't answer, didn't react, just stood there and stared.

Giving up on getting anything out of him, Xander ducked into the bathroom, where he splashed his face, urinated, and washed his hands. He didn't want to just give up so easily. He'd always prided himself in trying to resolve issues he'd had with people. For that reason, he decided to try again.

"You've never given me the silent treatment before, so I guess that's why I'm reacting the way I am," he called out to Dwayne, drying his hands on a towel.

They were red and chapped, probably from the cold weather. There was lotion in his suitcase, so he went to get it.

On the way, he looked over at Dwayne, who was still standing beside the bed, but staring directly at him.

This is too much for me to deal with right now, he thought.

He squirted lotion onto his hands and rubbed it in, closing his eyes to enjoy the sensation and the pleasant scent.

When he opened his eyes, Dwayne was standing in front of him.

Xander started to speak, but his words became a gurgling scream as Dwayne raised the knife he'd been holding and slashed it across his throat. Blood spewed from the wound.

Xander raised his hand to his neck, confusion on his face and tears in his eyes.

He collapsed, bleeding, to the floor. Dwayne just continued to stand there, emotionless.

Since marrying Dwayne, his life had been a fairytale, but now that fairytale had turned into a nightmare! He pleaded with his eyes. *Please help me,* he thought. *Please Dwayne, don't let me die. Our life together isn't over. It can't be. I don't know why you did what you did, but I know you didn't mean it. Please, save me.*

Xander watched as Dwayne's gaze shifted to the knife, as if he were admiring it. It was covered in slick, red blood. He turned it over and over, looking at one side and then the other, fascinated. He brought the blade to his nose and inhaled deeply.

Then, Dwayne -- this thing that was *not* Dwayne! -- ran his tongue down one side of the blade, then the other, until he'd licked every drop of blood from it. He smiled.

Xander went still, his pupils dilated, that terrible smile the last thing he ever saw.

Chapter 31

Amalie hummed as she ran her duster along the baseboard of the second-floor hallway. She was halfway finished with her cleaning duties for the day, and was looking forward to her break.

When she thought she heard someone cry out, she hesitated for a moment, trying to make up her mind if she wanted to investigate. She knew from experience that, sometimes, ignorance was the better option. Working in this castle, one just never knew what they'd find, should they go poking around.

Making up her mind to go and have a look anyway, she moved quietly down the hall. The door to the guest room occupied by the male couple wasn't completely closed, so she went to take a peek inside just to check ...

What she saw nearly made her lose her balance.

One of the men was standing over the body of the other, licking what looked like blood from the blade of a knife.

Amalie backed carefully away from the door, but she only made it a few paces before bumping into a pillar, knocking over a stone statue atop it. The clatter and crash as it hit the floor was quite loud. The statue shattered into pieces.

She looked around her for a place to hide, but all of the other doors were closed. Then the man -- Dwayne -- appeared in the doorway. Amalie turned to run, but he grabbed her from behind, covering her mouth to keep her from screaming.

Amalie struggled, but he was much bigger than she was, and she knew it was of no use to continue trying to get loose. He took her back into the bedroom, closed the door, and hurled her into a chair in the corner. The minute his hand was off her mouth, Amalie tried to scream, but he hit her as hard as he could, and Amalie was knocked out, cold.

When she came to, her head was killing her and she couldn't see out of her left eye. Her hands were tied behind her back. She felt sick to her stomach. She tried to remember where she was and what had happened. Then it came back: Dwayne, licking the bloody knife ... and Xander, dead on the floor.

She raised her head enough to see Dwayne rolling Xander's body up into the bedspread. She quickly lowered it again, not wanting him to realize that she'd regained consciousness.

If I'm going to get out of this, I'm going to have to come up with a plan, she thought to herself. She quickly took inventory of her surroundings. Her feet were not tied, which was advantage number one. Secondly, her arms were not secured to the chair, even though they were tied behind her back.

Very subtly, so as not to draw attention, she moved her hands and wrists around, trying to gauge how tight the rope was tied. She quickly realized that it was too tight for her to be able to work free of it, so she'd have to try an escape attempt without the use of her hands.

She risked a glance at Dwayne, praying he wasn't looking in her direction. Fortunately, her prayers were answered. He was still working on getting Xander's body rolled up in the bedspread. She shifted her gaze to the door and found another win. The door was open!

Slowly, Amalie scooted her bottom to the edge of the chair. It was painful going this slow, but she had to make sure Dwayne didn't realize she was awake.

From where she sat, it was about eight feet, but the good news was that it was a straight shot to the door. She wouldn't have to go around anything, or pass Dwayne to get out.

Finally, deciding to make her move, she eased silently to her feet, lifting her bound arms over the back of the chair. As she took a step toward the door, she looked over again ... and saw Dwayne staring right at her.

It was now or never. All prior thoughts of staying silent and going slowly went right out the window. Amalie raced for the door as fast as she could, Dwayne right behind her.

She opened her mouth to call for help as she ran, but before she could utter a word, her foot slipped and her head hit the bare floor very hard, and she was knocked unconscious once again.

***

The thing that was not Dwayne dragged Amalie back to the bedroom by the ankles, moving as if he had no fear of being caught. His face showed no emotion whatsoever.

Dumping her onto the bed, he bound her again, using more rope and tying her feet this time. He also stuffed a washcloth into her mouth, securing it with one of Xander's neck ties.

No more escape attempts for Amalie.

The thing that used to be Dwayne then began working on the final tasks he needed to do before moving the bodies to their designated locations.

Once everything was in order, he picked up Xander's body as if it weighed nothing. He carried it downstairs, across the courtyard to the chapel, where he finally laid it on the altar.

As he passed the pit, it began to glow. He stared into it, as if he were receiving secret messages that were meant only for him. Finally, he retraced his steps and lifted Amalie. She was much lighter than Xander had been.

This time, he didn't go out into the courtyard. Instead, he went down another set of stairs. This time, he was headed for the basement, better known as Satan's Office.

The door was not locked. He pushed on a rock in the wall behind the throne, and a section opened. Dwayne himself must have had no idea how he knew about the secret room; if anyone outside had been watching, they'd guess he'd been given the information while at the pit.

Carrying Amalie inside, he set her body down on the ground and took the gag from her mouth. She didn't need it now. No one would ever find her in here.

She was stirring. She opened her eyes and looked at him.

***

"Where am I?" Amalie asked. "Please, let me go. I won't say anything, I promise."

He didn't reply, just went about securing the area as she continued to beg. On his way out, he mumbled something, but she was only able to make out a single word.

Sacrifice.

He closed the secret entrance, leaving Amalie trapped and all alone. Her eyes adjusted to the darkness, and she was able to see a little bit.

The first thing she noticed were the shackles and chains hanging from the stone walls. It dawned on her that this must be the dungeon she'd always heard rumors about, the one said to exist within the castle's walls, but no one had ever located it.

Dread filled her. If no one had been able to locate the dungeon before now, how was anyone going to be able to find and rescue her? Amalie focused on her breathing and tried to calm down. *Think*, she told herself.

Her back was wet from leaning against the wall. The whole place was damp, and stank of rotten things, things which Amalie didn't want to begin to speculate about. Her head was pounding, both from Dwayne punching her, and then, from falling when she'd tried to escape.

Something was scraping against her hip but she couldn't work out in her mind what it was. She scooted away so that whatever it was, it wasn't touching her anymore, but then felt something on her other side, poking at her like branches.

Great, she thought. Her hands were still tied behind her back, but she was able to turn and feel around. The objects felt the same on both sides. Smooth, but hard, kind of pointy at the ends, and ...

Suddenly she realized what she was touching.

Bones. To confirm her fear, she leaned her head closer to try and make out the details.

Bones. Rib cages. She was wedged in between two human skeletons.

She tried not to panic or get sick. She took deep breaths. But it was just too much for her. She began to scream as loud as she could, not knowing if anyone could hear her, or how thick the walls were; she didn't care. She would keep screaming until she lost her voice.

She wanted *out* of this place.

What had she done but be in the wrong place at the wrong time? A victim of circumstance. She thought about her parents and her younger brother and sister at home, and wished so much to be there with them. She'd only been working at the castle for less than six months. Everyone had warned her not to, but she hadn't listened. It paid more than the pub she'd been working at in Prague.

How long would it be before anyone would realize she was missing? Her parents would be expecting her home that evening, she supposed, but they knew sometimes she'd meet up with friends after work.

Would Dwayne come back to kill her? Or was he going to leave her there to starve to death, or die of thirst?

She continued to scream until she ran out of energy. Eventually, she curled up on the ground, and slept.

Chapter 32

Jakub arrived back at the castle and immediately sought out his sister. He found Klaudie in her room, reading a book.

"How's Mother?" she asked.

"She's fine. Irenka has everything under control, as usual."

Klaudie set her book down on the night table beside her. "That's good to hear. Was she having one of her good days?"

"As a matter of fact, she was," he told her. "Which is what I wanted to ask you about. We had a strange conversation regarding the castle. You know she's always been terrified of this place, and warned us against it?"

"Yes, of course, even before she fell ill."

"Well, she told me a story about when she was here once, as a child, with Grandpap." Jakub related what their mother had told him.

"That's insane," said Klaudie, when he was done. "Our mother is 84 years old, and she's never told either of us this? I wonder why?"

"She must have thought we were better off not knowing," Jakub said.

"Did you ask Irenka about it?"

"No. I didn't want to worry her."

There was a knock at Klaudie's door. Jakub opened it to find Sharon standing there, holding a mug of tea that looked to be piping hot.

"Come in," said Klaudie with a smile.

"Oh, thanks, that's okay, I don't want to interrupt. I just wanted to let you know I think I used the last tea bag."

"Thank you so much for letting me know. I will call Marek and have him pick up another box to bring when he drops off our dinner this evening. I have a secret stash too, just in case someone wants a cup between now and then." Klaudie went over to her dresser, opened it, and took out a small container. "I'm just going to run this downstairs."

As she made to do so, Jakub offered to walk Sharon back to her own room. Klaudie gave him a look over her shoulder, and Jakub knew exactly what his sister was thinking. They'd always had a close bond, and she could clearly tell he was falling for Sharon.

On the way, they noticed a toppled pillar and a broken statue.

"I'd better let Klaudie know so she can tell Amalie," Jakub said.

They arrived at Sharon's room and went inside. She set her mug on the night table and climbed onto the bed, curling up in a ball. Jakub sat in the same chair, still placed where he'd kept watch over her until she slept.

"Have you heard from Maxwell?" he asked.

"Nothing," she said. "I've texted several times, and all my calls go straight to voicemail."

"Please excuse me if what I say offends you, but ... Sharon, you don't deserve to be treated this way. Not only you, no one does! I may have only met you yesterday, which seems impossible to me already, but I can tell that you are a warm and kindhearted person, as well as beautiful."

Jakub stopped in his tracks, mentally kicking himself. He hadn't meant to say that last part. It had just slipped out.

"You think I'm beautiful?" she asked, as if she might not have heard him correctly.

"I'm sorry, I shouldn't have said that."

"But you do think so?"

"If I'm being completely honest, you are the most beautiful woman I've ever seen in my entire life. I keep having to force myself to look away from you."

"I ... no one has ever said something like that to me before."

"I'm sorry," he said again. "I've overstepped my boundaries. You're married. I don't want you to think badly of me."

"I'm married to someone who doesn't want to be with me," she said. "And I've just found out that someone I find extremely attractive thinks I'm beautiful."

Their eyes met.

I have to get out of here, Jakub thought. He leaned forward to get up from the chair, with intentions of leaving the room, but Sharon leaned toward him at the same time and their faces almost collided.

Unable to resist the temptation, he kissed her. Rather than draw back, she closed her eyes and melted into the kiss. He put his arms around her, parting her lips with his tongue. Sharon groaned with pleasure, returning the kiss passionately.

Finally, Jakub pulled back. Guilt crawled up his spine.

This woman was hurting. Her husband had just left her. Of course, she would respond to another man's affection. She was thirsty for any attention she could get.

He couldn't take advantage of her. He needed to be there for her as a friend, and someone she could trust.

She looked at him, confused, as he stood up, gently squeezed her shoulder, and left the room without another word.

Chapter 33

Instead of looking like they'd had an enjoyable afternoon, everyone looked haggard and unkempt when they gathered for dinner. Keeping up appearances was no longer of concern for anyone. Klaudie noticed it straight away when she came in to join them.

The pot roast and mashed potatoes Marek had brought sat mostly untouched in the center of the table. Laila seemed distraught, and Nigel seemed to be comforting her, but Klaudie was unsure why. Sharon picked at a bit of food, seeming fidgety and nervous. Every once in a while, when she thought it would go unnoticed, she'd glance in Jakub's direction.

Jakub himself ate his dinner, but was careful not to look at Sharon, which Klaudie also found odd, since he normally couldn't take his eyes off of her.

Xander and Dwayne did not even put in an appearance, evidently deciding to skip the meal altogether. Hopefully, they had made up for their disagreement earlier, and everyone would soon be themselves again.

Klaudie had also noticed the broken statue in the second-floor hallway, and cleaned it up after being unable to find Amalie. She did hope the girl hadn't quit and left without telling anyone. Although she had worked there for only a short time, she didn't seem the type to do something like that.

"Has anyone seen Xander or Dwayne?" she asked.

Jakub, who had been gone part of the day to check on their mother, just kept eating his food. The others glanced around at each other.

"We haven't," said Nigel. "Not since breakfast."

"They must still be up in their room," offered Laila.

"Xander was pretty upset," said Sharon. "I hope they worked it out. Maybe we should make them plates and take them up?"

"That's a wonderful idea, Sharon," said Klaudie.

Laila nodded. "I'd be happy to help. I do like those young men. I hope they are finished with that silly fight. Xander was so upset that Dwayne wasn't speaking to him. Poor lads, they definitely need us to check on them."

***

Jakub wanted so badly to look at Sharon, but he made himself focus on his food.

After leaving her room, he'd gone back to his own. Kissing her that way had aroused him and left him feeling very frustrated. He'd made up his mind before coming down to dinner that he was going to back off from the situation, give her some space.

However, the minute he was in her immediate vicinity again, he felt helpless.

Then she spoke to him. "How was everything at the farm? Turned out alright?"

"Fine," mumbled Jakub, without looking up from his plate. He wanted to very badly, and he knew it must seem like he was being rude.

"Oh, that's good," Sharon said.

The entire meal continued that way, with occasional brief remarks back and forth, asking simple questions when nobody really cared what the answers were. When they were finished eating, or in some cases pretending to eat, Nigel stepped outside for some air while Sharon and Laila headed upstairs with plates for Xander and Dwayne.

Jakub watched them go, and stifled a sighing groan. Klaudie glanced at him with a mix of sympathy and amusement, but didn't say anything, except to ask Marek, when he arrived to clear the dishes, if he'd seen Amalie.

"Not most of the day," Marek replied. "I even tried calling her a few times, when I was on my way back to the castle to see if she'd be able to help me bring everything inside, but she didn't answer. I thought she must have gone home early."

"If she did, she didn't tell me," Klaudie said. "I looked for her earlier and I couldn't find her either. There was a broken statue upstairs I was going to ask her to clean up. I hope she didn't quit without telling me."

"With all respect, she wouldn't. I've known Amalie since she was a little girl, and I know her family. She wouldn't up and leave a job without letting anyone know."

"Well, she has to be around here somewhere, then." Klaudie shrugged. "She didn't just disappear into thin air."

Chapter 34

"So," Klaudie said, once Marek left the room. "Are you going to tell me what's bothering you?"

Jakub looked at her with an innocent expression. "What do you mean? If it's about Amalie, I'm sure she's fine. Probably got called away suddenly and didn't have the chance to say anything."

"That's not what I meant, and you know it. Though I hope you're right; if she quits, I don't know what I'll do. But I wasn't talking about that."

"Well, if you weren't talking about the maid, then I have no idea what you're talking about. Everything is fine."

Jakub rubbed his nose and looked away from Klaudie. She knew this as a tell-tale sign he was hiding something.

"If you aren't going to address it, then I suppose I should," she told him. "Jakub, I'm not blind. I see there is an attraction between yourself and Sharon."

"What in the world are you talking about, Klaudie? I barely know the woman; I just met her yesterday! She seems to be a nice woman, that's all." He spoke too much, too fast, and still wouldn't meet her eyes.

Klaudie rolled her eyes, unimpressed. It was just like him to try and sweep this under the rug. Although he had the kindest heart she'd ever known, he preferred to present a tough exterior to the world. It was nothing she hadn't seen before.

"You can deny it all you like, Jakub, but I know what I'm seeing. You moon over her like a schoolboy when you think no one's watching, and she follows you around like a lost puppy. I'm concerned your feelings will end up trampled on in the end. At some point, her husband is bound to come back. In the meantime, she may be relying on you as a crutch."

Jakub massaged his forehead. "I know you're always watching out for me, Klaudie. You've done it our entire lives. But you're making a bigger thing of this than it really is. Sure, Sharon has turned to me for comfort, just like she's turned to Laila. She just wants someone who'll listen to her and be a friend. She deserves to have friends, doesn't she?"

***

Jakub could see Klaudie wasn't buying it. He got up from the table and began pacing the room, wondering if it was that obvious to everyone.

He'd certainly tried to act normal around Sharon in front of the others. He tried not to stare, and keep conversations casual. But this was becoming a big mess.

Klaudie put her hands on his shoulders, which stopped him from pacing. "Jakub, I love you. I want you to be happy. And, you are right, I have always tried to watch out for you, as you've done for me. I know you are grown and can make your own decisions, but I wouldn't be a good sister if I didn't at least voice my concerns."

He hugged her, knowing she only had his best interests at heart. She always had. Even so, he didn't feel like he could discuss his feelings about Sharon with her, when he was trying to hide them from himself.

Klaudie ushered him back to his chair and then sat down beside him. "So, what do we do about the chapel?" she asked, changing the subject.

"A friend of mine knows a rabbi in Prague. I thought I'd call him and see if I could get the rabbi's contact information."

"That sounds like a great idea," said Klaudie. "Could you call him now, while we have a free moment?"

"My phone is in my saddlebag, but I need to check on Blesk, anyway." Jakub stood. "Don't worry, I'll take care of it."

Jakub walked to the stable. Blesk was happy to see him, and happier for the carrots and refill of fresh water. When the horse's needs were seen to, he pulled out his phone.

There was a missed call from Irenka, but no message. Which likely meant everything was fine, and she was just calling to make sure he made it safely back to the castle. He'd call her later.

He scrolled through his contacts until he reached Daniel.

"Jakub, it's been a long time!" Daniel said, picking up on the second ring. "How are you, my friend?"

"I'm doing well. How are you? How is your family?" Jakub asked.

"We are all doing very well also. Heidi is expecting our fourth child, can you believe it? Only a couple of months left to wait! And the other three are growing like weeds."

"That's wonderful news, congratulations to you both! Speaking of Heidi, I was wondering if you're still in touch with her rabbi?"

"Dr. Bartik? Yes, he's currently teaching Jewish history at a college here in Prague."

"Any chance you could give me his contact information? I'd appreciate it."

Daniel paused. "Is everything alright, Jakub? That's not the kind of question I'd expect from you."

"Yes, yes, everything is just fine."

Daniel paused again, clearly skeptical. "Well, if you say so, I've no choice but to believe you. I'll text it over to you when we're done here."

"Thanks so much. And let me know when the baby arrives, will you? I'd like to make a trip to come and see you all. It's been too long."

"I agree, it has been. I will let you know. Talk to you soon, Jakub."

"Bye, Daniel."

Moments later, his phone made the familiar sound to let him know that a text had arrived. He saved Dr. Bartik's information, intending to reach out to him tomorrow.

Feeling satisfied he'd done what Klaudie wanted, he started back to the castle.

A blood-curdling scream stopped him dead in his tracks.

It sounded like Sharon.

Jakub ran the rest of the way to the castle as fast as he could.

Chapter 35

Laila and Sharon carried the trays of food up the stairs, chatting as they went along. When they'd reached Xander and Dwayne's room, Laila knocked on the door. There was no answer.

"Hello?" Sharon called. "Xander? Dwayne? Are you in there? Laila and I brought you some dinner."

Still nothing. Just silence, and not a sleeping kind of silence.

She tried the door handle, which turned easily, but was sticky with some darkish substance that smeared onto her fingers. She frowned and wiped her hand on her skirt before pushing the door wide open and flipping on the light switch.

Neither she nor Laila were prepared for what they saw.

Is that ... blood? Sharon thought.

It was everywhere. All over the carpet, splashed onto the walls, covering the bedsheets. And it wasn't just confined to the room; she looked in horror from the doorknob to her hand, to the stain on her skirt.

They set down the plates and conducted a hasty search, but the room and the bathroom were both empty. Then Laila spotted a reddish-brown trail of droplets, and followed it, with Sharon sticking close at her side.

"Should we call for the others?" Sharon asked. "Jakub, Klaudie, Nigel?"

"Xander and Dwayne might need help now," Laila said, picking up her pace.

The trail led to the courtyard. Sharon felt a sense of dread, as if she knew what was coming was going to be terrible. She stopped.

"We shouldn't be doing this by ourselves," she said.

"No, but something strange is going on here. I'm frightened too. I didn't tell you what happened to me this afternoon, but it was awful. This is the last thing I want to be doing right now. But those young men might need help, might need *our* help, and I think we need to try to find them."

Sharon remembered Laila being more quiet than usual at dinner, and wondered what could have frightened her so, but this was not the time to ask. She pushed those thoughts aside and nodded.

They continued across the courtyard, following the blood. The chapel door was open, the chapel itself filled with lit candles, the effect beautiful and creepy at the same time.

The blood led them to the altar, where a long bundle lay rolled up in what appeared to be a bedspread.

Sharon thought of Dwayne and Xander's room, the bloodied sheets visible because the bedspread was missing. She looked at Laila and shook her head. This had gone far enough. Her instincts said it was long past time to get the hell out of there.

But Laila grabbed her arm.

"Please, Sharon. Don't leave me. I have to see what it is."

She wanted more than anything to run, but she didn't want to leave Laila behind, so reluctantly followed her closer to the altar.

The crack in the chapel floor had grown, forming a considerable-sized hole, with a glow emitting from it that hadn't been there before. Sharon tried to direct Laila's attention to it, but Laila, intent, pulled back part of the bedspread enough to see what was concealed within.

Laila staggered back, breathing heavily as if she were about to pass out. She covered her mouth with one hand and pointed at the bedspread with the other. Her wild gaze found Sharon without really seeing her, unable to focus on anything.

Sharon, though she didn't want to, risked a look and saw what Laila had uncovered.

Xander's lifeless, blank-eyed face and slashed, bloodied neck lay revealed amid the folds of the soiled bedspread.

She couldn't process what she was seeing. She opened her mouth and let out the loudest scream of her life before turning and bolting from the chapel.

Chapter 36

Jakub and Nigel found them in the courtyard, both having rushed toward the sound of the screaming. When Sharon saw Jakub she buried her face in his shoulder, crying. He put his arms around her and comforted her as best he could. Nigel did the same with Laila, and for several moments neither woman seemed to have the capacity to speak. They only pointed shakily in the direction of the chapel, but when the men made a move to go see what the fuss was about, neither Sharon nor Laila would let them go.

Klaudie was next to arrive, and when she took over, attempting to calm everyone down, Jakub went to take a look inside the chapel.

He saw the candles, saw the glowing pit in the floor. He saw the bedspread-wrapped body atop the altar, the blood, Xander's dead face and slashed throat. He went right back out and pulled Nigel aside, telling him what he'd found.

"Who would have wanted to kill him?" asked Nigel.

"Didn't he have a fight with his husband at breakfast?" asked Jakub. "Where is the husband?"

"Dwayne didn't do this, there's no way," said Laila, who'd overheard. Tears streamed down her face. "He loves Xander! And they didn't really have a fight per se ..."

"We need to notify the police," declared Nigel. "Immediately."

"Let's go back inside," Jakub suggested.

Sharon and Laila were quick to agree, both of them wanting to get as far away from the chapel as possible.

They gathered again in the great room, while Jakub called the police and Klaudie -- for lack of other ideas -- made tea. Sharon and Laila huddled next to each other in silence, Nigel standing over them.

"They are on their way," Jakub reported, ending his call. "Until then, we should all stay together, for safety reasons."

***

While they waited for the police, Sharon decided to let Maxwell know what had happened. She had no missed calls or texts from him, but sent him a message anyway.

ONE HELL OF A VACATION

JUST WANTED TO LET YOU KNOW THERE'S BEEN SOME TROUBLE HERE AT THE CASTLE. ONE OF THE GUESTS WAS KILLED. THE POLICE ARE ON THEIR WAY. NOT SURE WHAT WILL HAPPEN AFTER THAT. MAY BE GOING HOME EARLY.

Sharon pressed 'Send' and waited a few minutes to see if she would get a reply, but the screen stayed blank. Then she went over and sat beside Jakub.

"Why weren't you speaking to me this morning?" she asked him.

"I don't know what you're talking about," he said, but evasively, looking anywhere but at her.

"Was it the kiss? It made you uncomfortable? I'm sorry."

He hesitated, like he wanted to reply but didn't know what to say, and the timely knock at the front door heralding the arrival of the police was an obvious saved-by-the-bell relief.

One by one, everyone gave their accounts of what they'd seen. Their statements were taken, the chapel would be cordoned off to await forensics, and they were all asked to stay put for the time being. Sharon hadn't caught the officer's last name, but he'd said they could call him Boris.

Finally allowed to go back to her own room, Sharon checked to see if there had been any reply from Maxwell, but still, there was nothing.

That son of a bitch doesn't have thirty seconds to respond to me, she thought.

This was by far the worst vacation she'd ever been on and she couldn't wait to go home. She realized now that there was no saving her marriage. Her marriage had been over before she'd even won the trip. She'd just been too blind to see the truth.

Chapter 37

Maxwell read Sharon's message and wondered who'd kicked the bucket. Probably the old man who'd stuck his nose in their business the other night at dinner. Nigel, that was the man's name. He hoped the stupid fucking asshole was the one who'd died. It'd serve him right.

He was down in the bar area, having a couple of drinks. Monica was taking a nap, but he hadn't been tired so he figured he'd let her sleep for a while. The two of them had been going at it like rabbits since he'd arrived; the poor girl was worn out, and probably sore. He smiled, thinking about it.

Even better, he had finally come up with a plan to get himself out of his current mess. He just needed to have a discussion with Monica to make sure that they were on the same page.

Meanwhile, he wasn't going to answer Sharon's text. He didn't care if one of the others had died at the castle. The person he wanted to die at the castle was his annoying wife.

Finishing his drink, he ordered another, and took it with him to the elevators. Now that he'd had a few, he thought he might be able to lie down and relax.

He also reminded himself he'd need to try and score some more blow when they went out later. The little baggy he'd brought from home was almost gone.

In their room, he found Monica still sleeping peacefully, the sheets pulled up to her waist, but her beautiful breasts visible.

Damn, he loved those breasts.

He quickly undressed and got into bed beside her.

***

In the dungeon, Amalie woke to find that Dwayne had returned. She didn't know whether she was more or less scared to have him there. He sat on the ground staring at her, not saying a word.

She decided to try and speak to him instead.

"I'm thirsty," she said.

Dwayne didn't reply. He just watched her.

"If you let me go, I won't tell anyone. I will leave the castle, and never come back. I don't even know your full name."

It was clear she was not going to get a response from him. She wasn't sure why she'd thought she would. And hadn't the Asian man been upset because his husband wasn't speaking to him? Clearly, there was something very wrong.

She knew about the pit in the chapel, of course. She'd heard stories about it her whole life. When she saw the crack in the floor, she felt like she knew what was to come. She just didn't expect to be caught up in the middle of it.

Amalie wished she'd listened to her family and stayed away from the castle altogether, but she'd really needed the extra money, and it paid significantly better than the bartending she'd been doing.

Now she knew why. The castle was dangerous.

She wondered how much time had passed. Had she been here for an hour, several hours, or over a day? She couldn't be sure. She'd slept quite a bit, and had no idea what time it might be.

She really was thirsty, though; that hadn't just been conversation. But she wasn't hungry, so that was a blessing. She didn't know if she would ever be hungry, wedged in between two skeletons.

Dwayne stood up, never taking his eyes off her. He pulled out the knife and started toward her.

Amalie pleaded with him not to kill her. He reached out with the knife, and sliced at her leg, drawing blood. She screamed and pulled her leg away. He smiled at her, and attempted to cut her other leg. She pulled that one away, too.

Dwayne put the knife to his tongue and licked it clean, like he'd done before. He put the knife back in his pocket and went and sat down where he'd been.

Amalie didn't know how much more of this she could take. Not knowing what was coming next was the worst feeling. She hoped someone would realize she was missing and come find her, but she didn't see how that would happen, since no one had ever found the location of the dungeon before.

If that was the case, and she wasn't going to be rescued, she much preferred to die quickly than to die of starvation or thirst. So maybe if things got too bad, she'd ask this man to kill her. She didn't want to be toyed with.

Amalie watched the blood trickle from her leg and drip onto the floor. The cut stung, but wasn't very deep. She wondered how much blood had been spilled in this room. How many lives lost? Two that she knew of, because their bones were cozied up next to her on either side like best friends. Amalie wondered if the people they loved the most in the world knew what had happened to them, or if they were classified as missing.

She shook the dark thoughts from her mind and tried to keep herself in good spirits. Someone would find her. She had to believe that. It was the only thing that would keep her sane.

Chapter 38

After interviewing everyone about the incident at the castle, Officer Boris Jelinek radioed his boss. He hadn't learned anything to help him so far, except for learning that there had been a fight between the homosexual couple and now one of them was dead.

Boris headed to the chapel to investigate, since that was where the body was located. He certainly hoped he wouldn't be here for long, as his shift had been due to end fifteen minutes after the call had come through that they needed someone out here.

He'd had to drive an hour just to get to the castle, and it would take an hour to get back home; not to mention, it was after dark. The extra pay wouldn't hurt, but he'd just as soon call it a day.

As soon as he entered the chapel, he felt something wasn't quite right, though given he was here because of a possible murder, it was hardly a surprise. Nonetheless, Boris shivered as he walked up to the altar, pulling on a pair of latex gloves.

He lifted the edge of the bedspread and pulled it back. The dead man's eyes stared at nothing. His throat had been cut, with a very sharp blade, judging by how smooth the cut was.

He looked over the rest of the body, but didn't see any defensive wounds, so it must have been a surprise attack. One thing was blatantly obvious: this wasn't an accident, it was murder.

Feeling he'd done the best he could before the medical examiner looked at the body, he covered it back up just as he'd found it and started back toward the chapel door, only to stop after a couple of paces, looking at the hole in the chapel floor. Was it glowing?

He went over to it, and peered inside. The strange light seemed to glow only at the surface. Beneath that, there was only darkness.

Suddenly and unaccountably scared, he turned and left more hastily than he'd ever want to admit.

***

While the police officer was in the chapel, the rest of them decided to conduct a quick search for Dwayne. They started in the attic, Jakub leading the way. The attic yielded no results, nor did the rest of the third floor. They were careful to check each of the rooms, the ones that were accessible, that is. Over half of them were locked.

The bedroom Dwayne had shared with Xander was still a bloody mess. None of the other rooms on the second floor appeared disturbed, and the same went for the rest of the castle, including the trophy room, and the room adjacent.

Finally, they headed for the basement, and Satan's Office, but Sharon didn't hold much hope they were going to find anything there, either.

"I think he left," said Laila. "I bet he's not even here anymore."

"We still need to make sure," Jakub told her.

Again, they found nothing, and when they headed back up the stairs, Sharon saw Officer Boris in the courtyard. She touched Jakub's arm and pointed.

"Let's go see if he has found anything," said Jakub.

ONE HELL OF A VACATION

They all met up, and Sharon thought the police officer looked frightened. She wondered if he'd seen something in the chapel.

"We have searched the entire castle," said Jakub. "There is no sign of Dwayne."

"No one else is in the chapel either," Boris told them.

"What did you find out?" asked Sharon, feeling like he was omitting something.

"Just took a look at the body. It appears he was murdered. The murder weapon was most likely a knife. That's about all I gathered in there."

His eyes told a different story, but Sharon knew he probably wouldn't share it with them. He was in the middle of an investigation. He was probably used to not playing all of his cards at once.

"It's dark out here," said Klaudie. "We should go back inside."

Before they reached the door, Sharon saw something out of the corner of her eye. She turned her head to get a better look, and gasped in shock, clutching at Jakub's hand.

There, in the courtyard, stood a figure. It appeared to be a man. But this man didn't have a head, only a stump where a head should have been.

Sharon couldn't feel her feet and felt like she couldn't breathe.

Jakub and the others stared in disbelief at the headless figure. Laila even rubbed her eyes to look again, but the figure didn't disappear. Boris stood eerily still, his eyes as wide as saucers.

Still unable to breathe, Sharon felt her legs crumple beneath her, and soon, to her relief, her world faded to black.

Chapter 39

As soon as the headless apparition vanished from sight as inexplicably as it had appeared, Jakub scooped up Sharon and carried her to her room.

He was through denying his feelings for the woman. Anyone who had a problem with that, could take it up with him.

He'd known, the second she'd fainted, that he loved her. As impossible as it sounded, it was true. He felt his heart drop into his stomach at the thought of harm coming to her. He'd never felt this way about anyone else in his entire life.

Sharon woke up only a few minutes after Jakub laid her down on her bed. She opened her eyes and blinked foggily at him.

"Where am I?" she asked him.

"You're safe. You're in your room," he told her.

"But how did I get here? What happened?"

Before he could reply, he saw by the look on her face that she was starting to remember, and for a moment he thought she might faint again.

"It's okay, Sharon," he told her, stroking her hair. "You're safe now. I won't let anything happen to you. I promise." "

"Just, please don't leave me."

"Not a chance in hell. I wouldn't leave now if you asked me to, and that's a fact." He brought her a glass of water from the bathroom, which she drank immediately.

"What do we do now?" she asked.

"We stay put, stick together, and wait for more police to arrive. It's not safe out there."

"What I saw ..."

"Yes, we all saw it too, and then it disappeared."

"How did things take such a dark turn so quickly?" Sharon asked. "In only a couple of days, my husband may have opened a portal to Hell, then left me, and now Xander is dead! And to top it off, I'm seeing ghosts! I must be going crazy." She covered her face with her hands.

"You're not crazy. We all saw it," he repeated. "But you should get some sleep."

"What about you? Where will you sleep?"

Jakub didn't plan to sleep; he would keep watch over Sharon all night. Not that he was going to tell her that. "I can fall asleep anywhere; this chair will be fine."

She didn't argue, getting up and going into the bathroom to change onto her pajamas. When she came out, he couldn't help thinking how, even in such ridiculous attire, she looked gorgeous.

She climbed back into bed, curling on her side. Ten minutes later, Jakub heard the cutest sound to ever grace his ears since first hearing her laughter.

She was snoring.

***

"I say we pack our things and get the hell out of here," said Nigel.

"But the policeman said we needed to stay," countered Laila.

"Bother the policeman."

"And what about finding Dwayne? What about Sharon? We can't leave her here in this dreadful place by herself."

"We'll bring her with us to Prague, and help her check into a hotel room."

"I'm not sure she wants to go anywhere without her husband."

"Well, she doesn't have much choice. We're talking murder, love. We can't stay in a place where people are being murdered. We just can't. It's not safe. What if Dwayne has lost the plot and decides to murder the rest of us, too? Did you think of that?"

"Darling, we don't know Dwayne was responsible for what happened to poor Xander."

"Well if he wasn't, then who? Someone killed that boy, and that means we have a murderer nearby. I am afraid for your life, and mine."

Nigel knew he was going to lose this argument. Once Laila made her mind up about something, there was no stopping her. And she *was* quite fond of Sharon. Nigel was fond of Sharon too, but he felt certain that Klaudie, and especially Jakub, would look after her, should they decide to leave.

But he knew they weren't leaving.

He sat on the edge of the bed. Laila was already tucked under the covers.

"I don't want to fight about it, Laila," he said. "I do think we are in danger here, but I know that once your mind is made up, there is no stopping you. So, reluctantly, I'm agreeing with you. We'll stay. But only if you will listen to me, and stay by my side at all times. That's my only condition."

Laila smiled. "Thank you, Nigel. I promise to do exactly as you ask me to." She tried to lighten the mood with a smile. "But no funny business, mister," she said.

Nigel got into bed and they lay in silence, holding hands. He had never felt more thankful to have such a caring and considerate woman who loved him.

Chapter 40

The next morning, as Boris argued with headquarters about when backup would arrive, as well as forensics and a medical examiner, the guests for the most part remained in their rooms.

Klaudie brought everyone breakfast, not that they had much appetite. Jakub stayed with Sharon until she asked him to step out so she could take a bath, which he did reluctantly.

The afternoon passed much the same way, though Klaudie suggested they all meet downstairs for dinner.

Nigel, Laila and Klaudie were already seated around the dining table when Jakub and Sharon reached the great room. Everyone greeted each other and was friendly, but there was less enthusiasm than normal.

Marek brought in sea bass with orzo salad and fresh bread. Everyone helped themselves to small portions. Conversation was minimal, but Nigel finally spoke.

"Like the rest of you, I'm sure that the events that have taken place over the last couple of days have taken a toll on you, as it has on us. Laila and I strongly considered leaving this morning. However, my dear wife has convinced me that we need to stay. We want to help look for Dwayne, and of course,

Laila has become quite attached to you, Sharon, and doesn't want to leave you by yourself. So, we will stay until things are more sorted."

"Thank you, " said Klaudie. "I also wanted to let you know we are looking for Amalie, the maid I introduced you to on the day you arrived. She hasn't been seen since yesterday morning either. At this point, we don't know that she is actually missing. But we didn't see her leave yesterday, and she didn't show up this morning for her regularly scheduled duties. Marek and I have tried calling her and so far, we've only been able to leave voicemails."

"This is too much," said Sharon. She buried her head in her hands.

Jakub put his hand on her back and told her things would be okay.

"And what about last night?" she asked. "Are we going to talk about what happened? Did everyone else see what I saw?"

"If you are referring to the headless person in the courtyard with us, then yes, I saw it," said Laila.

"Now, given headless people normally don't walk around," said Nigel, "combined with what Klaudie told us about reported hauntings of the place ... well, I'd hate to say it, but we may have encountered an actual ghost."

Again, silence took over the table. No one had any better explanation for what they'd seen, and it had been truly terrifying.

"Let's try not to worry," said Jakub. "It's very important that we stick together now, more than ever. No wandering off exploring the castle on your own, or going outside for walks by yourself, either. Do you understand?"

Laila shuddered. "Jakub, you can't be serious. There's no way in hell I'd go anywhere without Nigel now."

"I wasn't so much speaking to you as I was my own sister," said Jakub, looking pointedly at Klaudie. "Do you understand?"

"Of course, I understand," she said. "But this castle isn't going to run itself."

"It will have to. At least for a while. Marek and I can stay here and help out, that way you'll have both of us to look out for you."

Klaudie nodded.

As everyone continued eating, Jakub told Klaudie he'd gotten Dr. Bartik's phone number from his friend, but hadn't had a chance to call him yet.

"I will soon," he promised.

After dinner, Marek came to clear the table, and Klaudie arranged for him to stay at the castle. They all retired early. Sharon couldn't wait to climb back into bed. She had slept most of the day but was still exhausted.

She felt guilty that Jakub insisted on staying with her. If she locked the door, she suggested, she should be all right, but he wouldn't hear of it.

He also wouldn't entertain occupying the other side of the bed and getting some sleep, though she'd told him several times it was fine

Instead, he took his usual spot on the chair. She gave him a small wave, and smiled to herself as she made herself comfortable.

It was only minutes before she drifted off.

Chapter 41

Maxwell was having the time of his life. He'd lost count of how many times they'd had sex over the last couple of days. But now, Monica was complaining about wanting to go out and do other things besides stay in the hotel room, so he booked a cruise down the Vlatva River, followed by dinner at a five-star restaurant.

As he expertly tied his tie around his neck before putting on a dinner jacket, he decided that tonight was the night he would discuss the plan with Monica, regarding getting rid of Sharon. He knew she'd be on board, he just had to make sure he worded things the right way. If Monica loved him the way she claimed to, it shouldn't be a big issue.

He turned around and Monica was standing in the doorway, in the hottest dress he'd ever seen her wear. It was silver, body-hugging, long-sleeved, and so short she'd have to be careful if she bent over. Not that Maxwell minded. If things worked out the way he hoped, he'd be the one to bend her over as many times as he wanted.

To show he could be romantic, Maxwell went over to her and began kissing her neck. She sighed with pleasure. He then took her hand and led her to the door, where he opened it for her.

The cruise down the Vlatva was incredible. Prague was a beautiful city with many more things to offer than Maxwell had initially thought. He was glad his wife had won this trip; it gave him the perfect opportunity to spend time with his girlfriend.

When the cruise was over, they took a taxi to the restaurant, where Maxwell spent well over two hundred American dollars on dinner. He even left a very generous tip for the waiter. Monica was impressed. He had her just where he wanted her. He needed to make sure she was in the perfect mood for what he was about to put forth.

Nor did it hurt that Monica was a little drunk. As soon as they were in their hotel room, she immediately began slipping off clothing. Off went her shoes, then her dress, then her stockings.

Oh yes, thought Maxwell, *she's going to be in just the right mood once I give her what she's craving.*

Monica sprawled the bed on her back. It wasn't very graceful, but Maxwell didn't care. He knelt between her legs, pleasuring her with his tongue while his hands explored her breasts, teasingly pinching her nipples. It only took a minute before she had her first orgasm. She moaned, and cried out his name. Maxwell wiped his mouth and smiled. Standing, he let his pants drop to the floor as he flipped her over onto her stomach and entered her from behind.

God, she felt good!

He fucked her hard and fast, and came in record time. Afterward, they both laid on the bed catching their breath.

Maxwell rolled over and propped himself up on an arm.

"Mon, I have to talk to you about something."

"What is it?" she asked.

"I have a plan for our future. I just need you to hear me out, and let me explain it in full."

"Okay, go for it."

"Sharon has a million-dollar life insurance policy," he said.

Monica's eyes widened.

"We took it out right after we got married," he went on. "There is one for me, too."

"Maxie, what --?"

"Don't interrupt me. So, here we are, out of the country, right? It'd be pretty easy to have an accident in a foreign country. And, since I'm here with you, you can give me an alibi. No one would be able to blame me for it. Then, we collect the life insurance, and live happily ever after."

"Why can't you just get divorced?" she asked. "I don't want anyone to *die*."

"I don't want anyone to die either," he lied, "but I don't see another way. I need that life insurance money for us to be able to make a fresh start somewhere else."

"I don't know, Maxie. I don't like it. We don't need a bunch of money. We can start over on our own. You're smart. We'll be able to make it."

"I won't be able to get another good job, Mon. There's some stuff I've done at the bank that's going to get me in trouble if I don't straighten it out. I need money to do that, too. Do you understand what I'm saying? It's not as easy as the two of us just walking away."

"What if you get caught? What will happen if you do?"

"I told you, Mon, I'm not going to get caught. I promise. I haven't worked out the specifics, but I'll figure it out as I go along. All you have to do is swear I was with you the whole time. I'll take care of business, we'll get the hell out of here, and be back in the United States in the next couple of days."

Chapter 42

It was still dark outside when Maxwell opened his eyes. He reached for his watch on the nightstand and read the time. Just past three in the morning.

He rolled over, expecting Monica to be beside him, but his hand felt nothing but empty sheets. He sat up, then noticed a light under the bathroom door and relaxed.

Then, he heard her voice from in there, speaking hushed but urgently. He crept over to listen, barely able to make out what she was saying.

"I have to get *out* of here, Cam," Monica insisted. "Yes, I know. I'll call a taxi the minute we hang up."

Maxwell's eyes got wide.

"No, he's still asleep. With any luck, I'll be gone before he wakes up."

He felt his blood pressure rise. He'd heard enough. Where the fuck did she think she was going? He threw open the bathroom door. Monica jumped, dropped her phone, and raised her hands.

"Maxie," she said. "I thought you were asleep."

"I'm sure you did. Who were you on the phone with?"

"My sister, Cameron. I promised to call her and I forgot to do it earlier, so I set my alarm for when it wouldn't be the middle of the night there."

Even if he hadn't heard her mention a taxi, it was obvious she was lying.

"Cut the shit, Monica. You're planning to leave? Why? Is it the plan I discussed with you? I thought you were on board with it. At least, you said you were before we went to bed."

Monica tried to move past him, but he blocked the door.

"Please get out of my way," she said.

"I'm not moving until we work this out."

"Maxie, we aren't *going* to work it out. I'm done. I can't be with a man who plans to kill his wife. What happens when you get tired of me? Are you going to kill me, too, at some point in the future?"

"I can't believe this." Maxwell put a hand to his forehead. Then, with one swift motion, he stomped hard on her phone with his heel.

"What the fuck?" she cried, and bent over to retrieve it. The screen was cracked, damaged beyond repair.

ONE HELL OF A VACATION

Stupid little bitch, he thought. He couldn't believe she'd turned on him so quickly. He couldn't believe he'd trusted her. She was just like every other bitch out there. She wasn't worth shit.

His anger continued to build, almost as if it had taken on a life of its own. He wrapped his hands around Monica's neck. Monica tried to push him away, and he squeezed.

Just a little at first. Just enough to see her start to panic. Then he let up and released her. He laughed.

"You're crazy," she wheezed, gulping for oxygen. She pushed forward again, trying to get past him, but he blocked her again. "Let me go!"

"If you ask me nicely, I might. Come to think of it, maybe we should fuck one last time before we part ways." He reached down to stroke his cock, which was already hard.

Monica's smile seemed hopeful and genuine. She knelt and replaced his hand with her mouth. Her head moved forward and back as Maxwell closed his eyes and enjoyed the blow job.

Damn, he'd miss this. She really knew what she was doing. Just as he was about to suggest they get back in bed and forget the whole argument, he felt her teeth bite down, and he howled in pain.

She was on her feet in no time, but he caught her by the throat, this time squeezing much harder. Her face turned purple.

"You fuckin' bitch!" Maxwell squeezed until she passed out, then shoved her backwards.

Her head hit the toilet with a sickening crack. Blood began to gush onto the floor.

Maxwell looked at his hands and back to Monica, trying to understand what he'd done.

Fuck, I killed her, he thought.

He immediately swung into action, putting on clothes and grabbing his belongings. Instead of taking the elevator, he took the stairs. Even at three in the morning, he knew there was less of a chance that way of bumping into someone who could identify him later. He exited the hotel through a side door and walked for two blocks, his mind racing. The plan had changed, but only slightly. Now there was just no future with Monica.

He hailed a taxi.

"Take me to Houska Castle in Blatce," he said.

"But sir, it's the middle of the night," said the driver.

Maxwell held up a wad of cash. Without another word needing to be said, the taxi sped off down the road.

Chapter 43

Silence permeated the room as Jakub kept watch over Sharon. He shifted uncomfortably in his chair, his back stiff from sitting too long, but he didn't get up, for fear of the floor creaking. She was sleeping so peacefully; he didn't want to disturb her.

He loved the way she looked, lying on her side, her hair cascading over the pillow. He listened to her soft breathing and watched her lips move, as if she was having a conversation with someone in her dream.

More than once, he'd stopped himself from joining her on the bed, telling himself it wasn't appropriate and that he need not complicate things any further than they already were.

But oh, how he longed to lie beside her and show her what it felt like to be genuinely loved.

Jakub lifted his hands to his face and rubbed his eyes, trying to make the thoughts go away. When he put them back down, he saw that Sharon had opened her eyes and was looking at him.

She blinked and then patted the mattress. "Come here. Lie down. Please, Jakub."

He tried with all his might to resist the temptation, but he couldn't. Not with her angelic eyes looking at him that way, and her voice pleading with him.

Jakub removed his boots, sighing with relief at how good it felt to take them off. He left his clothes on to help ward off further temptation, but he felt himself get hard as he stretched out beside her.

He lay there on his back, staring at the ceiling. He could feel Sharon's eyes on him. He tried to ignore her nearness, to enjoy just being able to lay down and stretch out for a minute, but it was no use. He could smell the perfume coming from her skin. It was intoxicating.

She took his hand, and he felt like electricity was shooting through his entire body, his heart beating rapidly in his chest. But still, he tried not to let her feel his reaction.

Then she let go of his hand and rolled onto her side, facing him. She draped an arm and leg over him, snuggling as close as she could get. Jakub lay there, stiff as a board. Finally, Sharon spoke, meekly.

"Jakub, would you ... hold me?"

Jakub groaned. He touched her arm where it lay on his chest, and ran his fingers along it, caressing her smooth skin.

"I don't know if this is a good idea," he said in a husky voice.

"I just need to be held."

"Okay, but, roll over to your other side," said Jakub.

Sharon did so, and he did the same, spooning their bodies, with his arm around her waist. He inhaled her scent and groaned again.

Then he realized his erection was pressed against her bottom. And, he could have been imagining it, but it felt like she was pressing herself back against it.

She giggled a little. No, he wasn't imagining it.

"I thought you said you just needed to be held," Jakub said.

"I don't know what you're talking about," she replied innocently, continuing to wriggle tantalizingly against him.

He wanted her so bad he could hardly stand it. This wasn't fair. He shouldn't have gotten in the bed with her. He rolled over, slid to the edge of the bed and got up.

"What are you doing?" asked Sharon anxiously.

"This was a mistake. Go back to sleep."

"Jakub, please, lie back down. I'm sorry, I won't tease anymore."

"It's not right, Sharon. You're married. And I am not that kind of guy. It's already gone further than I should have let it." He returned to his chair and sat down again, resolute.

"Fine." Sharon turned away from him, so that her face was hidden from his view.

Jakub knew she was disappointed. Hell, *he* was disappointed! He wondered about what kind of men Sharon had dated in the past besides Maxwell. He guessed none of them had ever had any respect for her either. He just wanted to show her the respect she deserved. If they were meant to be, the path would open up. And, if not, he'd love her from afar.

It wasn't long before he heard sniffles. *Great, I made her cry,* he thought. It was the last thing he wanted to do. He stroked her hair, letting her curls run through his fingers.

"Shhhh, don't cry. I'm sorry. I don't ever want to hurt you."

"I'm so confused," she sobbed. "My whole life is a mess. Maxwell is gone, maybe for good. He won't even answer my texts. I came on this trip with him, hoping I'd be able to save our marriage. But there was never any hope of saving it, because it would have taken both of us, and he didn't want to." Sharon wiped her nose. "And then something happened. Then I met you. I feel this ... unexplained connection with you. It's made me almost forget about Maxwell. It's made me not even care. Does that make sense?"

"More than you know," he said. "I've never had feelings for someone the way I do for you. I'm trying to be respectful. I want you to love me, Sharon, because the truth is, I'm falling for you. But it's not right to go to bed with you now. Not with the way things are. Just try and get some sleep, and I'll sit right here, where you can feel me close to you, okay?"

"Okay," Sharon sighed, and closed her eyes.

Chapter 44

Hearing banging coming from the front door downstairs, Jakub woke with a start. He quickly pulled his boots on and left Sharon's room, locking the door behind him.

When he opened the door, a policeman stood there. An unfamiliar one, not Boris. Had his backup finally arrived?

"May I help you?" asked Jakub.

"Good morning, sir. I am Officer Cermak. I am looking for a Maxwell Stone."

"He ... he isn't here," he said, as Klaudie came up behind him.

"What's going on?" she asked.

"This is Officer Cermak. He's here looking for Mr. Stone."

"We found a travel itinerary that indicated he was staying here," said Officer Cermak.

"Yes, he was here, but he left a couple of days ago," said Klaudie. "His wife is still here. What is this about?"

"Maybe it would be easier if you come inside and have a seat." Jakub stepped to the side.

Cermak nodded, and followed Klaudie down the hall to the trophy room, where she offered him a seat and inquired as to whether he'd like a cup of tea

"No thank you, ma'am. Now, you said Mr. Stone left a couple of days ago?"

"Yes," said Klaudie. "He sent a text to his wife and told her he needed to deal with some work issues for a while." She paused, weighing her words. "Mrs. Stone, she was very upset."

"I was upset about what?"

Everyone looked to the door, where Sharon stood, a robe over her pajamas.

Jakub ushered her to a chair, and introduced her to Officer Cermak.

"Mrs. Stone, I am here regarding your husband," said Officer Cermak. "Early this morning we had a call from the on-duty manager of a hotel in Prague. A maid noticed a door was partially open to one of the rooms on the fourth floor. After calling out, she went in to check. In the bathroom, she found the body of a young woman, deceased."

"But ... but what does that mean?" Sharon asked. Her hands were shaking.

"Are you familiar with a Monica Morris?" he asked.

"Monica? That's ... that's Maxwell's secretary" As she sat there, trying to keep her composure, Jakub moved behind her and rested his hands on her shoulders.

"Did you know that Ms. Morris was in Prague?"

"Wait, wait, are you telling me the woman in the hotel room was *Monica?*" Sharon shook her head to indicate that she couldn't believe what she was being told. "And ... and you think Maxwell ..." No, it was just too insane.

"The room was paid for by a credit card in his name," Cermak said. "Hotel staff report having seen a man matching his description."

Sharon's jaw dropped. She knew it could only mean one thing. Maxwell had been sleeping with Monica -- *an affair with his secretary, how cliche*, part of her mind thought wryly -- and had brought her to Prague to keep himself entertained. During the vacation she had won, to add insult to injury. And now Monica was dead, and the police suspected Maxwell might be involved?

Klaudie sprang up and offered to make some tea. Jakub told her to go ahead and do so.

Officer Cermak kept his gaze on Sharon. "Has your husband been acting differently since you arrived here at the castle, Mrs. Stone?"

"No differently than he normally acts," she said, subdued. "We've been arguing quite a bit. We came on this trip hoping to get away from our regular lives and rekindle things, but it was clear from the start that was just my wishful thinking."

"I'm sorry to have to ask you these questions, ma'am, and I'm truly sorry about your marriage troubles. But my focus right now is finding your husband."

"Do you... you don't think he killed Monica?" Sharon almost pleaded.

"That's not for me to speculate. We just need to talk to Mr. Stone, so we can get to the bottom of what happened."

"Oh my God." Sharon lowered her head into her hands and began to cry.

"I'm going to leave you with my card. If you hear anything, or if he turns up, please, give me a call."

Jakub took the card, then led the officer back to the front door. Officer Cermak turned around and spoke.

"It's my understanding that Officer Jelinek is here investigating a different matter?"

"Boris? Yes," Jakub said.

"The apparent murder of one guest and the apparent disappearance of another?"

Jakub winced. Hearing it put like that, along with this business of Maxwell and the woman in the hotel, did not sound at all good.

"I wanted to ask if there was an update," Officer Cermak continued.

"We haven't seen him yet this morning. But I will let him know."

"Very well, sir. Thank you for your cooperation, and please tell Mrs. Stone not to worry. We'll do our very best to find her husband." Officer Cermak turned and walked down the path to his car.

Jakub closed the door and returned to the great room, where Marek was setting up breakfast trays. He sat down beside Sharon, who hadn't budged.

"I'm taking a quick trip to Prague after breakfast," he told her. "Would you like to come with me?"

Sharon nodded dully. Jakub asked Klaudie to keep an eye on her for the next few minutes, while he went out to check on Blesk. The minute he stepped outside, he pulled out his cell phone and punched in a number.

"Dr. Bartik?" he said as a man's voice answered. "My name is Jakub Dvorak, and I need your help."

Chapter 45

"Where, exactly, are we going?" Sharon asked, as Jakub drove the car he'd borrowed from Marek away from the castle.

"To Prague," he said. "There's a rabbi there I need to speak to about what's going on in the chapel. If it's indeed the fabled pit opening up, we need to figure out how to close it." He glanced at the speedometer, and eased up on the gas pedal. He clearly wasn't used to driving a car, taking Blesk everywhere he needed to go.

"How will a rabbi be able to help?" asked Sharon.

"I don't know for sure that he will. But I wanted to meet him in person. And I thought it would be nice to get away from the castle for a bit. You definitely needed a break."

"Especially after the visit from Officer Cermak this morning," she said. If both of them were speculating whether the matters might be connected -- the chapel, and whatever had happened with Maxwell and Monica -- neither of them mentioned it.

They chatted of inconsequential things on the rest of the drive to Prague, making it seem like a short trip. Once they reached the city, it didn't take Jakub long to find Dr. Bartik's office. They knocked, waited, and the door opened to reveal an elderly man.

"Dr. Bartik? I spoke with you on the phone. I'm Jakub." He offered his hand to the rabbi and the rabbi shook it eagerly.

"Yes, yes, come inside my dear boy. I've been expecting you," said Dr Bartik, smiling. "Please, call me Herschel." He led them to a comfy couch in his office, where they both took a seat, and sat in an arm chair across from them. "Oh, where are my manners, would either of you like something to drink?"

"No, sir. But thank you for offering," said Jakub.

"Well, let's get down to business, then, shall we? Your phone call sounded quite urgent. What can I help you with?" asked Herschel.

"My sister manages Houska Castle. I assume you are familiar with the old legends?"

"Houska Castle. My, my. I haven't thought about that place in quite a long time. But yes, I am familiar with all of the folklore."

"We've had some disturbing activity recently. One of the guests found an old book hidden under a loose floorboard in the attic. The book was in Hebrew but included handwritten translations in German, with sprinkles of Latin throughout. Its title claimed it was a book of spells. Another guest stole it, and took it out to the chapel, where it seems he read some of the passages aloud. The next morning, the chapel floor was cracked. Since then, another guest was murdered, some more people have gone missing, and the crack appears to be getting bigger. My sister and I are worried that whatever was read aloud in the chapel may have opened the legendary portal to Hell."

Jakub and Sharon both watched Herschel closely for his reaction. He didn't laugh or throw them out, but looked thoughtful.

"Tell me more about this book. Do you have it with you, or any pictures?"

"I don't. I didn't think to take pictures before I left, but when I get back to the castle, I will email some to you," said Jakub.

"If this book is what I fear it might be, you are all in grave danger. It cannot be a coincidence that this hole in the floor appeared after words from a sacred book were read there. You are right to be worried. I am worried for you. For all of us. The longer such a portal is open, the stronger it gets. If left open too long, it will be impossible to close. If that happens, all of humanity could be at risk."

Jakub exchanged a glance with Sharon. She was frightened, he could tell. He was scared too, but put on a brave face for her. They'd figure out how to fix this, together, with Herschel's help.

"So where do we go from here, sir?" he asked.

"Straight back to the castle. I need to know more about this book immediately and do some research. I will work as fast as I can to find a solution for you. In the meantime, stay out of the chapel. Do not go in there for any reason. The pit is more dangerous the closer in proximity you are to it."

ONE HELL OF A VACATION

Jakub stood and Sharon followed suit. "We'll head back now."

Herschel went to his desk by the window, wrote something on a piece of paper, then handed it to Jakub. "Here is my email address. Send me the pictures as soon as possible."

He walked them both back to the door, where they exchanged goodbyes. As Jakub opened the car door for Sharon, he glanced back at the office, seeing Herschel, through the window. He watched the old man as he poured himself a stiff drink and downed it.

Then Herschel knelt on the floor, closing his eyes and bowing his head in prayer, and Jakub felt chills down his spine.

Chapter 46

Boris Jelinek sat on the front steps of the castle, smoking a cigarette. He was tired, hungry and frustrated. He'd radioed in again a few minutes ago to ask when the coroner was going to arrive, because as of yet, no one had shown up to remove the body from the chapel.

Headquarters told him they'd send someone as soon as they could. He also learned that prick Cermak had been there earlier that morning, nosing around for some reason.

Boris heard the door open and turned to see the guest called Nigel standing in the doorway.

"How's it going?" Nigel asked.

"Not too well right now, I'm afraid. The victim's husband must have fled the grounds. I've searched everywhere I can think of, and turned up nothing."

"But all of his things are still here. Anyway, where would he have gone? He didn't have a vehicle, and fleeing on foot in the middle of the woods seems far-fetched."

"I agree with you on that. But if he's here, then where is he?"

"I'd be happy to help you search again. Not much else going on right now. The ladies are having tea. I can pop in and remind them to stay together."

"I appreciate the offer. Are you sure you wouldn't mind? Normally I'm not on my own when there's been a crime, but they're shorthanded at headquarters."

"Not a problem. Give me just a minute to let the ladies know." Nigel went back inside.

Boris puffed on his cigarette. It was just his luck he'd end up with a case like this. He'd been looking forward to getting off shift and finding a pub to have a few beers. Instead, he was stuck at this miserable place, with no help and not even an ETA of when help was coming. Not to mention, when he'd decided to take this cigarette break, he'd pulled out the pack and discovered he only had three cigarettes left, one of which he was now smoking. Which left him with two.

He tried not to think about it. Couldn't be more than a couple more hours before someone arrived to relieve him.

He stubbed out the cigarette just as Nigel returned. "Everything settled?" he asked.

"Yes, Klaudie will stay with my wife. Marek, the chef, is here also, and planning to stay as long as he's needed."

Boris stood up. "Okay then, let's get going," he said.

They searched all of the spots Boris had already been over several times. Though both were a bit reluctant to go back into the chapel, it was necessary, but still turned up nothing. Same for the stables, and the rest of the outside parameters of the castle. Next, they went up to the attic again, then the third and second floors, looking in bedrooms, in closets, under beds, in the bathtubs.

But still, nothing.

Nigel turned to Boris. "Where to next?"

"Fuck if I know," Boris said, beyond frustrated. He hadn't truly expected this search to be any different than the ones before, but still had hope. He was beginning to think they'd have to use the hounds to sniff out Dwayne's hiding spot.

"The basement?"

"I hate it down there," Boris admitted. "I know I'm a policeman, but that place gives me the creeps."

"Me too," said Nigel, "but we can't have done a thorough search if we haven't been down there."

"Right you are. Lead the way, then."

ONE HELL OF A VACATION

Satan's Office was still as unsettling as ever. There were no cobwebs, but there might as well have been; it couldn't have gotten any creepier.

Nigel looked over at the stonelike throne and shivered. "I can't believe Maxwell had the nerve to sit on that thing," he mumbled.

"Huh?" Boris asked.

"Nothing, just thinking out loud."

Boris glanced around. There weren't very many places down here that a person could hide. He walked the perimeter, including behind the throne, but nothing was back there.

Then he heard, or thought he heard, a noise.

He looked at Nigel, who'd also evidently heard something.

"Hello?" Boris called.

Muffled sounds were coming from somewhere. Someone was yelling. It sounded like a woman, but the noise was very faint. Boris leaned his head against the wall behind the throne and listened.

"Someone is behind there!" Boris said.

"But how?" Nigel asked.

They closely examined the wall, running their hands over it. Whoever was behind the wall continued to cry out.

Finally, Boris noticed one stone in the wall that looked different from the others. He called Nigel over, then pressed it and felt it move underneath his hand.

The back wall behind the throne began to swing outward. Boris and Nigel stepped back, shocked.

A hidden room in the basement? The cries they'd heard before were louder now, and desperate. Boris feared what he would find once he went inside, but he had no choice, and even if he'd hesitated, Nigel was ready to rush right in.

Amid fleeting impressions of dungeon walls and hanging shackles, there, on the floor, wedged between two skeletons, was a filthy, bloodied young woman, looking up at them with wild, pleading eyes.

"Get me out of here, please!" she cried.

Chapter 47

Jakub and Sharon returned to find Klaudie and Laila chatting pleasantly and drinking tea, as if it were any ordinary day.

"How was the trip?" Klaudie asked.

"Where's Nigel?" asked Jakub, ignoring the question.

"With Boris, doing another sweep of the place," Laila said. "Dwayne still hasn't turned up. Why?"

"I need the book. We just got back from speaking with a rabbi in Prague. He's asked me to send him some pictures."

"It's in our room. I'll go and fetch it." Laila got up.

"I'll go with you." said Sharon. She turned to Jakub. "We'll be right back."

As they left the room, Jakub sat down across from his sister. It was amazing how well she was holding up, all things considered. He leaned back in the chair and stretched his legs. Driving would never be the same as riding.

"So, the meeting?" Klaudie prodded.

"I could kick myself for not taking pictures of the book before I left. I should've known he would need to see the passages."

"Ah, it's just as easy to snap a few now and send them to him. He'll have them in a matter of minutes. Would you like a cup of tea?"

"Sure," he said. A tray of biscuits was on the table, so Jakub helped himself to one. He had been in such a rush to get on the road earlier, he hadn't eaten much breakfast, and was hungry.

"Did he say anything that might help?" Klaudie asked.

"He told me we were right to think it's related to the pit of the legends. He said the bigger it gets, the more of a danger it is, and we need to close it as soon as possible."

Klaudie nodded, pouring Jakub a cup of tea and refilling her own.

Voices from the hall preceded Laila and Sharon. Laila gave the book to Jakub.

He pulled out his phone and activated the camera, snapping pictures of the cover and the title page.

"Do you remember which passages he said he read?" he asked Sharon.

"I think so. Klaudie was there too when he showed us."

They flanked him, and Sharon flipped pages until she stopped at one and glanced to Klaudie for confirmation.

"Yes, that's it," said Klaudie.

Jakub snapped some more pictures and then opened his email.

Herschel,

Attached are pictures of the book found in the attic here at Castle Houska. Please call me as soon as you have any information. I appreciate your help in this matter.

Regards, Jakub Dvorak

Jakub reread what he had written quickly and then pressed 'Send.'

"So now what?" Sharon asked as he picked up his tea and reached for another biscuit.

"Now, we wait," said Jakub.

"I'm wondering where Nigel and Boris got off to," said Laila. "I didn't expect them to be gone this long."

At that very moment, they heard Nigel's voice, shouting from the far end of the hall.

Laila went to the doorway and gasped. Jakub got up and joined her, Sharon and Klaudie close behind.

Boris and Nigel were making their way down the hall, but it appeared they were carrying someone between them.

"They must have found Dwayne!" Laila cried, and hurried toward the men, halting when she got a better look at the person with them, who most decidedly wasn't Dwayne.

"Amalie!" exclaimed Klaudie. "It's Amalie! Where did you find her? What happened? Is she hurt?"

They brought her into the great room and set her down in a chair. She looked dreadful, her face bruised and her hair tangled, her clothes stained, with a bloody cut on each of her legs. When Laila offered her a glass of water, she gulped it greedily.

Then, as the others gathered anxiously around her, she took a deep, shaky breath and told them what had happened.

Chapter 48

"I was dusting in the second-floor hallway when I heard someone cry out. It was from the room with the two male guests. To my regret, I decided to see what was happening."

"Xander and Dwayne," said Laila.

"The door was partway open, so I could see inside. I saw the Asian man..."

"Xander," said Sharon.

"I saw him on the ground, bleeding, and the other standing over him with a knife. And he was licking the knife! It scared me, so I tried to quietly retreat, but I bumped into a statue and knocked it off of its pillar. It made a huge noise when it hit the floor and he caught me. I tried to get away from him but he punched me in the face, and I guess it knocked me out because I woke up tied to a chair. I tried to get away again, and fell while he was chasing me. The next thing I knew, I was in the dungeon. He was there too, and at first, he just sat and stared at me. But then he cut my legs. He licked the blood from the knife again. It looked like he was enjoying it. Then he left me alone with the ... with the skeletons. I thought I'd never be found. I'm so grateful to you both." Amalie burst into tears.

As Nigel, Klaudie, and a hastily-summoned Marek arranged to come up with some bandages and disinfectant to treat Amalie's wounds, Boris continued questioning her.

"So, Dwayne killed Xander, is that correct?" he asked.

"I didn't see the actual killing, but he was standing over him with a knife." Amalie shuddered. "Licking the blood from it. He looked like a mental patient."

"It's all right, you're safe now," said Sharon. She took off the coat she'd worn on their outing and draped it over Amalie.

"Did he give you any information at all that might help us locate him?" Boris persisted.

"I don't even know when he left the dungeon. My head hurt so bad. I kept falling asleep and then waking up and then falling asleep again."

"You mentioned ... skeletons?" asked Sharon.

Nigel nodded grimly. "There were two human skeletons in the dungeon, one on either side of her. At a guess, they've been there for quite a while."

"They'll be removed and sent off for further examination," Boris said.

"You poor thing! This must've been awful for you," Klaudie said to Amalie. "Let's get you into a bath and some clean clothes, and then you can rest until someone from your family can come get you. I'll call them. I know they've been worried. And you should probably see a doctor; you could have a concussion."

***

"Thank God she's safe," said Sharon, once Amalie's father had driven off with her, promising to see her straight to a doctor.

She was also, under orders from Klaudie, to take at least the rest of the week off, to recover from her ordeal. Whether Amalie would decide to return to work at the castle or not would have to remain to be seen.

"My sentiment exactly," Laila agreed. "This place has turned into a circus."

"Well, if Dwayne was in the dungeon most of the time, that means he's had to find a new hiding spot now," said Boris.

Nigel nodded. "Exactly. We need to do another sweep right now and catch him before he tries to leave altogether."

Jakub looked at Sharon. "Will you be okay here while I help them search for Dwayne?" he asked her.

Sharon nodded her head. "Yes, I'll be fine."

"I'll go up with her," said Laila. "I'd quite like to have a bath myself. It's so chilly in this place and I think that would warm me up nicely."

With all arrangements made, Laila and Sharon headed upstairs, while Boris, Nigel and Jakub began their search.

"Are you sure you don't want me to wait in your room while you take your bath?" Sharon asked. "We aren't supposed to be alone, Laila."

"Don't be silly, my dear." She gave her a hug. "My room is only two doors down and I promise, I'll lock the door. And our good man Marek is stationed right here in the hall. It'll be fine."

Chapter 49

From underneath the bed, the thing that was not Dwayne watched as Laila's feet crossed the bedroom floor. He squeezed the knife in his hand tightly. Laila hummed a tune as she went into the bathroom and took off her clothes. Soon, he heard water being poured into the tub, and the scent of lilac hit his nose.

The thing that was not Dwayne waited for her to get comfortable before crawling out from under the bed. He slowly got to his feet. Laila was immersed in the bath, with a wash rag across her eyes. She breathed evenly in and out.

The thing that was not Dwayne crept closer, but there was a wet spot on the floor he didn't see. His foot made a squeaking sound as it slipped in the puddle. He had no time to hide. Laila pulled the rag from her face and saw him, standing over her with the knife raised.

Laila screamed in terror. He swung the knife down, hoping to penetrate her flesh, but she moved out of the way just in time. She grabbed his arm, struggling to keep him from trying again, still screaming.

The locked bedroom door rattled furiously, then crashed open. Someone charged in, burst into the bathroom, and grappled the thing that was not Dwayne from behind. He slashed the air, aiming at nothing and everything all at once.

***

Nigel, Jakub and Boris were in the courtyard when they heard someone yelling and turned to see Sharon running toward them.

"Come quick! It's Laila!" she cried, barely able to catch her breath.

Nigel didn't wait for the others. He took off running for the bedroom, his head full of fear and worry for his wife. He reached the second-floor landing in no time and raced down the hall. The bedroom door was open, its lock broken. A commotion was going on in the bathroom.

His mouth dropped open in shock when he saw Marek struggling with a knife-wielding Dwayne, as Laila cowered, naked and screaming, in the tub.

Boris shoved past him, drawing a billy club. He swung at Dwayne's knee, dropping Dwayne to the floor. Marek and Boris then managed to wrestle the knife away from him and pinned him.

As Marek and Boris, with Jakub's help, successfully restrained Dwayne, marching him into the bedroom and tying him to a chair with neckties and torn strips of sheet, Nigel helped Laila out of the tub and put a towel around her. She was crying hysterically. He wrapped his arms around her and held her as she continued to cry.

"There there, darling, it's alright. I'm here now. No need to be afraid any longer," he said.

"Nigel, I don't know what happened. One minute I was taking a relaxing bath, and the next, that maniac was standing over me with a knife. I thought I was going to die!" Laila said, looking up at her husband with her tear-stained face.

"I know, sweetheart. Everything is alright now. Let's get you into some clothes before you catch a cold."

***

At Nigel's request, the men dragged Dwayne and the chair out of the room, then Klaudie and Sharon took charge of helping Laila get dressed.

Klaudie then sat her down at the vanity, picked up a hairbrush, and swept it through Laila's damp silver hair to remove the tangles.

Laila felt the adrenaline beginning to wear off, replaced by exhaustion.

"I'm so tired. Do you think I could lie down for a little while?" she asked.

"Of course," said Sharon. "We will stay with you the whole time."

She tucked Laila in, then made herself as comfortable as possible while she waited and kept watch.

Klaudie prayed this was the end of the nightmare, but knew that, until Maxwell was found, and the pit in the chapel was dealt with, it was far from over.

Chapter 50

Once they'd gotten Dwayne downstairs, tied more securely to a heavier chair in the trophy room with ropes Jakub fetched from the stable, Nigel walked right over to Dwayne and punched him in the face.

They all heard Dwayne's nose crack, but he showed no reaction, the blank expression on his face unchanged.

"Now, no call for that," said Boris, more as if he knew he was supposed to than because he meant it.

Jakub studied Dwayne, surprised he hadn't put up any more of a fight or spoken a single word. He just sat there, bound, saying nothing, staring straight ahead with an unsettling blankness.

"I think we should keep him locked in here," he said. "Away from the women, so they don't have to see him. And we'll take turns watching him, until your backup arrives, Boris."

Boris nodded, wiping sweat from his forehead. "Agreed, but first I need a smoke."

Leaving Marek and Nigel to keep an eye on Dwayne ... as well as Marek to keep an eye on Nigel in case he got free with his fists again, not that anyone could have blamed him ... Jakub tagged along outside with Boris.

Boris took his pack of cigarettes and lighter out of his pocket. He opened the pack and peered into it with dismay, having forgotten he was running low. Only two left, soon to be only one. He lit the second-to-last, took a long drag, and blew out the smoke, contemplating everything that'd transpired in the last few hours.

It had been an intense afternoon, that was for sure.

Jakub interrupted his thoughts.

"Do you find it strange Dwayne hasn't said anything at all? Or resisted when we tied him up, or tried to escape?

"Maybe he knows he's been caught and there's nothing he can do about it," suggested Boris.

"Of all the people you've arrested, how often does that happen? They just let you take them into custody, and they don't say a word?"

"Actually, come to think of it, even the blatantly guilty ones usually have something to say."

"I don't understand why he's doing this. If he had a beef with his husband and they argued and he killed him, that's one thing, but why kidnap Amalie?"

"Because she saw him kill the husband."

"Then why not just kill her too, instead of imprisoning her? And why try to kill Laila? She hadn't done or seen anything."

"I have no explanation for any of that." Boris stubbed out his cigarette, already craving another, but he needed to save his last one, in case it was a while before he could get more. "Or how he found, or even knew about, that secret room in the basement."

"The dungeon," Jakub said. "There were rumors, like with the chapel, but I don't think Klaudie mentioned it when she told them the history"

"I guess we should try and get some answers," said Boris.

They went back inside. In the trophy room, Dwayne didn't appear to have moved a muscle, Nigel and Marek watching him.

"Has he said anything?" Jakub asked.

Nigel shook his head. "Not a word."

Boris dragged another chair in front of Dwayne, sat down, and cleared his throat.

"Sir, do you know why we've detained you?" he asked.

No answer.

"Can you tell us what happened between you and your husband that resulted in his death?"

Still no answer.

"What can you tell us about the maid, and the room in the basement?"

The silence and blank stare continued.

"This isn't working," Nigel said. He stalked over and loomed threateningly. "Listen here you fucking piece of shit, why did you try to kill my wife?"

At that, Dwayne's gaze moved to Nigel, and his blank expression twisted into an evil grin.

With a cry of rage, Nigel lunged for him, putting his hands around his throat. Boris and Jakub pulled him back.

"I said, none of that," Boris repeated, sounding more like he meant it this time. He made Nigel sit down. Nigel's face was bright red with anger, but he complied.

Jakub decided to try a different tack, one Boris had seen done often enough before.

"Hey Dwayne," he said, mildly. "What's going on? My sister says this isn't like you at all. Is something wrong? Something we can help with?" He was taking a gentler approach, trying to gain trust.

But Dwayne remained silent.

It was obvious that they weren't going to get anywhere with him, so they decided to wait until other officers arrived.

At that point, Dwayne would be their problem.

Chapter 51

With Boris taking first watch over Dwayne, Jakub went upstairs to the guest room assigned to him, not that he'd had much occasion to use it what with watching over Sharon all night.

He sometimes found it easier to communicate if he wrote out his thoughts first. He wanted to talk to Sharon about how he felt toward her, but didn't trust that his brain would come up with the right words in the moment. So, he figured he'd take this opportunity to try and organize them properly.

Putting pen to paper, he wrote:

Sharon,

We've known each other only a few short days, but, in that time, I feel like I've known you for a lifetime. The first moment I ever saw you, I felt like I was about to pass out. I'd never seen such a beautiful woman in all my days. Your hair black as night with curly tendrils that I'd love to run my hands through, your gorgeous brown almond shaped eyes that I could get lost in... I could go on and on.

But then, I got to know you. And your inner beauty far outweighs your outer beauty, which seems nearly impossible, but it is true. I never stood a chance. I fell in love with you instantly.

Love is a strange thing. I've never experienced it, I don't think. Not beyond my love for my parents and my sisters. I've had a few girlfriends in the past and growing up. Klaudie will tell you that none of them were special, not like you. I'm normally a very level headed man, but all logic and reasoning are thrown out the door when it comes to you and the lengths I would go to in order to make you happy. I'd move heaven and earth.

I hate that we met under these circumstances, but I feel as though no matter the circumstances, the outcome would still be the same. I am a smitten man. I hope you feel the same about me.

I don't know what the future will bring. It's very selfish of me to worry that your husband will return and wish to work things out with you. I don't want that to happen, which is awful because I know your heart is broken because he left you. But I know that, if given the chance, I could make you happier than he ever did. I would treat you like a princess. I'd even move to the United States just to be with you. Or if you decided you wanted to stay at the farm, that would be okay with me too.

Wherever I go, though, you know I must take Blesk with me, so if I do move to Connecticut, we must have a backyard big enough for him. This is a joke, Sharon. I hope you laughed.

Your husband didn't treat you the way that you deserved to be treated. And even if we aren't meant to be together, I want for you to know this. You deserve the best in life. Do not ever settle for less. The worst possible thing that could ever happen would be for you to be with someone who doesn't treat you well. If I'm the person who's meant to be with you, you will never have to worry about whether I will love you forever because the answer is yes. I will love you forever, Sharon. That, I promise.

Jakub read back the words. *Rubbish*, he thought. Even trying to write it down hadn't helped him express the love within him.

Maybe now wasn't the time to worry about it. There were so many things going on, it seemed like it could wait for a while.

He sat and thought about everything that had transpired that day, from finding out that Maxwell was missing, the dead woman in Prague, going to see Herschel with Sharon, Boris and

ONE HELL OF A VACATION

Nigel finding Amalie, Dwayne trying to kill Laila... it just seemed to be never ending.

He just wanted some peace and alone time with Sharon, where things were normal. He wasn't sure if that would ever happen.

Jakub wondered where Maxwell had gone, and if he was responsible for killing the woman in Prague. It certainly seemed like he must be involved in some way.

He also wondered where Boris's backup was, and why they hadn't arrived yet. He'd been here since yesterday, and yet, no one had shown up to relieve him. How could the police department be so short on help?

His thoughts wandered to Laila, hoping she'd be all right. He felt terrible for her and for Nigel. He couldn't imagine what must have been racing through her head as she struggled in the tub to keep Dwayne from stabbing her. It was lucky Marek had been right outside in the hall and heard her scream. If everyone else had been downstairs, they'd have had another dead body on their hands.

Most of all, he still wondered why Dwayne wasn't speaking. It was almost as if he was in some sort of trancelike state. None of it made any sense. Klaudie said he'd seemed fine when he first arrived at the castle. It wasn't until the morning he and Xander seemingly had some sort of issue between them that his demeanor had changed drastically.

Jakub looked down at his note again. He shook his head. *This is just embarrassing,* he thought. He wadded the paper up and tossed it in the waste basket. Then, he stood and left the room.

Chapter 52

The longer Boris sat keeping watch over Dwayne, the more aggravated he became. It had been over twenty-four hours since he'd arrived at the castle, and still no word on when his backup was going to arrive. This was beyond ridiculous.

He paced the length of the trophy room to give his legs something to do. He'd been sitting for too long, and become stiff and uncomfortable. The movement also helped him think. He wished he could smoke in here.

The room was silent. Dwayne sat motionless with his eyes staring straight ahead like a zombie. Which was another reason for moving around; Boris couldn't take the both of them just sitting there. It was disturbing to say the least. Something was seriously wrong with the man.

Examining some of the old weapons that were laid out on display, it dawned on him that the knife they'd taken from Dwayne could have come from here. He would have to check into that later, making a mental note to ask Klaudie. She would surely recognize the knife if it belonged to a collection owned by the castle.

Boris paced the floor a few more times and finally he couldn't stand it any longer. He needed to smoke. He didn't care that it was his last cigarette. He'd make another phone call to headquarters while he was outside.

He glanced at Dwayne, wondering if he should call for one of the others to take over while he stepped out, but decided that, no, Dwayne was securely tied up. There was no way he could get loose. He'd be fine by himself for a few minutes while Boris took a few puffs.

He slipped out of the castle, finding a stand of trees so as not to be immediately noticed by anyone else if they were to come outside.

He looked at the lone cigarette with both longing and despair, knowing that after he finished it, he'd regret having smoked his last.

Before he lit it, he pulled his mobile phone out of his pocket and pressed the speed dial for headquarters. The phone rang twice before someone picked up on the other end.

"Officer Jelinek, we've been meaning to call you."

"Who's this?" asked Boris.

"It's Michael. I got stuck watching the phone this shift."

"Michael, where the fuck is my relief? I've been on location at Houska for over a day now!" Boris tried to control his temper.

"I'm really sorry. Officer Cermak was supposed to tell you when he came out there earlier; we had five people call in with the flu. I guess it's getting to be that time of year. I sure hope I don't catch it."

"Why didn't Cermak stay to help, then?"

"He said he had to get back. The missus was having a cocktail party."

"Are you joking? A fucking cocktail party? I have a dead person here, a woman was kidnapped, and another woman was almost killed. I have a suspect in custody now as well. This is ridiculous!" Boris yelled, staring at the cigarette in his other hand. God, he couldn't wait to light it.

"I'm just relaying information, Officer Jelinek."

He felt bad that he'd sworn at the boy, who was only doing his job.

"I'm sorry, Michael. I shouldn't have lost my temper. But please tell the captain that I need someone out here immediately. If he needs to call a neighboring unit to help out, then do it. I have things under control at the moment, but I don't know for how much longer."

"I'll do it, sir." Michael said, and ended the call.

Boris put his phone back in his pocket and raised the cigarette to his mouth, lighting the end. He inhaled deeply. He already felt himself relaxing.

When he heard a noise behind him, he took another quick drag and turned around.

"Who's there?" he asked, not seeing anyone.

He listened for the sound again, but there was only silence. He shrugged his shoulders, thinking it must've been an animal. He went back to enjoying his cigarette.

The second time he heard the noise, he didn't have time to turn around; something hard and sharp struck him on the back of the head.

He fell to the ground, dazed but still conscious. Through blurred vision, he saw the shape of a man standing over him, holding what looked like a large rock.

The man raised the rock high and brought it down again.

ONE HELL OF A VACATION

Boris released the cigarette he'd been holding. It was only half smoked, but he no longer wanted it.

He no longer wanted anything, because his brain had been bashed to bits.

Chapter 53

Maxwell was huffing and puffing by the time he got the cop's body all the way to the clearing where he planned to bury him. Thankfully, he'd found a shovel in the stable and scoped out the location prior to executing (no pun intended) the plan, so it was waiting for him there.

As he started to dig the hole, he was grateful it had rained quite a bit, so the soil was loose, and easy to move. His back hurt from sleeping on the ground in an unused stall at the very back of the stable all night. He was used to much better accommodations.

After paying the cab driver to bring him to the castle, he'd ultimately decided to be dropped off about a mile out, walking the rest of the way. He was exhausted when he arrived, but the horse in the stable didn't make much noise, and he was able to get some rest.

The next morning, he'd heard a car pulling up, and went to see who it was. He got nervous when he saw it was another cop, because he hadn't counted on them finding Monica's body quite so fast. It was only logical for them to follow up at his last known location.

He'd watched the cop get out of his car and go to the door. The guy that led the outside tour let him inside.

Maxwell contemplated what to do. If he stayed in the stable, he ran the risk of being caught if they decided to search the grounds. But if he left, where would he go?

He'd opted for hiding in the forest. It was while wandering around that he discovered the clearing, and now he was pleased that his exploration had ended up coming in handy.

The hole got deeper and deeper the longer he dug. When he was finally done digging, he rolled the cop's body into the hole and sat down, needing a break. He was hungry and thirsty, having had nothing to eat or drink but a few carrots he'd taken from the horse's saddlebag.

Once it was dark, he would sneak into the castle and make his way upstairs to the room he'd shared with Sharon.

She'd be sleeping in their bed, without a care in the world. It would be as easy as picking up a pillow and covering her face until she quit breathing.

Maxwell thought about his future, what it would be like to be free of Sharon, and to have paid back the money to the bank. He could do as he pleased, go anywhere and do anything that he wanted. It was sad Monica wouldn't be able to join him, but hey, that's the way things went sometimes.

Maybe he'd go to Costa Rica anyway. He had always wanted to. It was warm and the women didn't wear a lot of clothes. He'd have a girlfriend in no time. Hell, he might even have two, or ten.

As the sun started to set in the west, Maxwell got up and picked up the shovel. He started moving piles of dirt back into the hole, covering the body.

He'd hated to kill the cop, but didn't see a way around it. Having him there would make it nearly impossible to get away with killing Sharon, so he'd only done what he had to do This cop's presence probably had something to do with the text Sharon had sent, about a death at the castle. But it didn't matter why he was there; it only mattered that he was, and Maxwell had to get rid of him.

And now, it was done. Maxwell patted the dirt down with the shovel and smiled with satisfaction. It was nice to feel a sense of accomplishment.

He thought about just tossing the shovel in the woods instead of taking it back to the stable, but reconsidered. He needed Sharon's death to look like an accident, like she'd simply died in her sleep. If the police discovered a shovel in the woods during whatever investigation they conducted, they might suspect that there was yet more foul play going on. Better be on the safe side and put it back where he'd found it.

His tongue felt like sandpaper. He was so thirsty. He'd give anything for a drink of water, but it would have to wait. Only a few more hours, he thought. He'd be able to get some water from the great room before or after he went upstairs.

He started the trek back to the stable. With little sunlight permeating the deep shadows, the woods were dark and ominous. He picked up his pace, eager to get out of there, and away from the fresh grave, as soon as possible.

Chapter 54

With Nigel now keeping Laila company, and Klaudie looking after Amalie, Jakub was able to go downstairs for a while with Sharon, to make some tea.

As they sat together in the front room, waiting for the kettle to whistle, it wasn't lost on him how companionable and easy it was, whatever was going on between them. It felt like he'd been doing it all of his life.

When the tea was ready, he poured two cups, and they both sipped in a comfortable silence. Finally, Sharon spoke.

"What's going on with Dwayne? Where did you take him?"

"He's in the trophy room. Tied to a chair. Boris tried questioning him earlier, but we didn't get anywhere with it. He just sits there and stares into space."

"Do you think he's on drugs?" she asked.

"I suppose it's a possibility," said Jakub. "But if he was, eventually it'd wear off, I'd imagine."

"Have we heard more from the police?"

"Boris still hadn't heard anything the last time I saw him."

"That's strange," said Sharon.

"A bit. He said he'll try calling them again. Right now, he's watching Dwayne."

They continued to chit chat while they finished their tea, and when they were done, Jakub asked Sharon if she'd like to go with him while he checked on and fed Blesk. She said she'd love to, so he escorted her out to the stable.

Blesk was happy to see both of them, and more importantly, happy to have his dinner, though the supply of carrots in the saddlebag was smaller than Jakub had remembered. Had he not been paying attention? In the meantime, Blesk would have to get by on only a couple of carrots and some hay to munch on.

While Jakub was refilling the trough with water, Sharon showed Blesk some love, stroking his mane, and planting a kiss on his nose.

"I wish I had half the luck of my horse," said Jakub, laughing.

Sharon chuckled as well. "Are you jealous?" she asked.

"I'll admit, I am a bit."

"Well, I don't want you to be jealous of your own horse." She leaned forward to give him a kiss on his nose, too, but Jakub lifted his head and pressed his mouth against hers.

They kissed hard and passionately, arms around each other. Then she rested her head on his chest, and they stood there just enjoying being close to one another.

"It's getting late," Sharon murmured after a while. "Will you come back to my room with me?"

He only hesitated for a heartbeat. "Of course."

***

The love they had for one another would have been quite obvious to anyone who happened to see them.

At least, it sure was to Maxwell.

That cheating little bitch, he thought.

With this rustic hillbilly, no less? Klaudie's farm boy brother -- *Jacob? Jakub? Yeah, Jakub* -- who'd played tour guide for the guests exploring the castle grounds?

Whatever was going on between them seemed to have been going on for quite a while, because they seemed to be very familiar with one another. He'd watched them kiss, and seen Sharon lay her head against Jakub's chest, smiling with contentment.

They spoke briefly, but Maxwell couldn't make out the words. Whatever she'd said, the guide seemed to go along with it because he took her hand and they started walking back to the castle.

That's fine, he thought. *Let her have her fun.* After all, he'd had his fun with Monica. Besides, she didn't have long to live. She might as well enjoy the last few hours of her life.

He cupped his hands and drank deeply from the horse's water trough, which wasn't ideal but was better than nothing. He decided he'd try to rest for a couple of hours and try to regain his strength. Digging the cop's grave and burying him had taken a lot out of Maxwell.

He made a bed of hay and laid down, but he couldn't get comfortable and his mind wouldn't shut off. The wheels in his brain continued to turn. Maybe he could find a spot inside the castle that would be safe to rest and more comfortable? Perhaps on the empty third floor?

TARA TANNENBAUM

He decided to take the chance.

Chapter 55

Luckily, the castle's front door was unlocked. Maxwell opened it, thankful it didn't make any noise. Everything was quiet. He guessed they'd all gone to their rooms. He tiptoed to the great room, found himself some water and drank until he was no longer thirsty. Seeing some biscuits left over on a tray from earlier in the day, he quickly ate five of them. His stomach instantly felt better.

Now that he'd tackled hunger and thirst, Maxwell thought it might be better to look for a place to sleep on the first floor, rather than risking being heard on the stairs. He was eighty-five percent sure he'd seen a couch in the room with all the animal heads, when he'd taken the boring tour on the first day. He doubted anyone had been inside the room since then.

That doubt was dashed as soon as he looked in. The light was on, and someone -- one of the guests, the black member of the homosexual couple -- was ...

Was *tied* to a fuckin' *chair*?

Determining the room was otherwise unoccupied, he crept in, curiosity overcoming his good sense. What the hell was going on here? What had happened in the couple of days since he'd been gone?

"Hey," Maxwell whispered, unable to remember the man's name. "Hello? Why are you tied up?"

The man didn't respond, but his eyes bored a hole into Maxwell. Something about him, his posture, his expression, just wasn't right.

"Can you hear me? What's wrong with you?" He bent over so they were at eye level.

Still, the man didn't reply. Maxwell was getting tired of this.

"Listen, asshole, if you want me to help you --" Maxwell started.

Beams of white light shot out from the bound man's eyes and penetrated Maxwell's, leaving him frozen in place. The man's mouth opened and black liquid spewed from it like a fountain, soaking Maxwell's face and chest.

Maxwell didn't cry out or try to move away. He simply stood there, anchored, until the rays of light and surge of black liquid ceased.

ONE HELL OF A VACATION

The bound man's body slumped forward in the chair. He groaned, blinked a few times, and lifted his head as Maxwell straightened to his full height.

"Where ... am I?" he asked, shifting his hands and feet, trying to free himself from the ropes. He struggled some more while looking at his surroundings, as if trying to figure out where he was and how he'd gotten there.

Maxwell, meanwhile, walked calmly away, the black liquid dripping from his clothing as he went. His feet took him to the other end of the room, where he paused to examine the contents of a cabinet.

"What the hell is this? What's going on? Why can't I remember anything?" the man babbled, panic in his voice.

"I wondered the same thing when I found you," Maxwell said, turning to him. "But now, everything is clear. I have the answers, and I know what I must do."

He returned to the chair, a gleaming two-foot-long machete in hand.

The bound man, frozen in terror by what he was seeing, didn't cry out before Maxwell swung the weapon at his neck.

The blade was sharp, quite sharp. Maxwell hadn't expected the man's head to come clean off in only one swing, but there it was, on the floor, confused eyes still blinking as his brain died and blood jetted from the stump of his neck.

Maxwell sighed with pleasure. He felt wonderful! Something was inside him, something powerful. He felt it controlling him, but he didn't care. He'd gladly let it control him, if it felt like this. Better than any drug he'd ever taken!

He closed his eyes and listened to the instructions being given to him, nodding in compliance.

His plan to get some rest would have to be put aside, but that was okay. He didn't mind. He didn't feel like he would ever need to rest again. Maxwell smiled as the thing inside him praised him, not only for the killing, but for reading from the book of spells.

Listening to the words the thing was speaking inside his head was magical, almost sexual. He craved to hear the voice. It promised him eternal life for the favors he was about to do. There would be more killings, oh yes, plenty more, but when it was done, he would get to live with this thing inside him forever.

He had an erection just thinking about it. This was much better than his plan to go to Costa Rica. Sharon would still die, and many others, but that was okay. The thing inside him told him he'd be living somewhere the weather was hot year-round.

Exactly what Maxwell wanted.

He looked around the room. He was eager to get to work. The faster he accomplished his tasks, the faster he'd get to go to his tropical destination. He continued to nod as the thing inside him whispered words of encouragement.

Firstly, the dead man would need to be taken to the chapel and placed on the altar. Once he'd accomplished that, he could start on his second task. He untied the body from the chair, and, with strength he hadn't had before, he lifted it with ease, making sure he grabbed the head on the way.

Chapter 56

Jakub's phone rang just as he and Sharon reached the second-floor landing. Seeing who it was from, he waved for Sharon to go on ahead to the room; he'd catch up.

"Dr. Bartik?" said Jakub. "Herschel?"

"Yes, Jakub. I'm sorry to call so late in the evening --"

"Not a problem at all. It's good to hear from you." Jakub sat down on the top step. "Were you able to come up with anything that might help the situation here at Houska?"

"Yes. After doing some digging, and speaking with a few of my colleagues, I've come up with a couple of options that may solve your problem. I'll warn you though. None of those options are good," Herschel said in a grave tone.

They spoke for several minutes, Jakub with a deepening a frown on his face. Herschel wasn't exaggerating when he said that the options weren't good.

"I wish I had better answers for you, my friend. Don't hesitate to call me again if I can help you further."

"Thank you, Herschel. I appreciate all you've done." They said their goodbyes, and then Jakub sat there, thinking about everything Herschel had just told him and what it would mean.

He needed to speak with Klaudie. He turned and looked behind him, as he could see her room from where he was sitting. The door was closed. But less than a minute later, the door opened, and out walked Marek, in his boxers. Jakub's jaw dropped to the ground.

Marek looked up and saw Jakub sitting on the landing step. His face turned bright red.

"Jakub," he said.

Jakub picked up his jaw quickly and nodded at Marek as he walked past him, and down the stairs. So Klaudie was sleeping with Marek? Jakub's mind was blown. Marek was half her age!

Well, that's fine, he thought.

He was happy for Klaudie. She'd struggled to find the right person her entire life. If Marek made her happy, then so be it.

He couldn't wait to give her a hard time, though. She'd teased him plenty about the girls he'd dated in the past, so it was only fair to do the same thing to her. He smiled.

Just thinking about how much fun he was going to have with this brought Jakub joy.

***

Sharon wondered who'd called Jakub with something important enough to make him wave her to go on to the room without him.

None of them were supposed to be alone, though that wasn't the only reason she hoped he would stay with her tonight.

While he was on the phone, though, she decided to make the best use of her time. She undressed, pausing at the mirror to examine her body, running her hands over her smooth skin and turning from side to side.

Still looking damn good for fifty-two, she thought.

Going into the bathroom, she freshened up with a damp cloth and gave her legs a quick shave, then went to her suitcase. When she'd packed for the trip, she'd optimistically put in some lingerie, just in case things with Maxwell went very well indeed.

All that now seemed like it had happened a hundred years ago. So much had transpired since then.

She pulled a silky black teddy and matching panties out of the suitcase and slipped both of them on, then went back to the mirror to inspect herself again.

The teddy revealed just enough, and perfectly complemented the mocha color of her skin. *This should do the trick*, she thought.

If, that was, Jakub still came to her room, and didn't change his mind or let his nobility get the better of him again. As she thought about the kiss they'd shared at the stable, her body became warm and she felt a lovely tingling between her legs.

As well as being physically attracted to Jakub, he possessed many other qualities that she loved about him. He was warm and kind. He always put her first. He asked her opinions on certain subjects, and listened. He never belittled her, or called her names, like Maxwell.

This was all so confusing. Two days ago, she'd wanted to reconcile with her husband. Now, all she wanted from Maxwell was a divorce ... and to see him locked up if he really had been responsible for Monica's death.

She also wanted, needed, to make Jakub understand how she felt about him. She had no idea how she'd fallen totally head over heels for someone she'd only just met, but she had.

And, more than that, she knew it was the real thing. It was the love she'd been looking for her entire life and thought she'd never find. Jakub made her feel like the only woman in the world. He made her feel loved and appreciated.

Waiting for him was driving her mad. She tried to clear her head. He'd be there soon enough; she was sure of it.

At last, she heard a small knock at her door, and then, there he was. The look in his eyes as he saw her was priceless.

He didn't say a word, and his gaze never left her, as he came into the room and let the door swing shut behind him.

Chapter 57

Maxwell trekked across the courtyard with a headless corpse thrown over his left shoulder, carrying the matching severed head by the hair in his right hand.

It was very dark outside, and unseen creatures watched from the castle's rooftop, though he knew they were there.

Inside the chapel, he hoisted the body onto the altar, next to the other body. He tossed the head between the two.

Maxwell looked around. The chapel felt like home. The pit had grown immensely since he'd seen it last. He gazed into it with longing. He wanted to join his master now, but knew he had to complete all of his tasks before he was allowed to.

Closing his eyes, he imagined what his life would be like in his new tropical home. He'd sit in a lounger beside a pool with crystal clear blue water, sipping from an exotic drink.

Surrounding him would be tons of women, all of them nude, with huge breasts and asses. The women would cater to his every desire, including but not limited to food, drinks, and any sexual positions or favors that he could come up with.

He imagined lying there on the lounge, as a hot blonde walked up, with luscious tits and a bald triangle between her legs. She'd tell him her name was Candy, and ask him if he'd been serviced lately. He'd shake his head no, and she'd immediately apologize, dropping to her knees beside him. Gently, she'd wrap her small hands around his penis and lower her mouth to it, kissing the tip and swirling her tongue along the shaft.

He watched Candy's head bobbing up and down as she hungrily sucked on his cock. He was almost there. Just a few seconds more. *Keep going, Candy baby,* he thought to himself.

Suddenly, the visions vanished, and his mind went blank.

Maxwell understood what that meant. His master wanted him to quit fuckin' around and complete his tasks.

There would be plenty of time to play with Candy in his own tropical paradise once he'd finished the job he had to do. It was time to get to work.

***

Marek crept back up the stairs quietly, hoping he wouldn't run into anyone else. He made it to Klaudie's room and slipped inside.

Klaudie was still on the bed. She'd put her robe on while he was gone, though hopefully he could get her to take it off again. He handed her the biscuits and tea he'd brought from downstairs.

"I saw Jakub in the hall when I went out," he told her as she bit into a biscuit.

Klaudie looked up at him, crumbs on her lip. "Did he see you?"

"Yes." said Marek, sheepishly.

"Did he say anything to you?"

"No. I said hello to him when I walked by him, and he nodded at me."

"Shit." said Klaudie. "Did he seem upset?"

"No. To be fair, I think he was just as embarrassed to see me coming out of his sister's room as I was." Marek climbed into the bed with Klaudie and ran his hand up and down her leg.

Klaudie swatted at him, playfully. "This is a disaster! I'll never hear the end of it."

"Are you embarrassed to be with me?" asked Marek.

"No, of course not."

"Then why do you care if Jakub knows? He probably just wants for you to be happy. Does it matter if I am younger than you? We've talked about it before, and I was under the impression we were on the same page about age just being a number. I love you, Klaudie. That's all that matters."

Klaudie blushed. Marek wasn't one for sentiment. He showed her physical affection, but rarely had he spoken the words. Her heart glowed with warmth. She leaned forward and kissed him.

"I love you, too. And no, you know I'm not bothered by the age thing. And it doesn't really matter if Jakub knows about us. But he will tease me to death about it." She laughed. "It's just the way our family is, and poor Jakub has had the worst of it, being the youngest and the only boy. Oh, we tortured him over anyone he brought home to date. It might be why he's still single. Although, I have a feeling he won't be for long."

"You mean, Sharon?" asked Marek.

"You've seen the way he looks at her, the way he acts around her. He's completely smitten."

"But what about her husband? Isn't he wanted for the murder of that woman in Prague?"

"He's wanted for questioning," Klaudie said, "but the police aren't sure he did it. What if he didn't? That's what worries me. What if he comes back and decides he wants to work things out with Sharon? Where does that leave my brother?"

Marek nodded in understanding. "Let Jakub handle his own business and we'll handle ours." He scooted closer to Klaudie, and traced her collar bone with his finger. "Now, where were we? Oh yes, I was going to ask you to please remove that robe, if you don't mind. It's the least you could do after I traipsed all the way downstairs to get you biscuits and had to endure the humiliation of running into your brother with nothing on but my undershorts."

Klaudie giggled like a school girl and untied her robe.

Chapter 58

Klaudie woke suddenly, disoriented. Marek wasn't there, but she was unbothered by it. She knew he'd have had to leave early to get breakfast for the guests, to be ready by the time they came downstairs.

Hearing a noise from the hall, she got up and put on her robe. Investigating was probably a bad idea, but she went anyway. As she took a few steps down the hall, toward the stairs, the noise sounded again, from behind her.

It sounded like... flapping?

The hair on Klaudie's neck rose. She swallowed and turned.

A tall, winged creature stood in the hallway, solid black with red eyes. Klaudie opened her mouth to scream, but the creature rushed toward her so quickly all she could do was run.

It chased her, so close she could feel the heat radiating from its body.

She dashed downstairs and out into the courtyard. Halfway across, she tripped and fell, badly buckling an ankle. She lay on the ground, covering her face and head with her arms. The creature had stopped running, but she felt it looming over her and could hear it breathing.

"Please don't hurt me," she said meekly.

The creature leaned down and inhaled deeply, as if smelling her. Klaudie tried to stay calm, hoping it would leave her alone if she held still.

She heard more of the flapping sounds and decided to risk peeking through her fingers, then instantly wished she hadn't. Instead of one winged creature, there were now four. She covered her eyes again and began to pray, something she hadn't done since she was a young girl.

The one that had initially chased her continued to sniff her skin. The others joined in. They seemed to find her smell satisfactory because the first creature flicked out a forked tongue and licked her arm. Klaudie shivered with revulsion.

It worsened as she felt four loathsome tongues tasting her skin, her sweat and her fear. Tears rolled down her face. She was too scared to scream, afraid of their reaction.

After what seemed like an eternity, one of the creatures gave a commanding shriek, and they all sprang up, flapping their wings as they took to the sky and circling above her. Klaudie flinched, but they only continued to circle for a bit, then veered off to land on the roof of the castle. Their red, beady eyes watched her.

Afraid to stand up, she got to her knees and began to crawl. Every time she heard a flap or a rustle, she stopped, afraid they'd come after her again.

Ages passed before she reached the door, crawled through it, and closed it behind her. She made it to the great room and hauled herself into a chair to inspect her ankle. She didn't think it was broken, but it certainly hurt. She rubbed it. It was a little swollen, but she was sure she'd be fine.

She couldn't remember the last time she'd been so frightened. Even seeing the headless person in the court yard the other day hadn't been as bad as this. Perhaps because the other incident had been more like seeing a ghost, while this was something else. Something evil.

Whatever had chased her was related to the pit in the chapel. Those creatures came from Hell, she was sure of it.

But what was she to do? She wanted to go back upstairs, but her ankle hurt too much to walk far on it. And once she was up there, then what? Marek was gone, and she didn't want to be by herself.

She'd go to Nigel and Laila's room. They'd let her in.

Now having a firm plan in her head, she limp-hopped to the stairs, then sat and boosted herself up the steps on her butt. It was slow, but it worked, and she got a good arm workout into the bargain.

She listened to the stillness of the castle as she went, imagining she heard the flapping of wings but knowing it was her mind in overdrive, a natural reaction to what happened earlier.

She rested about halfway up. *Just a little further*, she thought. She couldn't wait to be safely in with Nigel and Laila. Sweat dripped from her forehead, and her upper back and arms ached, but she made it to the landing. She lay flat for a moment, catching her breath. *Now just crawl to their door,* she told herself.

Sitting up, she glanced back down the stairs and saw a pair of red eyes glowing up at her.

No, no, no, this can't be happening! her mind screamed.

She twisted her body and got on her knees, crawling as fast as she could down the hall.

Chapter 59

A sudden desperate banging on their door jolted Nigel and Laila awake. Nigel sprang up and went to it, pulling it open, and Klaudie fell at his feet.

"Shut the door!" she gasped as she dragged herself inside.

Nigel did so without pause or question, instinctively locking it as well.

"Klaudie, my God, are you all right?" asked Laila, clutching the covers to her chest. "What happened?"

Shuddering, Klaudie let Nigel help her up, clearly favoring an injured ankle. They got her situated as comfortably as possible, propped up by pillows with her leg elevated, as she told them about demonic winged creatures chasing her through the house and courtyard. When she was finished, she looked at them closely for a reaction, clearly expecting them to think she was insane or had been dreaming. Instead, they both glanced anxiously at the door, and then at each other.

"I think you should tell her," Nigel said to his wife.

"It doesn't seem so strange now, does it?" Laila turned to Klaudie and described encountering some strange doppelganger of Nigel, and how it had led her to the attic and locked her inside.

Klaudie listened to Laila's story in growing horror.

"I believe we are in real danger," she said. "It must be connected to the pit in the chapel. The legends just might be true. If it's a portal to Hell, it would explain the demonic creatures I saw tonight, and probably also whatever the thing was that locked you in the attic. It might even explain what's been going on with poor Dwayne, forcing him to do what he did to Xander and Amalie."

"How can this be real?" asked Nigel, sounding frustrated. "None of it makes sense. There has to be a reasonable, scientific explanation for everything. Maybe some sort of gas leak, or a chemical inside the castle that's causing all of us to hallucinate."

"I wish that were the case," Klaudie said, "because the alternative is terrifying. But I know there is no chemical or gas problem. Something has come out of that hole in the chapel. Something evil. And now, we are going to have to figure out how to get rid of it before it gets rid of us."

Nigel shook his head. What she was saying went against everything he'd ever known. All of this talk of demons and winged creatures and ghosts was silly. Like stories he and his childhood friends had made up around campfires to scare the pants off each other. Such things didn't exist in real life.

"You mentioned earlier Jakub was consulting a rabbi?" said Laila.

"Yes, that's why he and Sharon went to Prague this morning and why he needed to take those pictures of the book of spells."

"That again," Nigel muttered. "Wish I'd never found the bloody thing." He ran his fingers through his hair. "Maybe I should go downstairs and take a look around,"

Both Klaudie and Laila instantly shook their heads.

"That's a terrible idea," said Laila. "This isn't the time to be stubborn, dear."

He could see from the look on her face that she was reliving the frightening events in the attic, and when Dwayne tried to kill her while she was in the bath. He took her hand, comforting her, and she smiled at him with appreciation and affection.

"What do you propose we do, then?" asked Nigel. "It's the middle of the night, and it'll be my turn on guard duty soon anyway."

"I think we should all try to get some more rest," said Laila. "The bed's big enough. I'll be in the middle. It might be a bit cramped, but we'll make it work."

The three of them lay in silence, each thinking about what had transpired. Laila was the first to fall asleep, followed by Klaudie. It took Nigel quite a bit longer; in his mind, he kept thinking he heard the flapping of wings outside the bedroom door.

Chapter 60

All the blood had rushed to Jakub's loins when he walked into the room to find Sharon on the bed, wearing black, silk lingerie. He couldn't think of any way around this, short of turning and leaving, and he didn't want to. He couldn't resist her.

"Cat got your tongue?" she asked, smiling at him.

He forced himself to look at the floor, the furniture, anything but the tempting image before him. This wasn't fair. He was trying to be respectful, but she was making it damn near impossible.

"Jakub, it's okay. I want this." She approached, taking his hands.

He gave in, pulling her to him, hungrily kissing her like there was no tomorrow. Sharon melted in his arms. He ran his hands over her soft skin and the silky black teddy, gently easing her back onto the bed.

Her breasts were soft under his fingers. He squeezed them slightly and Sharon exhaled in a low moan. As he lifted the teddy up her body, she raised her arms to help and he slid it over her head. Once it was off, he tossed it aside and admired her. She was just as beautiful as he'd imagined.

Jakub lowered his head to her breasts and began to pleasure her nipples with his tongue, playfully licking and sucking, teasing and stroking one and then the other. Sharon ran her hands over his back, chest, and abdomen, before lowering them between his legs to feel his hardness. She stroked him as he continued to suck on her breasts.

When she undid his belt and his pants, and closed her fingers around him, Jakub groaned. He drew back long enough to kick off his shoes, let his pants drop to the floor, and pull his t-shirt from his body. Sharon watched him, admiring his muscled physique.

Climbing back onto the bed, he urged her to roll over on her stomach, peeling off her tiny black panties to reveal her ample backside. Fondling it with one hand, he worked the other hand beneath her, finding her warm and ready. He teased her sweet spot with his fingertips, then slid his fingers inside her. Sharon cried out with pleasure as he continued to rub and caress.

Her first orgasm came fast and hard. Jakub rolled her over again. She called his name as he pushed into her. He kissed her face and neck before claiming her mouth.

He wanted this moment to last forever. He'd never experienced an intimacy like this. Sure, he'd had sex plenty of times, but all of those times paled in comparison.

But he soon felt himself building up to a release as he moved faster inside of her. Sharon's body rose to meet him with every stroke. Finally, he couldn't hold it in any longer. He felt the earth shatter as he came, filling Sharon as she throbbed with her second orgasm.

After a few moments, Jakub removed himself and lay by her side, cradling her in his arms as they both tried to catch their breath.

Sharon curled against him, practically purring. Jakub kissed her hair and smiled. Nothing between them had changed for the worse. They were stronger than before. Now, they'd joined as one, a team.

"Can we do that again?" she asked.

"Just as soon as I'm able," he replied, laughing.

Which didn't take long at all. The lovemaking went on for hours, both of them enjoying each other's bodies like nothing they'd ever known before. Sprinkled with the sex, they held each other and talked.

ONE HELL OF A VACATION

When they were both spent, she fell asleep in his arms, and he watched the moon through the window and wondered where their future would lead.

He hoped he got to keep her for himself. Now that things had gone this far, he didn't know if he would be able to let her go. He hoped he wouldn't have to.

Had it been like this for his parents, each knowing this was the one, from the moment they met? He'd never asked his mother, mostly because after his father died, he was afraid of upsetting her. Perhaps Klaudie knew the answer. He'd have to remember to ask her sometime.

The night was silent but for Sharon's soft snoring as he played with her curly tendrils. He knew he needed to get some sleep, but didn't want this time with her to end. What if he never got this chance again?

He thought of his sister and Marek and wondered how long the two of them had been seeing each other. He wanted Klaudie to be happy, to feel the way that he felt about Sharon.

Chapter 61

Jakub wasn't sure when he'd fallen asleep, or for how long, but he woke to feel Sharon kissing his hand. He turned on his side toward her, so they were facing each other.

"I didn't mean to wake you," said Sharon.

"It's alright."

"So where do we go from here?" she asked.

"Wherever you'd like," said Jakub. "There's no pressure."

"I feel more like I've been the one pressuring you," said Sharon. "This has all happened so fast, I'm glad it has, but it's such a change."

"People deserve their chance to be happy," Jakub said, then chuckled. "Oh, not that I'm trying to take the focus off of us, but I didn't tell you about Klaudie and Marek."

"What about them? Is everything alright?" she asked.

"Everything's fine. When I was in the hall earlier, after that phone call, I saw Marek come out of Klaudie's room."

"Maybe he was just checking on her."

"He was in his boxers." Jakub grinned.

Sharon's eyes got wide. "Do you mean...?"

Jakub nodded. "Marek is sleeping with my sister."

"I can't believe it! I never would have guessed."

"Me neither. The two of them are certainly better at playing it casual than we are."

"Are you alright with it?" asked Sharon.

"So long as he treats her well. If he doesn't, he'll answer to me."

"And, what do you think about the two of us?" Sharon asked, changing the subject back to what they had been discussing.

"Are you asking if I like you? Meh, I guess so," he teased.

Sharon playfully smacked his arm. "Do you think we have a future together?"

"I hope so. But that's not up to me, it's up to you. I don't ever want you to be unhappy."

"I was so confused at first. Meeting you was like being pointed in the right direction. It's hard to believe, but now, I can't imagine what my life would be like without you."

Her words were like music to Jakub's ears. He wanted nothing more than to be with her, and to hear that's what she wanted too was like a huge weight being lifted from his shoulders. Whatever happened from this point on, they would face it together.

"I meant to ask earlier, but we were ... busy." She smiled and kissed his shoulder. "The phone call, who was it?"

"Herschel."

"I thought it might be. Did he have any news?"

"He suggested a few options, all of which were awful."

Jakub quickly went over everything Herschel had told him. When he was done, Sharon shook her head in frustration.

"What are we going to do?" she asked.

"I haven't figured it out yet. I need to have a conversation with Klaudie, and then, maybe between all of us, we'll figure out the best way to proceed. There has to be something."

"I agree," she said, snuggling closer to Jakub. He rolled onto his side and pulled her to him, spooning her body, wishing they could stay this way forever.

Once again, he grew hard against her bottom, and once again she pressed it firmly to him. His breath quickened. Sharon reached behind and grasped him, guiding him inside. Slowly, they moved together. As Jakub kissed her neck, he draped an arm over her, placing his hand between her thighs, rubbing her most sensitive spot.

The combination of him moving inside of her while also touching her soon sent her over the edge and she orgasmed hard. Jakub pumped harder and faster, as she pushed her ass back against him.

He tried to hold on as long as he could, but the pleasure was too intense, and he let himself release, groaning her name.

They continued kissing and lazily touching for some time, but both were exhausted and eventually sleepiness overcame them.

Wrapped in each other's arms, they both felt as if they were one, united in love. Each had found their special person, the love of a lifetime.

***

All was quiet in the night's stillness. The moon watched over them while they slept.

Neither had any idea of the danger lurking right outside of the door, but it was there all the same, waiting patiently.

Chapter 62

They'd been fucking for hours, napped a bit, fucked again, and finally seemed to have gone to sleep for real. Maxwell wanted to go for it then, but the voice in his head had directed him to wait a bit longer.

So, he did. He waited another couple of hours more, hiding when the cook had emerged from Klaudie's room -- was *everybody* in the place getting some tonight? -- and again when Klaudie herself went for an unplanned little excursion. Though, in that case, he had been hard-pressed not to laugh while watching her scuttle on her ass up the stairs and crawl down the hall, to escape what was, for the moment, just toying with her.

Finally, he heard Sharon's farm boy get up from the bed and go into the bathroom, followed by the sounds of water filling the tub. He waited yet a bit more, giving the man time to settle into his bath, before quietly slipping into the room he'd formerly shared with his wife. Although it was dimly lit, he saw her clearly, on the bed, asleep.

Maxwell wasn't emotional at all about what he needed to do. He'd planned to do it anyway, even before his new master had offered him such a great deal. The only difference now was that he wouldn't have wait on the money from the life insurance policy. He'd be able to leave for his tropical destination as soon as his tasks were complete. That was what had been promised to him.

He crossed to the bedside, grabbing an extra pillow and lowered it toward her face.

Shouldn't take but a second, he thought.

Then, of all the bad luck ...

He sneezed.

***

Sharon opened her eyes at the sudden sound of a familiar sneeze and saw Maxwell standing over her.

She blinked, thinking that she must be dreaming, or imagining things, but then her instinct kicked into gear and she screamed at the top of her lungs.

From the bathroom, she heard a splashing sound and Jakub's alarmed voice, but before she could scream again, Maxwell brought a pillow down over her face.

She struggled to breathe as he pressed the pillow down as hard as he could. She tried to fight, thrashing and kicking, but he was too strong, holding her pinned to the mattress. Just as she was about to pass out, the pressure let up. Sharon flung the pillow from her face, inhaling deeply.

Jakub, soaking wet and naked and looking absolutely ferocious, had Maxwell in a choke hold. Maxwell's fists pummeled at him, connecting with Jakub's ribs, causing him to loosen his grip enough to let Maxwell escape, rounding on Jakub with more vicious blows.

As they fought, Sharon jumped from the bed. Jakub yelled for her to get out of there, but she was not about to leave, looking around for something to serve as a weapon. But nothing useful was within reach.

Jakub managed to clamp his hands around Maxwell's neck and forced him up against the wall. Maxwell's arms flailed, first trying to remove Jakub's hold, then groping out to the side, reaching for a heavy lamp on the dresser.

Sharon realized what was going to happen a split second before it actually did. She saw Maxwell swing the lamp at Jakub's head. It made contact with a sickening crack. Jakub crumpled to the floor and Maxwell went down with him, continuing to bludgeon him with the lamp's solid marble base, over and over.

She saw herself running at Maxwell, but it felt like it was happening in slow motion. She heard herself screaming at him to stop, her own voice sounding distorted in her ears, as if underwater.

Then she was on him, and everything went back to real time.

Still screaming, she punched and hammered at him as hard as she could.

Maxwell, barely affected by her attack, spun and struck her in the face. Pain exploded through her head. Seeing stars, she fell, landing in a puddle of blood that covered the floor. Jakub's blood.

She looked up at her husband, but the man she married a year ago was no longer there. Something else had taken over his body. Something evil was inside him.

Maxwell raised the lamp again, and Sharon cringed, expecting him to hit her with it. Instead, he paused, lowered it to his side, and dropped it to the floor. He gazed off into space, as if he was listening to someone she couldn't hear.

Sharon crawled to Jakub's side. He was battered and motionless, barely recognizable. She tried to wipe away some of the blood, but there was too much. She felt for a pulse and couldn't find one.

Sobbing uncontrollably, she buried her head in his chest.

This couldn't be happening. She wished Maxwell had killed her. She had nothing to live for now.

***

Sharon's screams woke Klaudie, Nigel, and Laila. They raced down the hall, Laila helping Klaudie hobble, fearing the worst.

The screams were joined by the sounds of a struggle, and Jakub's voice shouting for Sharon to run, followed by a series of hideous crunching noises.

The door was ajar and they burst through, the first sight meeting Klaudie's eyes that of the bloodied wreckage of her brother, with Sharon huddled over him, crying hysterically. Both of them were naked, and a heavy lamp lay on the floor nearby.

Standing off to the side, with a faraway expression, was Sharon's husband. He seemed to be lost in some silent conversation.

For a stunned moment, nobody moved. Then Klaudie began to lurch toward Jakub, and Laila caught her wrist, holding her back, as Maxwell's gaze cleared and he turned to look at the newcomers.

Chapter 63

The stunned moment didn't last long. Nigel sprang into action, lunging toward Maxwell, but Maxwell was too fast for him. Shoving Nigel aside, Maxwell bolted for the door. Klaudie and Laila dodged out of the way to avoid being knocked down.

Maxwell took off down the hall and Nigel ran after him.

"Nigel!" Laila cried. She let go of Klaudie, who dropped to her knees and crawled to Jakub.

Laila knew she had to do something, but didn't know what. She pulled the bedspread from the bed to cover Jakub's nudity, then wrapped a blanket around the hysterical, weeping Sharon.

"I'll go get Boris," Laila said.

She hurried downstairs, alert and wary. She had no idea where Maxwell had gone, with Nigel off chasing him. It occurred to her, as she reached the trophy room, the amount of noise and commotion certainly should have gotten Boris' attention by now.

She opened the door. The light was on, but the room was empty. The chair she presumed Dwayne had been tied to was upended, surrounded by cut lengths of rope and a splattering of blood, but there was no sign of either Boris or Dwayne.

This was bad, really bad. Laila didn't know where to turn. Marek must have already gone to start preparing for breakfast. She wanted to sit down and cry, but it was a luxury she couldn't spare. Thinking instead to find someone's phone and call the police, she started back for the stairs, then heard footsteps as Nigel, puffing from exertion, came in the front door

"Thank God you're all right!" She ran over and flung her arms around him. He squeezed her tight.

"This has been one hell of a vacation," Nigel said. "Next time, we'll just stay in the comfort of our own home."

"If there is a next time," she replied. "Where's Maxwell?"

"I lost him. This old body can't keep up anymore. How are Klaudie and Sharon? And Jakub ... is he ...?"

"I think so," Laila said, choking up. "Such a nice man. Klaudie and Sharon are beside themselves."

"Poor chap." Nigel bowed his head.

"Not only that, Boris is gone! I went to fetch him, and the trophy room was empty."

"Dwayne was gone too?"

"There was a chair turned over, and cut ropes and blood next to it."

"Good God!"

"Then I was going to find a phone, call the police. What time is it?"

Nigel looked at his wrist, but didn't have his watch. "It must be almost six. The sun will be up soon."

They went up the stairs, soon able to hear sobbing from Sharon's room. "She'd gotten so close to him," Laila murmured with sympathy. "In just a few short days, she seemed to genuinely be in love with him. Such a sad thing. And her husband! What on earth was wrong with him? He seemed.... different. Not because he'd just murdered someone, but because he didn't seem like himself. He had madness in his eyes."

"He didn't wield a single insult at me as I gave chase," Nigel agreed. "He didn't appear to even know who I was."

"Almost like Dwayne," Laila said, shuddering.

Reaching the doorway, they saw neither of the women had moved, both still sitting with Jakub.

With Jakub's *body*; about that, there no longer appeared to be any doubt.

Klaudie lifted her head as they came in. Laila went to her and hugged her, but Klaudie seemed to be in shock.

"Come, love," Laila said, coaxing her up from the floor. "Let's get you more comfortable. Maybe you'd like to go back to your own room for a bit?"

Klaudie complied and let Laila guide her toward the door.

"Sharon, dear --" Laila tried.

"I'm not leaving him," Sharon said, her face buried against his chest.

Laila threw Nigel a stricken look.

"I'll stay with her," he said. "But lock the door, and call for me if you hear anything, anything at all."

Chapter 64

Laila pressed the end button on her cell phone and let out a sigh of frustration. The incompetent person who'd taken her call at the police station told her they were still shorthanded and would send someone to assist Boris as soon as possible. When she told them Boris was missing, they didn't even seem to care.

Marek had returned with breakfast, only to be greeted by the shocking news of what had taken place while he was gone. He went immediately to Klaudie to comfort her, while Laila and Nigel managed to get Sharon to at least wash Jakub's blood from herself, and put on some clothes.

Then Nigel, against Laila's wishes, insisted on taking another quick look around, in case Maxwell might be lingering. She made him promise to be careful, and take a weapon from the trophy room. He agreed, though he said it made him feel a bit absurd.

As he went out, she and Marek tried to talk Sharon and Laila into going downstairs and having something to eat, but neither would. Sharon was adamant about not leaving Jakub, and Klaudie, further distraught after calling to inform her sister, only wanted to be alone. They had decided it was best, for now, to not let their mother or the rest of their family know, but sooner or later it would have to be done.

There was nothing Marek and Laila could do but agree. No sense upsetting either of them further by making them do something they clearly didn't want to do. They decided they'd let them each rest for a bit, and then try again.

Nigel returned, looking pale and clammy. Laila rushed over to put her arms around him.

"Anything?" asked Marek.

"No sign of Maxwell." Nigel gulped. "But I did find Dwayne."

Laila gasped, and he hugged her reassuringly.

"He's dead. With Xander, on the altar in the chapel. I have no idea how he got there or why, but..." Nigel paused, and made to motion Marek aside, but Laila stopped him.

"Whatever you have to tell him, please tell me too," she said. "Even if it's terrible, we all need to know what's happening."

Nigel took a deep breath, unable to look at her as he spoke. "Dwayne's head had been cut off. It was lying next to his body."

Laila's expression remained calm. It was one more awful thing in a string of awful things. Sadly, she was getting used to them. She glanced at Marek, who also showed little reaction.

"And Boris?" she asked.

Nigel shrugged and shook his head.

"He has to be here somewhere," said Marek. "His car is still parked out front, or at least it was when I arrived with the food this morning."

"Do you think Boris killed Dwayne?" Nigel asked.

"Only if he was defending himself, but even if that were the case, it wouldn't have been like *that*."

"And he certainly wouldn't have put him on the altar," added Laila. "Someone else must be responsible for Dwayne's death."

"Maxwell?" Nigel suggested. "Maybe he killed Dwayne, and did something to Boris too. Were you able to you call the police?"

Laila huffed. "They were less than helpful. Told me that they were short staffed and they'd get someone out here as soon as they could. They didn't even seem to care when I told them Boris was missing."

"So, what do we do now?" asked Nigel.

"We have to stick together," Marek said. "And keep checking on Sharon and Klaudie."

***

Eventually, they were able to persuade both Sharon and Klaudie to go downstairs and at least try and eat something. The breakfast Marek had brought was stone cold, and he wasn't about to leave again, so they made do. Not that any of them had much of an appetite.

It took far more strenuous effort to convince Sharon not to return to her room, where Jakub's body lay stiffening with rigor mortis. The police, if and when they bothered to arrive, would need to go over the crime scene, and they'd probably tampered with evidence enough already. In the end, she agreed, and stayed with Klaudie while Laila and Nigel ventured in to retrieve some of her belongings.

For a few minutes, the air was filled with silence, both of them sitting awkwardly, not knowing what to say.

Jakub had been such a strong link between them, having loved both of them in different ways.

"I'm so sorry, Sharon," said Klaudie at last. The words caught in her throat. "I know you cared very much for my brother."

"I never knew anyone could be so kind and loving. I didn't know the kind of love he gave me even existed. Last night was the first time ... he stayed with me because I asked him to. I think he was worried it would ruin everything, but I assured him I wanted to be with him."

"I saw the way he looked at you. It was very obvious he'd fallen madly in love."

"Do you really think so?" asked Sharon, looking up at Klaudie imploringly, fresh tears shining in her eyes.

"Yes, I believe he loved you," said Klaudie.

"Oh Klaudie, I'm so sorry too. This is all my fault! If he hadn't been with me, he'd still be alive."

"Don't say that. He was exactly where he wanted to be. And if he hadn't been, you'd be dead in his place."

"I'd trade my life for his in a heartbeat," Sharon said. "I would. If I'd known what was going to happen, I wouldn't have screamed. I would have let Maxwell smother me with that pillow. I wish he had. I have nothing to live for now."

"Don't say that, Sharon. It's not true. You have plenty to live for. My brother gave his life for you. He did that because he wanted you to live."

They embraced, tears flowing freely. So much love, so much hurt; Jakub had been taken from them far too soon.

"I don't know how much longer I can stand to be in this place," Sharon admitted, wiping her eyes.

"I don't blame you. I don't think I'll be staying either. Too much has happened." Klaudie tried for a weak smile. "And the pay is terrible on top of that."

"We'll get through this, together," said Sharon. "I'm going to find Maxwell and make him pay for what he's done."

***

In one of the other second-floor guest rooms -- the one that had technically been Jakub's, giving her an extra pang to the heart -- Sharon lay on the bed. She tried breathing techniques to calm herself and help shut off her mind, but they weren't working. Her every thought was of Jakub, only a few doors away in what used to be her room.

Her heart felt broken in two.

She'd turned down offers to stay with either of the other couples, adamant despite their objections. She just couldn't face being with anyone, and needed to be alone. Finally admitting sleep wasn't going to happen any time soon, she found her phone and began searching flights. She needed to get out of this place, as soon as possible. Needed to be back in the comfort of her own home, where she would be able to pretend she'd never met Jakub ... and pretend she'd never married Maxwell, for that matter.

Booking a flight and arranging a car service to pick her up and take her to the airport in Prague occupied some of her time. She thought about starting to pack, but the rest of her things were still in the other room, and the door had been locked with Klaudie hanging onto the key.

For her own good, they'd said, and she supposed they were right. And did she even need or want her clothes or suitcase, or any reminders of this disastrous trip?

Maybe what she did want and need was a drink. She remembered seeing a decanter of whiskey downstairs in the great room. Maybe that would help relax her enough to go to sleep.

She went to the door, giving only a brief pause to thoughts of danger if she left her room. At this point, she didn't care. With Jakub gone, she felt she had nothing left to live for, so she decided to chance it.

Her feet were freezing on the icy hallway floor as she hurried to the stairs and tiptoed down, hoping not to awaken anyone else.

With possession of the whiskey and a glass, Sharon made her way back upstairs to her new room, locked the door, sat down, and poured herself at least two fingers of whiskey.

Nice start, she thought.

She liked the way the amber-colored liquid warmed her as it traveled down her throat. She finished it off and poured another. Then another.

Soon well on her way to being drunk, but still nowhere near sleepy, she thought of Jakub. What would he think of her if he could see her now? Running away like a coward. He'd been dead only a matter of hours, and she'd already made plans to go back to the United States and forget he'd ever existed.

Tears of shame spilled from her eyes. Could she really be abandoning him so soon after his death? But was it really abandonment, since he *was* dead? She thought of Klaudie, and Jakub's mother and other sisters. They wouldn't be able to run away. They had to stay and face the ugly truth that Jakub wouldn't be there anymore.

Hating herself, Sharon reached for the whiskey again, but instead of refilling her glass, she drank straight from the decanter itself.

She wanted all of it to go away. The pain she was feeling hurt worse than any physical pain. She didn't think she would be able to live without Jakub. She knew she had to, but was afraid of life without him.

Her anger resurfaced, all of her hatred focused on Maxwell. He'd been nothing but a mean, cheating asshole, and could now add murderer to that list. If she never accomplished anything else in her life, she vowed to take Maxwell down. That motherfucker would pay for what he'd done to Jakub, and for what he'd done to her.

***

"I know it's awful to say," said Nigel, climbing into bed, "but I am looking forward to getting a good night's sleep tonight."

"It does sound awful, doesn't it?" Laila replied. "But I'm hoping everyone will have a nice rest, and things will look up in the morning. Perhaps the police will finally be able to make it out here."

"Are you still adamant about us staying, given the recent occurrences?" he asked.

She thought for a moment. "I don't know."

"I know you want help Klaudie and be there for Sharon, but if our lives are at risk...is it worth it?" He reached out and took his wife's hand.

"I'd feel like I'm abandoning them if we just leave and go back to England. I'd never forgive myself. How could I act like everything is all right and move on with my life, if we left now, with things the way they stand?"

"I figured that was what you were going to say, and much as I hate to say it, I think I agree with you," said Nigel.

Laila chuckled. "I know, I know. It's difficult for you to admit I might be right once in a while, you old coot."

"I'm certain that damned pit in the chapel is responsible for what's been going on here. If we could get rid of it, we'd have a chance of things returning to somewhat normal."

"Tomorrow, we should try to contact that rabbi Jakub spoke to. Maybe he can help."

Nigel pulled her closer to him. She rested her head against his chest while he ran his fingers through her hair.

He loved Laila more than anything. Keeping her in harm's way seemed absurd, but she had the biggest heart he'd ever known, and he knew she wouldn't want to abandon their friends. She'd do anything for anyone; she always had. It was only one of the thousands of reasons he loved her so much.

They lay there in silence, the night still and quiet. They welcomed the peace. Finally, sleep overtook them, which was a relief. They would need all the rest they could get for what was to come.

Chapter 65

Outside the castle, Maxwell listened to his master's commands. It was almost time to put the final plan into place.

Then, off to tropical paradise with Candy he would go!

The wind picked up, some rain droplets falling from the sky, but Maxwell didn't care. He just stood there, nodding his head and listening.

The storm gained strength, rain pouring down. Wind whipped at the trees. Thunder rolled closer, lightning putting on a spectacular display.

In the stable, the horse was so badly spooked it broke loose from its stall. Kicking open the stable door, it took off galloping across the countryside, swiftly lost to sight,

Maxwell watched it go, smiling to himself. Even horses knew when bad shit was about to go down.

The castle's exhausted inhabitants slept like the dead, missing the show. They didn't hear the crash of uprooted trees toppling onto and blocking the roadway, which was already washed out in places by the torrential downpour.

Maxwell's smile widened. Mother Nature was on his side, making sure that no one at Houska Castle was going anywhere soon, and no help would be arriving for quite some time.

Chapter 66

Sharon woke up and didn't recognize her surroundings, but within a few seconds it started coming back to her. She was in the other bedroom, the one that had been Jakub's.

Also, she was very drunk, and she had to pee.

She got up and wobbled to the bathroom to attend to business. On her way back to bed, she detoured to the whiskey decanter she'd left on the dresser, but was disappointed to find it empty.

Well, there has to be more alcohol in this castle somewhere, she told herself, venturing into the hall.

But, halfway to the stairs, she knew she'd never be able to make it, far too dizzy and unstable. She retraced her steps, sat down on the bed, and covered her face with her hands. She felt awful.

Unfortunately, she wasn't feeling the least bit tired anymore. Switching on a lamp, she made her way to the vanity table and stared at her reflection in the mirror.

Ugh, she thought.

Underneath her bloodshot eyes were puffy, unsightly bags, caused from lack of sleep and crying. Dark, discolored blotches showed on her face from when Maxwell had struck her. Her skin was dry, and her hair was a disaster. She did what she could, but it felt like she was only going through the motions. There was a gaping hole in her chest.

How could she do this? How could she make it through this awful time?

She sat up straight, and wiped her eyes. This was ridiculous. She needed to pull herself together.

Yes, she'd loved Jakub, but she had no idea how serious his feelings really were. They'd slept together, but what did that mean? For men, especially, it didn't necessarily mean anything.

She'd known him a total of four days. Not even a week, in the grand scheme of things. Klaudie had known Jakub her entire life. Sharon had to stop being so selfish and set aside her own grief to be there for Klaudie. Suddenly, her stomach rebelled. She ran to the bathroom and vomited into the toilet.

Serves me right for drinking so much, she thought. She continued to retch until there was absolutely nothing left for her to throw up. She felt weak and tired.

Rinsing her sour mouth, she then drank some water, letting the cool liquid run down her burning throat. It tasted good, better than the whiskey had, and helped clear her head.

Her hands were still shaky, spilling a bit down her front. She blotted at it with a tissue, went to toss the tissue into the wastebasket, and missed by three feet. Groaning, she bent and picked it up, then stood directly over the basket to drop it in.

It landed beside a wadded-up sheet of paper covered with what looked like handwriting. On a curious whim, she retrieved it, smoothed it out, and twitched in shock when she saw her own name written at the top.

A quick scan told her it was a letter to her, from Jakub.

She dropped the paper like it was hot and backed away from it, shaking her head.

She didn't want to know. What could Jakub have written that was so bad he'd decided to throw it away?

He didn't love her. Maybe he was planning to tell her that in a letter and then leave, before she'd gone and seduced him and gotten him killed.

She stared at the crumpled paper on the bed.

She went back to the bathroom and washed her face.

She didn't need to read it. It probably contained things she didn't want to know.

She returned to the bedroom, feet feeling as if they'd been dipped in cement.

She was going to look. She had to know what it said, even if it was bad. For closure, she told herself, as she picked it up and began to read.

Sharon slowly walked back into the bedroom. When she reached the bed, she picked up the piece of paper, knowing these were the last words she'd ever receive from Jakub, and she began to read.

***

"Sharon," said Jakub. "Sharon, wake up."

Sharon opened her eyes. "Jakub? Is that you?"

"It's me."

"I don't understand. You died. I saw you die."

"You're dreaming, my love," he told her. "I can still visit you in your dreams."

Dreaming or not, she began crying again. "I read your letter."

"I know."

"Why did you throw it away? It was beautiful! And you did love me!"

"And I always will."

"I miss you so much," she sobbed.

"I miss you, too. Things didn't turn out the way we'd planned. We didn't have enough time together, but I'm grateful for the time I did have with you. I found true love, if only for a few days."

"It's cruel, it's not fair. I found you and fell in love with you and then you were taken away from me. That's not fair!" She touched his cheek.

"Life isn't fair. It doesn't go by the same rules we humans have to. But those who are still alive must go on. Sharon, you have to go on, I need you to do that."

Sharon nodded to show she understood, though she had no idea how she'd be able to go on. Jakub took her in his arms, holding her tight. She buried her face in his chest and cried.

"Look at me, Sharon," he said. "Listen to me. This is important. You have to help the others. Everyone is in grave danger. The pit in the chapel needs to be closed. It needs to be done as soon as possible. More than just the castle is at risk. The pit will continue to grow. The chapel walls will not confine it. Time is of the essence."

"You said all the options are terrible, Jakub. I wouldn't know where to begin."

"Talk to Klaudie. She will help you. My sister is very resourceful. I'm sure Nigel, Laila and Marek will pitch in as well. You *have* to get rid of it. Please. If you don't, it will destroy of all of you."

"I'll ... I'll try," Sharon said, sniffling.

"Another thing, stay away from Maxwell. He's dangerous. I know that seems silly and obvious to say, under the circumstances, but it's more than that. He's possessed, Sharon. Dwayne was possessed first, and that's why he killed Xander. The demon that was inside Dwayne wore out his body, so it left and found a new host."

"Actual demons? A real portal to Hell? I ... I can't ... it's too far-fetched," said Sharon.

"You must believe me, Sharon. I would never lie to you. I want you to be safe and go on to live a happy life."

"I trust you. I know you wouldn't lie to me. I just don't know how I'm going to do anything."

"Believe in yourself. You're clever. You're strong. You can do this." He hugged her again, then reluctantly withdrew. "I have to go now, my love. I'll see you again soon."

"Wait! Jakub! No! Don't go!" Sharon called, but it was too late. He was gone.

***

Sharon woke with a start and sat up.

The dream had been so real! She swore she smelled Jakub's scent in the air.

Through the window, she noticed the storm raging outside and was amazed it hadn't wakened her sooner. Thunder and lightning were putting on a show, the rain poured down in buckets, and from here it looked like several trees had been blown over, blocking the roadway. A couple might have even landed on Boris and Marek's cars.

That meant she was stuck here. She couldn't leave, even if she had a choice.

She crawled back in the bed and pulled the covers around her, thinking about what Jakub had said in her dream. She had to see Klaudie, first thing in the morning, so they could come up with a plan,

She pulled the covers up over her head and tried to pretend that Jakub was there with her in the bed. That she was loved. That she was safe.

Thunder cracked again, and the power went out, plunging the castle into darkness. Sharon had no doubt their phones would soon be rendered useless as well. The storm had destroyed any ties to the outside world they might have had.

Mother Nature is angry tonight, she thought. A line came into her head and she couldn't recall if it was from a song or a poem, or she'd just made it up, but it seemed to fit.

Tonight, the earth is crying, for the end is nigh.

Chapter 67

Morning came, but the sun did not. Sharon climbed out of bed and stretched, then put on some of the clothes Laila had brought from her old room and went downstairs.

With the power still out, Sharon drank a cup of cold tea and ate a now stale biscuit from a tray on the counter. She wasn't hungry, but knew she should eat something.

The others began trickling in, looking as tired as she felt, though they all claimed to have gotten at least some sleep. They remarked on the weather, the power outage, and the shortage of food.

"I'll go into town and bring back --" began Marek.

"Bring back, nothing," said Nigel. "I say we all pile into a car, tight fit or no, and get away from this wretched place."

Seeing hope rise on Klaudie and Laila's faces, Sharon hated to dash it, but had no choice.

"We can't," she said. "A tree fell on the cars, and the road is blocked and washed out. There's no way to leave at the moment."

ONE HELL OF A VACATION

"What?! Are you joking?" Marek ran to the window and looked outside.

The others followed. Sharon watched them take in the dismal scene. The thunder and lightning may have eased, but the wind and rain hadn't let up, not even a little bit.

"Well, this changes things," said Laila, sounding like she was trying to keep her chin up. "We'll need to gather whatever food we can find, and maybe start a fire."

"If the worthless police would just get here," grumbled Nigel. "It's been over two days."

"If they even could." Marek nodded at the downed trees and flooded road.

"We can't worry about any of that right now," said Sharon.

They all looked at her, quizzically.

"We need to close that pit," she declared, pointing in the direction of the courtyard and chapel. "It's what's behind all of this misery. We take care of it, and everything else will fall into place."

By their expressions, even those who didn't want to agree couldn't really argue.

"But how?" asked Klaudie. "I don't know if Jakub ever heard back from the rabbi. I didn't have a chance to talk to him, before..." Her words trailed off.

"He did," Sharon said. "As we were on our way upstairs. He sent me ahead to my room, while he stayed to take the call." She couldn't bring herself to mention his encounter with Marek in the hall. "He told me what Dr. Bartik said."

"Go on then. Tell us," said Klaudie.

"Dr. Bartik only found a couple of options, neither of them good, and neither of them guaranteed to work. The first involves taking the heart and liver from a dead fish, and sacrificing it into the pit while reciting a specific prayer."

Nigel glanced to the window again. "Not the best day for a fishing trip, but, if needs must ..."

"I may have an answer," said Marek. "The sea bass you had for dinner the other night, a friend of mine knows a local fishmonger. I could call him --"

"How would he even reach us?" protested Laila.

"And that's only if our phones work," Klaudie added.

.

"It's worth a try," Marek said. "I'll walk down to meet him, swim if I have to. Thomas is a good friend. He owes me. He will not let me down. And he could bring extra food, and other supplies."

"So." Nigel clapped his hands together briskly. "That's a definite maybe; what about the second option?"

Sharon took a deep breath. "We'd have to sacrifice the person who opened it in the first place."

For a moment, the room was silent except for the rain lashing the windowpanes.

"You mean Maxwell," said Klaudie. "Your husband."

"And when you say 'sacrifice' ...?" Laila hesitantly drew a finger across her throat.

Sharon nodded at both of them. "Along with, as with the fish, reciting specific prayers."

For another moment, the room was silent again.

"And that's it?" risked Laila. "We only have those two options?"

"They're what Dr. Bartik told Jakub," said Sharon.

"All right, then." Nigel repeated his brisk clap. "At least we have something to work with. Where is that bugger, Maxwell? He must still be around here somewhere, though I'm surprised he hasn't tried to attack us again."

"If he were in the castle, I'm sure we'd know by now," said Marek. "I suppose he might have tried hiding in the stable --"

"Oh no, Blesk!" Sharon cried, suddenly beside herself with worry. "Has anyone been to check on him?"

"We gave him some food and water yesterday," Marek told her. "I'll go again, right now if you like."

"I'll go with you," said Nigel. "We need to be especially careful, since that might be where Maxwell is hiding."

***

Within minutes, the rain soaked Marek and Nigel to the bone, even with the rain slickers Laila had insisted they wear. The wind battered relentlessly at them, and they splashed through mud and puddles nearly knee-deep.

When they reached the stable, they found the main door wedged wide open by a fallen branch, and Blesk's stall empty.

"He must have gotten loose during the storm and bolted," said Marek. "The thunder must have frightened him."

"Nothing we can do about it now." Nigel shook water from his hood. "Maybe he will make his way back."

"I hope so. Sharon is going to flip out."

"Then let's not tell her. What she doesn't know won't hurt her, at least for now. We'll just wait out here for a few minutes, and say everything went fine."

***

It wasn't long until both men were back, having changed into dry clothing, and settled into seats with their own cups of cold tea. They assured Sharon that Blesk was just fine, and they'd fed him and given him some fresh water.

"No sign of Maxwell?" she asked.

"He wasn't in the stable, as far as we could see," Marek said.

"Shit," said Klaudie, and they all looked at her in surprise. She looked back, defiant. "What? It's no secret where I stand. We find, catch, and sacrifice that fucker. He killed my brother. I want him to pay."

Sharon's eyes widened further. She'd never heard Klaudie be so blunt before.

"Hear, hear," said Nigel, lifting his teacup. Laila poked him, though her expression suggested her sentiments were similar.

"Look ..." Sharon folded her hands. "Believe me, I'm not disagreeing, but I have more to tell you."

"What do you mean?" Laila scooted closer to Nigel, and he put his arm around her.

"I had a dream last night," she began, then added hastily, "But I swear, it wasn't just a dream. Jakub was really there."

The others exchanged glances anyway. Sharon could read their skepticism from their faces.

"He told me the pit actually *is* a portal to Hell. It has to be closed. Right now, with no more delays. He said we are in great danger, and all of humanity is at stake."

ONE HELL OF A VACATION

Nigel spread his hands. "Then let's get on with it. Deal with Maxwell, close the evil Hell portal ... two birds with one stone."

"Except Maxwell isn't really Maxwell anymore," said Sharon. "He's possessed. So was Dwayne. Jakub told me a demon came from the pit and took control of him. That's why he murdered Xander, abducted Amalie, and attacked Laila. He wasn't himself."

"I knew there was something wrong!" said Laila. "When they first arrived, Dwayne was just the sweetest young man, and then he ... changed."

"So, Maxwell is also possessed?" Klaudie asked.

Sharon nodded. "Somehow, the demon transferred itself from Dwayne into Maxwell."

"And then Maxwell killed Dwayne and moved his body to the chapel," said Nigel. "Now it's all starting to make sense!"

"Which is why, when he ..." She couldn't bring herself to say it. "When he did what he did, he acted the same strange way Dwayne had been acting. He isn't responsible for his actions. Sacrificing him would -- I can't believe I'm saying this -- it would be wrong." Sharon shook her head.

"Like hell," said Marek. "If he hadn't read from that damn book, we wouldn't all be in this mess. He deserves whatever he gets."

"I know. I understand where you are coming from, but there should be no more death. We've all lost too much. If we have a way of getting the fish from your friend, I think we should try that first, and see if it works."

"What about the woman in Prague?" said Laila. "Maxwell's assistant? Didn't he murder her? But he couldn't have been possessed at that time, if what you are saying is true. He had to know what he was doing."

"And he came back here, after," said Nigel. "Also before he could have been possessed, and I daresay he wasn't planning to apologize to you and kiss and make up."

Sharon knew they were right, and dearly wanted to see Maxwell suffer and pay for his crimes, but ... "The police will find and deal with him," she said, though it sounded like desperate wishful thinking even to her own ears. She turned pleading eyes to the others. "We can't just kill someone. Not even him. It's too much."

Klaudie sat in silence for a moment, then spoke. "I've changed my mind. I agree with Sharon. There's been too much death. Marek, see if you can arrange for the fish?"

Relieved, Sharon smiled gratefully at Klaudie. "We'll have to do it without Maxwell knowing. If he, or the demon inside him, has any inkling, he'll do everything in his power to stop us."

***

Nigel caught up with Marek in the hall. "You know this is rubbish," he said in a low voice. "Fish or no fish, whether it works or it doesn't, if we get our hands on that bastard ..."

Marek nodded. "The women may not want more violence, but it may be necessary."

"Good. I'm glad you and I are on the same page."

He watched Marek head upstairs, presumably to get his phone and call his friend. And perhaps it wasn't very charitable of him, but he found himself hoping the phones didn't work, leaving them with only the second option. He wanted Maxwell Stone dead. He'd caused all of them grief, and was likely get away with everything he'd done. That didn't sit well with him. He believed in justice and he also believed in revenge.

Chapter 68

As the plan came together, Klaudie saw the overall morale of the group improve dramatically. Suddenly, they all had a purpose again, something to give them hope. Something to help them climb out of the darkness they'd been trapped inside of.

She was still heartbroken over Jakub, and dreading having to tell their mother and the rest of their sisters. She was worried sick about Marek, who'd miraculously been able to get ahold of Thomas and agreed to meet him at a halfway point.

Her ankle still hurt, but the swelling had gone down and she could move about without too much difficulty. At Nigel's suggestion, they each armed themselves from the cases in the trophy room.

Then there was nothing left to do but wait.

Marek had hugged and kissed her before he left, telling her, "I'll be back soon. I promise."

Then, he'd been gone, and she feared she'd never see him again.

***

The rain continued its merciless onslaught. Marek kept his head down and stuck to higher ground, if possible, but all too soon there was no more higher ground. He was trudging through ice cold water up to his knees. It didn't help matters that the temperature was only in the high forties, and the wind was bitter.

Shivering, he forced himself to keep going, trying to concentrate on other things.

He thought of Klaudie, and what he planned to say to her when they got out of this mess. He thought about the diamond ring he'd purchased, safely tucked away in his dresser drawer at home.

If only he had it with him now. He was finally ready. The last few days had taught him time was the enemy. He'd take Klaudie away from this place.

They'd met, ironically enough, while Marek had been doing a favor for Thomas. Delivering meals to the castle had originally been Thomas' job, but when his mother had been in the hospital, he'd asked Marek if he could take the task on for him for a week or so.

Marek, not having any other pressing business at the time, had agreed. When he'd first arrived, Klaudie greeted him at the door. Despite the age difference, her stunning beauty hooked him from the start; once he got to know her, he fell in love with her heart as well. When Thomas was ready to take his route back, Marek had offered to keep it permanently, which was fine by Thomas, as he didn't like the thrice-daily drive anyway.

In turn, Thomas had told Marek if he could ever do a favor for him in return, he'd be happy to help. Which was why Marek knew his friend would show up for him today.

The water was to his thighs, and his feet had gone numb, but Marek finally caught sight of Thomas's red truck waiting on the road.

He slogged uphill, noting the rain had finally lessened, and all but stopped by the time he and Thomas clasped hands.

"You look like a drowned rat," Thomas said.

"I feel like one," Marek replied. "Thank you for coming."

"The drive wasn't bad at all. I thought it would be, because of the rain you mentioned, but it's barely sprinkled the whole time I've been on the road. I guess you got the brunt of it."

"I guess," agreed Marek, inwardly wondering how the storm could be so localized.

Was there more to it than just a quirk of weather patterns? Could it be a deliberate force, somehow, an attempt to keep those at the castle trapped and unable to send for help?

He pushed all that from his mind. "Were you able to bring everything?"

"In these packs." Thomas handed him two waterproof backpacks, stuffed full.

Marek hung one on his back and the other on his chest to even out the load. The packs would grow heavier the longer he wore them, and he knew getting back to the castle with them was going to be no small feat.

"Are you sure about this?" Thomas asked, eyeing the dark clouds. "I could just give you a lift home --"

"No, they need me. Klaudie and the guests." He didn't want to, or have time to, go into details, because the explanation would have sounded insane. "Thank you, Thomas. You have no idea what you've done for me."

"It's no problem, my friend. I'm happy to help, anytime."

They shook hands again, and then Thomas got into his truck while Marek faced the long, waterlogged road back to the castle.

All too soon, the rain came down in torrents again, and the wind tried to push him off his feet. It really did seem as if something or someone didn't want him to make it back, but he was determined.

He pushed forward with everything he had.

The water, which had previously only reached thigh-deep, now came up to his waist, then his chest. At one point, it was up to his neck, and he was swimming with all his strength. The thunder and lightning returned, adding electrocution to his litany of fears.

The castle was in sight, candlelight flickering from a front window. He knew the others must be watching for him, though he doubted they could see much of anything.

Almost there. Almost there. Just a little further, and he'd be safe. He'd make it back alive.

Just a little further ...

***

Klaudie wept with relief as Marek stumbled through the front door.

Thank God! She wasn't sure what she'd have done if he hadn't made it. She'd lost her brother; she couldn't lose him, too.

He practically collapsed against her as she reached him. She helped take the heavy packs off, then left those for the others to deal with while she led Marek upstairs.

He was soaked, shivering from head to toe. She got him out of his wet clothes, dried him off, brought him a spare outfit from the things he'd been keeping at the castle since spending so many nights there with her.

"I thought I'd never see you again," she said, embracing him once he was dressed.

"I told you I'd make it, didn't I?" He said it lightly, but she could hear the strain in his voice, and feel the shivering still wracking his bones.

"Yes, you did." She kissed him.

"I won't lie; it was rough going. Like something was trying to stop me. Once I reached Thomas, the rain had all but stopped and I swear I thought the sun was going to come out, but as soon as I started back, it was pouring again, the water much deeper!"

"Well, it's over and you are back here with me." She took his face in her hands and leaned forward to kiss his lips again.

This time, Marek took her mouth in his. The kiss was passionate and long and left Klaudie swooning.

"Get away from me, woman, or we will never get out of here," he said, chuckling.

Klaudie laughed too, and they went downstairs to meet the others.

***

The contents of the backpacks had been unpacked and strewn across the table. Thomas had done as Marek asked, and the waterproofing had done a good job. There were crackers and cheese, bread and jam, beef jerky, and other non-perishable items, as well as a sealed package containing three whole fish.

As the rest of them ate, Marek insisted there was no time to waste and got started gutting and cleaning the fish, separating out the hearts and livers into individual baggies.

"Are we ready to try this?" he asked the others when he was done.

Everyone else nodded. Most of them had selected weapons from the trophy room, even if only to make themselves feel more secure. Marek carried one of the packs, and Sharon the other, each loaded with a first aid kit, a flashlight, a couple bottles of water and granola bars just in case, and some bagged fish parts. God forbid, if something happened, at least they'd be as prepared as they could be.

"I'll hang onto these, as a last resort," Nigel said, tucking the last two baggies into his pocket.

"To recap," said Sharon, "Laila, you are going to create a diversion. Nigel will be the lookout. Once Maxwell comes out, or if he doesn't, Marek, Klaudie and I will go straight to the chapel to perform the ritual. Everyone got it?" They all nodded again. It was going to be dangerous, but they had to try.

ONE HELL OF A VACATION

***

Nigel and Laila headed out the castle's front door, while Marek, Klaudie and Sharon made their way into the courtyard to hide. The rain was still falling hard, drenching them instantly. Thunder rumbled and the wind howled. Yet, even through the storm's chatter, it wasn't long before they heard Laila screaming for help at the top of her lungs.

Sharon shivered. The screams sounded so real. She couldn't wait until this was over.

Laila cried out again and again, each time louder and more desperate than the one before. If Maxwell was in the vicinity, there was no way he wouldn't hear her.

But still, there wasn't any sign of him.

"What if he's already gone?" Klaudie whispered. "Should we start the ritual?"

Marek shook his head. "I'm almost positive he's still here, somewhere."

Yes, thought Sharon. *But where?*

Chapter 69

Did they really think he'd fall for such an obvious, amateur trick? The squawking old bitch was a distraction, meant to lead him away. Possibly into a trap, possibly so the rest of them could try whatever idiotic plan they'd cooked up.

Maxwell stayed as quiet as a mouse in his hiding place, among the stand of trees where he'd clocked the cop. However diligent they thought they were being in their searches, he'd slipped past them with ease, time and time again,

Of course, it helped that his master told him where to hide and what to do.

As well as what these fools planned to do. Fish guts? They honestly expected fish guts and some stupid prayer had a chance in hell -- so to speak -- of stopping him?

He knew he could readily take out the old bitch and her annoying fart of a husband, who was playing lookout from a not-so-great hiding place of his own. Armed, even, with some weapon from the trophy room collection. And probably just itching to try it out on Maxwell, as if he'd stand half a chance.

Yes, he could have taken them both out, but that would have alerted Sharon and the other two to his presence, and he wasn't ready to do that yet. Let them wait, let them wonder and second-guess themselves. They wouldn't have the nerve to try anything until they knew where he was, and with any luck, they'd give up and go back inside, or split up for another 'search.'

***

Laila looked at her phone, which she'd been using to stay in text contact with Nigel while trying to lure Maxwell, and saw with dismay that its battery had died. But with the power having gone out during the storm, it wasn't as if she could have recharged it in the first place.

Still, she couldn't believe the luck.

Not that it seemed the plan was working, anyway. All she'd accomplished was to scream her throat sore, and get soaked to the skin from the pounding rain. At this rate, pneumonia would be posing more of a threat than the elusive Maxwell. He'd probably long since made himself scarce, and was somewhere warm and dry while they all mucked about in the storm.

Feeling wretched, defeated, and more than a little foolish, she trudged toward the spot where Nigel had said he would be standing lookout.

He came to meet her. "Laila, what's the matter?"

"My phone's dead, and all we're doing is getting drenched and freezing our backsides off. Either he's not out there, or he knows we're up to something."

"You're probably right," Nigel said. "Let's rejoin the others and try the original option. Much as I'd like to see the bastard get what's coming to him, first things first."

"We can't leave that portal open," Laila agreed. "The longer we do, the worse things will get." Shivering, she glanced at the ominous clouds. "And it's more than bad enough already."

***

ONE HELL OF A VACATION

Maxwell watched them head back toward the castle, holding hands as they slipped and splashed through puddles. They looked half-drowned and totally miserable.

To be sure, he was none too dry himself, even with what little shelter the trees offered. But that was okay, because most of his mind was already in his tropical paradise, lying on a lounge chair, with a drink beside him and a cigar in his hand.

And Candy in front of him, dancing for him, twirling in circles, her bikini barely covering her privates as she bounced up and down.

He commanded her to remove her top, and just like that, Candy reached behind her and popped the clasp on the bikini top that had barely contained her in the first place. She threw the top aside and continued to dance, smiling because her big luscious boobies were finally free.

Maxwell sighed, enjoying the show in his mind's eye. He crooked a finger at her, and she bounced over to him. He reached up for a grope --

And she vanished, along with the drink, cigar, lounge chair, and tropical paradise. He frowned, disappointed to find himself alone in the dark, rainy stand of trees again.

Then, unsurprisingly, he heard the voice in his head.

Every time he tried to have a little fun, that damn voice told him he still had tasks to complete. He needed to just get all of this bullshit over with, so he could head to his promised reward.

***

When Laila stopped screaming, Sharon's heart jumped into her throat. She was suddenly certain the worst had happened, Maxwell had found and killed her and Nigel despite their best efforts, and it was all her fault for insisting they risk their lives. Now she'd have more deaths on her conscience.

Then reason set in, and she realized Laila had probably stopped screaming because there was no point. Either Maxwell wasn't out there at all, or he'd seen the ruse for what it was and wasn't taking the bait.

She hoped it was the former. She hoped he'd gotten as far from the castle as he could after killing Jakub, knowing the police would soon be on his trail for not only one but multiple murders. Let the courts deal with Maxwell. The rest of them had bigger problems.

ONE HELL OF A VACATION

***

The storm was his ally, as it had been all along.

A huge crack of lightning shattered the sky, accompanied by a thunderclap loud enough to rattle Maxwell's bones. The bolt struck a tree, splitting it with a shower of splinters and sparks, and roughly half of it fell right on top of the old fart and his wife as they neared the front steps.

If the screams before had been convincing, these were award winners. A massive bough flattened them both into the mud, under a pile of broken branches and smoldering bark. Not killing them outright, but they had to be hurt, and were definitely stuck.

They'd wanted to be a distraction? Well, okay, but now the shoe was on the other foot. *See how they like that.*

***

Sharon, Klaudie, and Marek all jumped at the simultaneous flash and blast, and the sounds of destruction, fear, and pain immediately following.

"That's Laila and Nigel!" Klaudie said.

"Lightning must have hit one of the trees," said Marek. "If it landed on them --"

"Come on!" Sharon cried. "They might need help!"

"What about Maxwell?" asked Klaudie. "And the plan?"

"Later!" She pelted across the courtyard, back into the castle, and toward the front door.

Marek and Klaudie followed, all three of them stopping short on the porch to gape at the scene before them. One of the trees was indeed a smoking ruin, not fully on fire thanks to the rain, but laced with glowing embers. The rest of it was a jagged woody mass on the ground, beneath which two figures struggled and shouted.

Without another thought, Sharon shrugged off her pack and let it drop at the top of the porch steps. She ran down them and over to the pile of branches, calling Nigel and Laila's names.

Marek did likewise, with Klaudie keeping up despite her sore ankle. They began heaving debris aside, working to uncover the trapped, injured couple.

"It's all right," Sharon told Laila, grasping her hand. "We'll get you out of there."

"My arm," Laila sobbed. "And Nigel ..."

Nigel had gone silent, driving a spike of alarm into Sharon. She could see him, bleeding from a gash to the scalp, and hoped he'd only been knocked unconscious.

The three of them made quick work of it, and were soon able to pull first Laila and then Nigel to safety. They were both scraped and bruised. Laila cradled her left arm to her side, she and Klaudie supporting each other, but her main concern was for her husband. Who was, thankfully, still breathing as Sharon and Marek lugged him up the steps.

"What about Maxwell?" asked Klaudie again.

"If we're lucky, a tree fell on him, too," said Marek, nudging aside one of the packs with his foot.

"Wait, the packs," said Sharon. "We can't forget those."

"I'll come right back for them," he told her. "Let's take Nigel inside first."

***

Sometimes, they made it almost *too* easy.

Maxwell gave them a couple of minutes, then crept up the steps, pausing only briefly to see to one of his tasks before making his way into the castle. The door to the great room stood ajar, spilling a wedge of lantern light. From beyond it, he heard a bustle of voices and activity as they tended to the old couple's wounds.

Sounded like both of them would pull through. Too bad. But, on the plus side, it meant he would still have the pleasure of killing them himself.

He tiptoed past the door and continued along the hallway, not concerned about any wet footprints he might be leaving because the floor was already a mess from everyone else's back-and-forth.

Crossing the courtyard, he entered the chapel, and felt the welcome sensation of coming home. The glow from the pit bathed him in its eerie light, and the images in the murals smiled.

After setting up all the candles, he went to the altar, and picked up the severed head of the man he'd decapitated with the machete. He turned the face toward him. The dead eyes bulged wide open in a permanent look of terror. Maxwell laughed, then tossed it into the pit.

Next, he undressed the headless body. His master had no interest in clothes, preferring the sacrifices to be naked. Maxwell liked to think of it as similar to shelling peas. Once he'd removed the clothing, he dragged the body over to the pit, giving it a final push with his foot so it tumbled down.

He repeated the same procedure with the other guy. Off go the clothes, over to the pit, and bloop! Down you go!

Dusting off his hands with satisfaction, he practically skipped to his chair and sat to wait for the others to arrive. Then the party could really start.

He had never been very good at waiting, but he knew if he didn't do as he was told, his master would punish him, and being this close to leaving for his tropical paradise kept him from stepping out of line.

Soon now, soon.

And he couldn't wait to see the expressions on their faces when they figured out just how fucked they were.

Chapter 70

"We'd better get going," said Marek.

Nigel's head had mostly stopped bleeding, though some still seeped through the gauze pads Sharon had taped over the wound. He'd regained consciousness, and although woozy, utterly refused to stay behind.

And if he wouldn't, Laila wouldn't either, despite having her left arm bound to her body in a makeshift sling. They were all in this together, and it was time to finish it, once and for all.

Outside, the sky was darker than ever, and thunder was so loud, it seemed to rattle the castle. The rain was pouring down in sheets, stinging their skin as they entered the courtyard.

"Look," Klaudie said quietly, pointing.

The door to the chapel stood slightly ajar, with flickering candlelight dancing in the gap. Someone was in there, and they all knew who that someone had to be.

"What do we do now?" said Laila.

"We face him," said Sharon.

"That's right. It's time to take him down." Marek glanced at her. "We may still have to kill him."

Sharon nodded, firming her jaw.

Every step felt like a step towards their doom. She tried to push the feeling away, but it was nearly impossible. There was still a chance they could come out of this on top. There had to be. At the very least, they had to try.

Sharon moved past Marek, taking the lead. *Now or never,* she thought, pushing the door the rest of the way open and stepping inside.

She ignored the glowing pit, the candles, and the creepy murals on the walls.

Her gaze went straight to Maxwell, who was relaxing. He was sitting in a chair by the altar, and looked to be enjoying a snack.

"Oh, hi, honey," Maxwell said, between bites. "I've been waiting for you. What took you so long?"

Sharon stopped. So did the others, spread out behind her.

Maxwell nodded cordially at them. "Well, well. Looks like the gang's all here. I was beginning to think you guys were never going to show up."

"We're ready to put this to an end," Sharon said, sounding more confident than she felt.

"As am I, my dear wife," Maxwell said, swallowing the last morsel of whatever he was eating. He wiped his hands on his pants and stood up. "You know, I never dreamed you'd fuck around on me. But, when I saw that you did, it didn't bother me one bit. Gave me immense satisfaction to smash his skull, though."

Anger built inside of her, but she tried to keep it at bay, guessing from the harshness of Klaudie's breathing she was doing the same.

"Tell us what you want, Maxwell. What will make you leave us in peace?"

He chuckled. "I think it's obvious peace is not an option. Furthermore, I've already won. I just ate your plan for lunch, literally." With a maniacal laugh, he threw a handful of empty plastic baggies to the floor, baggies that had contained the fish hearts and livers.

"You son of a bitch," said Marek, hastily checking his pack.

Sharon didn't bother, her spirits sinking. She realized he must have been lurking outside after all, watching them rush to help Nigel and Laila. Watching them drop their packs on the porch, unattended for long enough that he could steal the vital organs.

"Oh, it wouldn't have worked anyway," Maxwell said. "None of you have the first idea of what you're dealing with."

"Actually, I have a rather good idea what we're dealing with," snarled Nigel, hefting the metal mace or club he'd chosen from the trophy room cabinets.

Laila, with her good arm, held him back.

"That would have been a real stupid move, old man." said Maxwell, as he picked up a wicked-looking ax. "I've already beheaded one idiot this week; don't think I won't behead another." Maxwell danced around the altar, swinging the ax all around him.

Sharon could hardly believe what had come over him. How could he turn into such a monster? Yes, she knew he was possessed, because she believed what Jakub had told her in her dream, but seeing him this way was hard to digest. Maybe he hadn't been the nicest person before, but now he was completely evil and unhinged.

Klaudie plucked at Sharon's sleeve, subtly. Sharon glanced at her and Klaudie shifted her gaze to the scattering of baggies littering the floor.

Yeah, so? Sharon thought. *All four are empty; that isn't going to do us any ...*

All *four* were empty.

She caught on, doing her best to keep her reaction from showing.

Four baggies, but Marek had parceled out six, and the leftover pair had gone into Nigel's pocket. With everything else, and his head wound, he as well as the rest of them had clean forgotten!

So, their plan wasn't completely foiled. If they could lure Maxwell away from the pit, they could still perform the ritual. They just needed to keep Maxwell talking, and distract him.

"But why?" she asked, figuring he couldn't pass up the opportunity to gloat.

"Why?" Maxwell sniggered. "Sharon, Sharon. I already had it all planned out. Get rid of you, start a new life with Monica ... well, that last part didn't quite go the way I wanted. Can you believe it? She wasn't on board with killing you." He shook his head in mock sorrow. "I guess she wasn't the person I thought she was."

As he went on, Sharon nudged Nigel, signaling him with her eyes. It took him a confused moment before the penny dropped. Klaudie was busy trying to direct Laila's and Marek's attention without being too overt.

"So, I came back here to take care of things once and for all. I needed you dead, Sharon. No offense, but I'd gotten myself into some trouble at work, and the insurance money would have bailed me out. I couldn't have cared less that you were fuckin' that dude. It didn't matter to me at all. But he got in the way."

"That 'dude' was my brother, you piece of shit," Klaudie said.

Maxwell smirked, shrugging. "But, before I came looking for you, I found one of the gay boys all tied up in the trophy room. It seems he was being used by ... well, someone else ... but had outlived his usefulness. So, that someone else hopped a ride on the Maxwell Express, and now here we are."

Sharon sidled closer to Nigel, who'd managed to surreptitiously dig the baggies of fish organs from his pocket. To keep Maxwell's mind occupied, she scoffed. "I thought banging your secretary was cliche, but killing your wife for the insurance money, too? Real original, there, Maxwell."

His eyes darkened. "You want original? How about this? After I feed all of you to my master, He's sending me to a tropical paradise. With a new girlfriend already waiting for me." He licked his lips. "Her name is Candy. She has the best body I've ever seen. Beats Monica's all to hell, let alone yours."

Closing her hand around the baggies, feeling the slimy lumps slide around, Sharon shook her head again. Laila, aware of what she was trying to do, chimed in.

"Classic midlife crisis, if you ask me," she said. "He'll be wanting a sports car or motorcycle next."

"Nobody asked you, you dried-up old bitch!" Maxwell glared at her, and Sharon used the moment to tuck the baggies into the back of her pants. He recovered his composure with a visible effort. "Anyway, the sooner we get this party started, the sooner I can be doing tequila shots out of Candy's belly button. So, who wants to go first?"

When none of them volunteered, he raised his eyebrows and crossed his arms, the ax dangling from one hand.

"I promise, it won't hurt," he said. "You just come kneel in front of me, and, bloop! Your heads will come right off. You won't feel a thing. The blade is super sharp."

"If you want to kill us, then good luck; we won't go down without a fight!" Nigel lunged, swinging his mace.

"Nigel, no!" Laila cried, but there was no stopping him.

Marek grabbed for him, missed, swore, and joined the fray with his own weapon, a solid-looking iron bludgeon. Klaudie was right beside Marek, teeth bared, screeching, "This is for Jakub!"

***

They had him outnumbered, but Maxwell was ready, and faster. He side-stepped and dodged their attacks, maneuvering to keep the gaping portal between them.

"The ritual!" Laila urged Sharon. "Do it now, hurry!"

Marek landed a glancing blow, to which Maxwell responded with a kick to the midsection. Grunting, winded, Marek staggered back. Klaudie lunged blade-first, aiming for the heart; Maxwell swatted her arm aside so she missed, and the weapon went flying. Nigel launched another tremendous swing. Maxwell ducked under it, the mace's passage riffling his hair.

As the momentum pulled Nigel around, he overbalanced and went to one knee, and in that instant Maxwell swept the ax in an arc, shearing through Nigel's neck. His head, the eyes still aware and shocked, rolled into the pit. His body slumped forward, blood streaming from the cleanly sliced stump.

Everyone else froze in horror. Laila made a horrible noise, then wailed aloud as Maxwell casually booted the headless corpse into the pit as well.

Marek struggled to catch his breath. Klaudie looked around wildly for her weapon. Laila collapsed like a rag doll, still wailing.

And Maxwell, after briefly cocking his head to the side as if listening, leapt at Sharon, tackling her to the chapel floor, groping roughly and crudely over her body. She writhed and fought, but he was too strong.

"Ah-ha!" he proclaimed, holding up the baggies. "Sneaky-sneaky, naughty girl."

He backhanded her across the face, stunning her, and got to his feet. No one could, or dared, move. Sharon tried to do something, say something, but the world was spinning around her.

"Killing always gives me an appetite," Maxwell remarked. "Don't mind me if I have another little snack."

He dumped the heart and liver into his mouth, chewed, swallowed, and smiled.

"Mmmmm," he said. "Really hits the spot."

***

"You ... can't do this, Maxwell." Sharon managed to hitch herself up onto her elbows. "We won't let you."

"I'm already doing it, and you can't stop me," he told her, in his condescending way. "Honestly, Sharon, don't you get it? I serve a higher purpose now."

"Higher purpose?" She cast a scornful look at the pit. "What, that?"

"*That*," he mocked, "is the gateway to the underworld. We're talking Hell here, Sharon, literal Hell. Lucifer, Beelzebub, Satan, Prince of Darkness, El Diablo, the big Numero Uno. I never knew what a favor I was doing Him when I opened it up again."

"I won't let you win, Maxwell. You've taken too much already. You thought I was just a small-town black girl when you married me a year ago, but it's time I showed you who I really am, deep inside of my soul. I let you walk all over me and I regret that. I should have never married you. I'm too good for you. I see that now. You ruin everything and everyone around you. Even your own brother warned me about what kind of person you really are. I should have listened to him. Now I see it for myself. And you're not so tough, you with your arrogance and your big mouth. Even now, with that ax, you're still just the Devil's bitch."

"Aww, honey, you hurt my feelings," said Maxwell, with a pout. "That is to say, if I had feelings, they might be hurt. But since I don't, well ..." He shrugged as a wicked grin spread on his face. "As for Graham, I could care less. He's always been a thorn in my side. My parents compared me to him the entire time I was growing up. It doesn't surprise me a bit that the puss decided to try and sabotage my marriage. But I guess in the end you should have listened to him, because now look at the situation you're in." He gestured around, including a wave of acknowledgment toward Marek and Klaudie, who'd crouched beside Laila. "Facing certain death, your lover got his head bashed in, and your husband's off to paradise to live the life he deserves. If I'm the Devil's bitch, I guess that makes you a pathetic loser, Sharon."

"She is not a loser." Laila pushed herself into a sitting position with her good arm. Her eyes were red from crying and she looked like her entire psyche might break at any second. "Sharon is a strong, lovely, wonderful woman, and she deserves much better than you, you pathetic prick."

"Laila, don't!" Sharon cried.

Laila laboriously got up, bracing herself on Marek and Klaudie. She looked right at Maxwell. "Pathetic prick," she repeated, enunciating clearly.

"I'm gonna stomp your face in," Maxwell said, more matter-of-factly than angrily.

When and where Laila had pulled one of the water bottles from one of the packs, Sharon had no idea, but there it was, in her good hand, and she hurled it like a cricket player at the pitch. It smacked into Maxwell and burst, splashing water everywhere, startling him into letting go of his ax.

As if they'd planned it that way, as if it was the moment he'd been waiting for, Marek charged with his bludgeon. Maxwell, unarmed but seemingly unconcerned, plunged forward to meet him. They collided in a brutal impact, rebounding from each other. Marek regained his footing and swung for the fences --

And Maxwell reached out one-handed, catching his wrist in midair and stopping the swing cold. Before any of them could react, he'd seized the bludgeon from Marek's grasp with his other hand and drove the bulbous iron end of it into his jaw.

***

Marek heard and felt the bony crunch, tasting blood and broken teeth as he fell to the floor. He was dimly aware of Klaudie screaming his name in the background.

This was it. He was done. He knew he wasn't going to make it, and it was his own fault. After everything, he'd still misjudged Maxwell's strength, underestimated whatever force was assisting him.

Maxwell stood over him, and Marek waited for him to strike the fatal blow. He deserved it. He'd been too hasty. They hadn't been ready for any of this.

"Please Maxwell, please don't hurt him!" Klaudie begged.

"Why should I show him any mercy? He meant to kill me. Shouldn't I show him the same courtesy?" Maxwell started to dance around Marek's crumpled body, thoroughly enjoying his position. "Besides, he has to die. You all do. I'm ready to get out of here and get my reward."

The bludgeon came down again and agony exploded through Marek's skull.

"There," Maxwell said in a satisfied tone. "That takes care of him. Now, you three be good little girls and let me take care of you as well."

Marek's whole world was pain, but somehow, to his surprise, he wasn't dead yet. He might have been dying -- shit, probably was -- but for now he held on, trying to lie as still as possible and not give himself away.

Klaudie, Sharon, and Laila clung together in a group, shuffling backward as Maxwell advanced on them. "Don't be like that," he chided. "It'll only take a second, and it'll all be over with."

Chapter 71

When Klaudie had been a child, she, Jakub, and Irenka, being the three youngest and only a few years apart in age, did everything together. Their elder sisters weren't interested in childish games.

Their favorite was one they called 'catch me if you can', in which Jakub would always be 'it' and chase after the two girls. At some point, the girls would separate, one of them leading Jakub while the other ambushed him, tackling him from behind. Poor Jakub never did catch on, falling for the same trick again and again. Klaudie smiled sorrowfully. Her heart ached for the loss of her brother. But, just maybe, thinking about the game they'd played as children would help them now.

"When he chases me back in," she whispered to Sharon and Laila, "get him!"

They both looked at her as if she were insane, but, what choice did they have? She spared one last glance at Marek, praying he wasn't dead and feeling terrible about not going to help him, then darted sideways and raced for the chapel door, sore ankle be damned.

Her sudden move caught Maxwell off guard; he must've thought he had them cowed and cornered.

"Hey!" he blurted, his tone accusatory, like she was cheating or breaking the rules.

"Fuck you!" she yelled over her shoulder.

And he was after her, hot on her heels, even faster than she'd expected. She dashed into the courtyard, the rain once again beating on her skin.

It occurred to her that she could leave. Just keep going, through the castle and out the front door. If the road was still flooded, so what? She knew how to swim.

But she couldn't leave her friends behind. Nor could she get the thought of Marek from her head.

She wanted to believe he was still alive. Maxwell had hit him hard, yes, and twice, but that didn't mean he was dead. He could just need serious medical attention. Though, given how the police hadn't shown up for days now, she couldn't very well count on an ambulance either.

Was that part of the larger plan? Was the pit creating all of these outside problems to keep others away, so Maxwell could finish Satan's bidding?

ONE HELL OF A VACATION

It seemed impossible, but she was quickly learning that anything was possible. If the Evil going on in this place was even able to manipulate the weather, why not?

All this went through her mind in an instant, as she ran in erratic circles around the courtyard, veering this way and that at random. Swearing, infuriated, Maxwell pursued.

Hoping the others had understood and were ready, she pivoted and made for the chapel door.

***

Okay, this one was seriously beginning to piss him off. When he caught her, he would break both her legs before throwing her headfirst into the pit.

Right as he was about to snag a fistful of her hair, she dove and rolled, and he barged through the doorway to find a knife pointed at his face. It brought him up short, his wet feet skidding.

At the other end of the knife was Sharon, looking scared but resolute.

"Maxwell, please, can we just talk this through?"

He could not fucking believe it. His own fucking wife.

"*Get* him!" the one he'd been chasing yelled.

Maxwell raised his hands, palms out. "This bullshit," he said, "has gone on long enough."

"Yes, it has," she agreed.

Quick as a snake, he grabbed for the blade. It cut him, drawing blood, but he felt no pain. He wrenched it from Sharon, hurling it across the room even as he seized her by the throat.

She clawed at his fingers, trying to pry them loose, but he got both hands around her neck and began to squeeze. Sharon gagged and choked. He could have ended it then with a good hard snap, but wanted to see her suffer for all the inconvenience she'd caused him.

***

"Let go of her!" Klaudie cried. Drawing her own knife, she ran over and drove it deep into Maxwell's side.

"You *stupid slut*!" he roared, releasing Sharon and clutching at the handle. He ripped it free of his flesh.

Sharon stumbled away, coughing, clutching at her bruised throat.

"I'll stick this so far up your --" he began, turning toward Klaudie.

"Oh, no, you won't," Laila said, flinging her arms around Maxwell from behind.

"Get off me, crazy old bitch!" He tried to buck her loose, but she held on with tenacious strength.

Laila smiled affectionately at Klaudie and Sharon, both of whom gaped in horror as they realized what she meant to do. "It's all right," she told them. "I'm going to find my Nigel."

Then she tipped backwards and let herself fall, pulling Maxwell with her, into the pit.

Chapter 72

Tears spilling down her face, Sharon approached the pit, unfolding the paper upon which she'd written the prayer Dr. Bartik had given Jakub. She wasn't sure it still needed to be done, with Maxwell gone, but she wasn't taking any chances.

Her throat throbbed, and her voice was hoarse and raspy as she read the words. "With the Aramaic and Jewish names of God, your Father and my Father, I close all doors of spiritual Evil. Amen."

She bowed her head. She felt Klaudie come up beside her and take her hand.

The glow inside of the pit dimmed and went out. The floor underneath their feet started to shift, the edges of the gap narrowing, the crack getting smaller and smaller until it was no more.

It was over.

They stood there in silence, the chapel seeming somehow brighter, the figures in the murals no longer as menacing.

Then Klaudie, stifling a sob, went over to Marek's body. He lay there, motionless, his face a mask of blood and a thick puddle of it forming a halo around his head.

But, as Klaudie crumpled, weeping, onto his chest, Marek groaned. His eyelids twitched, then just barely opened, dazed and unfocused. Through a broken jaw and a mouthful of damaged teeth, he mumbled her name.

Tears spilled down Sharon's face again, happier ones, overjoyed to see him alive. She couldn't help thinking of Jakub, wishing he could be here to know some of them, at least, had made it, and did what they'd set out to do.

She went to the chapel door. Outside, the rain had stopped. The clouds had disappeared, the sky a beautiful blue. Sunshine filled the courtyard.

She even heard, in the distance, approaching vehicles and sirens; Boris' backup had finally arrived, better late than never.

***

The next few hours passed in a blur of police officers, paramedics, and questions for which there were no good answers.

How could they possibly explain? Yes, several people were dead, but only one body -- Jakub's -- could be accounted for. They still had no idea what had happened to Boris, or any way to rationalize the freak storm. And, honestly, right then, Sharon had no interest in talking about it.

She wanted to savor the feeling of being alive as long as she could, for she knew that when things got back to normal, she might forget living was a privilege. Not because she was selfish, but because she was human, and that was what humans did; they took life for granted.

Marek was loaded into an ambulance, and Klaudie rode with him. Sharon followed a police officer to a cruiser. She got in, sitting quietly.

As they drove off, she looked back out the window at the castle, never taking her eyes off it until it was out of sight.

The evil may have been gone for good, but she hoped to never see the place again.

Epilogue

Sharon swung her leg over Blesk, and her butt landed firmly in the saddle. She signaled him to run, and away they went. She was thankful for the breeze on her face, as it was a warm June day, six months after the horrific events happened in the Czech Republic. Blesk was used to his new home in Connecticut, and Sharon enjoyed her daily rides. He had settled in nicely at Graham's place, where he lived in a big, comfy barn.

After the ordeal at Houska, she'd learned that Blesk escaped the stable and ran all the way back to Jakub's farm. She'd asked Klaudie if she could arrange to take him home with her and there were no objections.

Klaudie and Marek were engaged to be married, and planned to visit the U.S. next month while on their honeymoon, stopping at Sharon's for a day or two before heading south to Florida. Sharon couldn't wait to see her. The two had been in constant contact, as close as sisters.

Klaudie wasn't the only one that had been in constant contact with her, though. Sharon dreamed of Jakub almost every night, just as he'd promised her. She was content, if not happy.

Pulling on the reins, they came to a halt as Sharon heard the familiar chirp of her phone.

"Hello?"

"It's Herschel."

"What a pleasant surprise!"

"The book is gone."

"Gone?" she questioned.

Klaudie had relayed to her that Herschel retrieved the book from the castle for safe keeping before she locked it up for the final time. Everyone came to an agreement that the castle wasn't safe, no matter if the pit had been closed or not. And now Herschel was telling her the book was…. gone?

"I've no idea where it went. I know books don't walk off by themselves, but it's definitely not where I left it" he told her. "I've called Klaudie as well, and let her know. I'll keep searching."

"Thanks for letting me know."

Sharon ended the call, a feeling of dread forming in the pit of her stomach.

ONE HELL OF A VACATION

***

From the bushes, she'd watched the old man wave to Klaudie before getting in his car and driving away from the castle. When the coast was clear, she ran for the road, where she'd parked her own vehicle. She knew his name, and knew she'd be able to find his address.

The plan was to visit him under false pretenses, and get her hands on the book when he wasn't looking. When her father picked her up from the castle, she was pretty sure she was going to be jobless, but it was confirmed a few days later, when Klaudie called her to tell her that there wouldn't be guests staying at the castle anymore.

But she needed money, and was tired of living with her parents, earning a meager wage. She was pretty sure the old book would bring her a small fortune if she took it to an antique dealer. So she went back to the castle, searching for it, but found Klaudie and the old man there, instead.

As she raced toward Prague, and the old man's house, Amalie smiled. This would all work out in her favor, she was sure of it.

ACKNOWLEDGMENTS

I would like to thank the following people for their support:

Christine Morgan - for being a great editor.

Kealan Patrick Burke – for making an amazing cover

Marva Webb – for being the greatest English teacher in the world

My family and friends including, but not limited to: Patrick Shaw, Kathy Allison, Jane Poore, Mary Allen, Rhett Poore, Bryan Lenertz, Melissa Weaver, Jared Smith, Darryl Reilly, Stacy Duncan, Charmaine King, Tina Barnhill, Kayla Polak, and Julia Jurcisin

ABOUT THE AUTHOR

Tara Tannenbaum lives in Murrells Inlet, SC where she enjoys spending time with her son, Patrick, and her two dogs, Juno and Neptune. *One Hell of a Vacation* is her first novel.

You can follow her on Instagram @ttannenbaum or on her Facebook page- Tara Tannenbaum

Made in the USA
Columbia, SC
26 October 2023

f1cdc12d-ebda-490a-8406-4ae5eb19dce1R01